A SLAUGHTER OF IGUANAS

ANNE LOISELLE

A SLAUGHTER OF IGUANAS

ISBN: 979-8-9952133-0-7 (sc)

ISBN: 979-8-9952133-1-4 (hc)

ISBN: 979-8-9952133-2-1 (e)

Library of Congress Control Number: 2026906754

Winchester, VA, USA

Cover design by Anne Loiselle

Also by Anne Loiselle

Sleuth of Bears

To local restaurants, cafes, and eateries everywhere

It is always so cozy and wonderful to sit around the table in congenial company

Slaughter / ˈslȯ-tər / *noun*

1. The act of killing in a manner that is brutal or unnecessary, or in large numbers
2. (informally) The act of utterly demolishing or discrediting
3. (other, collective) A group of iguanas

Contents

Chapter 1

The Great Eastern Ultra Triathlon

They're all out there somewhere, 120-odd competitors stretched across four and a half miles of Chesapeake, but for the most part, I'm oblivious. The wind is blowing hard, and I'm trying to keep from tipping over, paddling furiously. It's slow going, as both the wind and the tide are against me, but inch by inch, we make our way to the state park. I'm in a kayak, one of the safety volunteers, and I have a woman in tow. We just met out there in the middle of the gray washing machine of the bay, when I spotted a swimmer drifting on her back with one hand held high. That is the signal for help, and when I came over to check on her, she grabbed onto the side immediately, saying, "Oh thank you, thank you. I can't see, I don't know where I am." Then she threw up, down her wetsuit and into the water.

When she can talk again, she tells me that her name is Kelsey, and that she got seasick swimming and bouncing through the chop. She felt dizzy and was afraid she would black out. I told her that if she could hold on to the back of the kayak, I would pull her to land, and that is what we are doing now. When we finally reach the shore, Kelsey crawls up until she gets to dry sand and stays on her knees, her head resting on the ground, cradled in her arms, essentially in what in yoga class we would call child's pose.

Exhausted, I slowly extricate myself from the kayak, pull it up the beach, and plunk down next to Kelsey, breathing hard until I catch my breath. Only then do I look around for the source of a loud and sustained motor noise and notice the helicopter, and the crowd of people a short distance away. As I watch, the helicopter lands, and something—or rather someone, lying on one of those stretchers you see lifeguards use—is quickly hoisted on board. Then it takes off again. Kelsey has turned around and is sitting up, watching too. The crowd begins to disperse and walk in our direction.

My name, by the way, is Lily Piper, and I make my living as a yoga instructor at the Eye of Horus studio in Bethesda, Maryland, about an hour's drive from here. Over the past year or so I've also become an aficionado of open water swimming, and getting a close-up look at this herculean one had seemed like a good idea a month ago. Now, I'm not so sure.

"What happened?" I call to one of the passing spectators.

"Someone drowned," he calls back.

"Oh, no. That's awful," says Kelsey.

I nod in agreement, and turn again to watch the helicopter until it disappears from view. I don't yet know who it is in that helicopter, or the details of what happened. But soon I will learn that the body is not that of some stranger, and that this is no simple drowning, no sad accident in what can be a dangerous sport. It is so much more awful than that.

For now, I concentrate on looking out across the vast estuary, where here and there I can still make out a few neon-capped swimmers bobbing far away, some of the other volunteers in their kayaks, and, just barely, a police boat following them all to the other shore. It was densely foggy at the start, as well as windy, and even now visibility is not very good. I think of my friend Tessa, who is probably still out there, and fervently hope that she is safe paddling through the waves. We signed up together to be escorts for this first leg of the Great Eastern Ultra Triathlon, a two-day event that comprises 240 miles of biking and a 30-mile run in addition to the swim across the bay. It's a legendary race that Tessa has been eyeing for years, wanting to take on the challenge but intimidated by the enormity of the distances.

When I brought up the idea of volunteering, she jumped at the chance. For my part, I wanted to watch and cheer on some friends of mine, members of a team from Pennsylvania who are trying to make a name for themselves on a national level. Being a volunteer sounded like more fun than just watching from the sidelines, and I, too, thought I'd see more of the race. As it turned out, the fog and the size of the waves whipped by the wind made it all but impossible to see much of anything from the low vantage point of our kayaks, not to mention the fact that it took all of our concentration to keep moving in the right direction while looking out for swimmers in trouble. This in itself proved easier said than done, as their black wetsuits disappeared all too easily in the dark water, with only the bright swim caps—different colors designating gender and age group—clearly discernible.

Bringing Kelsey back to the start meant I completely missed the transition to the first day's bike leg on the other side, my only chance of seeing any of my friends today. With Kelsey having assured me she is fine now that we're back on solid ground, I head over to the volunteer tent to check in. When I arrive, there's already a crowd milling around, eating and chatting, although everyone speaks in hushed tones. I help myself to a free can of soda and a banana, and listen to the surrounding babble.

Some people are comparing personal "war stories" about how tough the conditions were out there, but most of the talk is about the helicopter. I glean it was a guy who drowned, and that race personnel called the helicopter at first hoping to save his life, but it was too late. Nevertheless, his body was being rushed to Austin Hill Hospital in Bethesda, in case they find he'd checked the "organ donor" box on his registration form. There still might be something they can save.

My phone dings, and it's a text from Tessa: she's on the shuttle and should be here in about twenty minutes. I can't help but be relieved that she is out of the water, safe and sound, and I reply with a thumbs-up emoji. Tessa and I have been friends since I was a little kid and she was my babysitter. She is the one who inspired me to take up swimming and try some open water events, now a shared passion that has brought us even closer. We drove here together early this morning in Tessa's car, which already seems like an eternity ago. I wonder briefly about her impressions and whether she still hankers to take part in this competition one day. I can't fathom it myself; I'm already bone-tired.

Since I'm waiting for Tessa and still have my phone in my hand, I consider giving Karen a call. Karen Ellsworth is both a friend and a yoga client of mine, and she works as an administrator at Austin Hill. It's the weekend, but I'm sure she'll be interested to hear what happened.

"Hey!" Karen says, picking up on the second ring. "How's the race? Did you see any of our buddies?"

Karen also knows the team from Pennsylvania and knows I'm volunteering today. At first, she starts laughing when I describe how, no, I could see absolutely nothing and absolutely no one who wasn't within about a 50-foot radius of my kayak.

"It was really wild out there," I tell her. "They delayed the start and almost canceled the swim portion because of the strength of the riptides, and because the waves were making it so hard for all the safety boats, but the forecast was good and things were starting to calm down."

Then I tell her about the guy who drowned, and that his body was sent to Austin Hill.

"That's terrible," she says, her levity gone, and asks, "Do you know who it was?"

"No, they're not giving out any details. But I thought you'd want to know, since it's your hospital."

"I am curious, especially since you were right there and saw it. I'll check on Monday to see what I can find out," Karen replies. "I'm glad you're all done and that you're okay! Guess we'll have to wait to hear from the crew how they did when we see them. They're probably all on their bikes by now, right? I hope they do well."

"Yeah—me too!"

When Tessa arrives on the shuttle and we're finally on the road home, we also discuss the drowning but only in a vague, "can you imagine" kind of way. Tessa herself is strong, and smart, and always prepared when she competes, so the possibility that such a fate could ever befall her has never entered my head until now. I look over at her as she drives, her blond hair tangled from the wind, her cheeks sunbaked and salty, and yet as beautiful and vibrant as ever.

The thought is gone before it even fully forms, as I remind myself that accidents like these are rare.

When I get home, I check the event website. There is a brief blurb that says only that a fatality occurred, and that relatives are being notified. Facebook is equally unhelpful, because while there are a lot of comments about whether the organizers should have canceled that portion after all, there are no specifics on who the victim was or the definitive cause of death. There's a report about the race on the regular TV evening news, too, but they don't mention the name of the person who died, only that it was a man in his twenties.

As disturbing as it is to remember the sight of that helicopter, to know that someone in the race drowned, I have no doubt whatsoever that *our* friends, who are all so tough and who have so much experience, are fine, and that I will hear from them soon. My initial sense of real apprehension comes when Karen calls me at exactly 11:51 am on Monday morning. She knows the class I'm teaching ends at 11:50, so this is literally the very first minute that I might actually pick up.

Chapter 2
Whose Body?

"Have you heard from Aspire?" She asks, not bothering with preliminaries. Something is definitely wrong, and I feel those first tentacles of unease tighten their grip.

"Nothing," I tell her, realizing how strange that is. Aspire is the name of the team from Pennsylvania. I certainly should have received at least a text by now. "The race results aren't posted yet, so I was going to wait until after class and then call to ask how they did. Why? Have you?"

"No, not from any of them." She pauses. "I just spoke with Dr. Ben."

Dr. Benjamin Benton (known to all as simply Dr. Ben) is the medical examiner at Austin Hill, and it was through Karen that he and I met. The two of them are work pals who often eat lunch together in the cafeteria. Dr. Ben is a kindly soul, fiftyish, bald on top but otherwise gray-haired and bearded, with twinkling eyes and what I can't help describing as a merry disposition—really, he always seems to me to have an aura of Santa Claus about him. He is also meticulous, devoted to finding and defending the truth, no matter where it leads. The world is a sunny, congenial place for Dr. Ben at all times, except when he is in the throes of his work. Then, he is deadly serious.

"Dr. Ben?" I repeat, momentarily confused.

Karen pauses again and then says quietly, "It was Wryan."

I stand stock-still as I take it in. Of course, I suspected it would have to be something like this, that it had to be one of them for Karen to call. But I'm still shocked by the news, and by the reality of that name in particular. Even as I hear it, definitive and stark, I continue thinking there must be some mistake. It's just not possible. Wryan Burley is—was—one of the founding members of Aspire, his cousin Duke the team captain. Friendly, witty, on a break between medical school and starting residency, Wryan is the perfect all-around athlete for triathlon: powerful swimmer, technical biker, unstoppable runner. How could he have drowned? Aspire is an elite team, somewhere on the line between semi-professional and top-performing amateur. What could possibly have happened? How could Wryan be dead?

"Oh my God," is all I can muster as tears flood my eyes, and I wipe them hastily with the neck of my t-shirt to stop them running down my cheeks. Then, maybe because shock can send our brains scampering in a million nonsensical directions, I ask what is probably the most irrelevant question just at this moment: "Why Dr. Ben? Do medical examiners harvest organs?"

"No, nothing like that. He got involved because Wryan didn't die during the race."

"What? What do you mean?" She's not making any sense.

"It turns out he died hours before the race even began."

"Wait. No way. You don't mean…" I can't finish the sentence.

"Yeah." She breathes out one long, deep breath. "According to Dr. Ben, he was murdered, then placed in the bay to make it look like he drowned."

The news is so unexpected and so horrifying that at first, I just stand in the middle of our small reception area in silence, clutching the phone to my ear. Then, wiping tears again, I make my way around the desk to sit down, so shaken that I clumsily bump into it and tip over a cup full of pens before half tripping and then landing in the chair.

"Lily? Are you okay?"

Of course, I'm not okay; but she's asking about the noise in the background, maybe wondering if I've fainted or something, so I tell her I'm fine.

"How?" I ask. "I mean, what does Dr. Ben think happened? He was alive, he was happy, he was taking care of his mom…" My mind is listing a thousand reasons why it is impossible that Wryan could be dead, and ten times that why it is impossible that he was murdered. It doesn't compute, and I can't fully grasp the fact that none of those things matter. He is dead. Dr. Ben examined his body and pronounced the manner of death homicide, and Dr. Ben does not get these things wrong. My ears ring as absolute impossibility collides with immutable fact.

"I know," Karen is saying, "I know, I know, I know. I can't believe it either. He didn't give me any details, but he did say that they knew something was wrong as soon as they got the body into the helicopter."

She explains as gently as possible how the medevac technicians thought they could save the organs of someone who had supposedly drowned at the start of the race, but the body they picked up had clearly been dead for hours. She adds that they'd had a difficult time identifying him, too, since he wasn't wearing either his numbered swim cap or his ankle chip, and his body had not been marked with his race number either, which was usually done near the starting gate by volunteers with sharpic pens. It was suspicious enough that they got Dr. Ben involved. He eventually found Wryan's name inked on the inside of his wetsuit.

Hours. What does that mean? I wonder frantically. *When exactly did he die?* Out loud, I say, "Are the police investigating? I mean, they must be, right?"

"Yeah, they are. I just saw Detective Ridley at the Nook. I bet he's following up with Dr. Ben."

The Nook at Austin Hill Hospital is an area next to the lobby with a coffee kiosk and comfortable seating. It's busy in the morning and after lunch, when everyone wants a dose of caffeine, but it can be a quiet place to talk at other times. Karen and I have met there more than once. As for Detective Ridley... there's a reason Karen knows him by sight; I know him too. He is a homicide detective for the Montgomery County Police. If it wasn't Wryan—Wryan!—the realization that we are all here again, converging on the periphery of a murder, would have stopped me cold. How many people find themselves enmeshed in a murder investigation even once in their lifetime? It can't be many, but for Karen and me, this is the second time around. We discuss this scarcely credible reality later, when we're together with the whole gang, but the only reality reverberating in my head right now is this: Wryan is dead. Murdered. The police are investigating. I put the phone on mute for a second as she talks, grab a tissue, and quickly blow my nose before speaking again.

"Ridley, huh? Interesting. I'm sure that's no coincidence, but I'm a little surprised. He's county police; the race was at the state park. I wonder why he's involved."

"Oh, yeah! I didn't think of that. There was a woman next to him, and I had the impression they were together. I assumed she was one of his colleagues, but didn't you say his wife is state police? Maybe that was her."

I pull my mind away from Wryan for a moment and picture the two of them: Detective Dan Ridley and his wife Toni, because I met her once, too. That occasion, at least, was innocuous enough. I'd bumped into them as they were going running late one afternoon, training for a marathon. They slowed to a walk, and Dan introduced us, both of them enjoying my chuckle at the revelation that she, too, is Detective Ridley. Washington, DC, is a huge, sprawling city, but the towns that make up its suburbs, Bethesda among them, can be surprisingly small when it comes to bumping into familiar faces.

"Did she look super fit, maybe five-five with dark shoulder-length hair and about the same age as Ridley?"

"Yep."

"Then that's her. They must be working together for some reason."

"I agree. Look, Lily, please don't say anything to anyone else yet. At least, not until the police start talking to people. I mean, I'm sure they're going to want to talk to Duke and the others, right? But Dr. Ben probably shouldn't have told me what he did, and I don't want to cause him any grief."

"I hear you. Not a word."

"Okay, good. You know, though, they might even come and talk to you. You were there on the scene, as it were. You also know the whole team better than any of us, so they might ask you about them, or maybe ask if you have any idea where Wryan was or what he planned to do the night before the race, stuff like that."

I know she's only trying to be helpful, randomly thinking out loud rather than pointedly trying to warn me, because Karen, friend and confidante for so many things, has been kept in the dark about a big one. Today has been a day of surprises, but Karen is in for a few more. While in all likelihood she is correct, and the Ridleys will come to ask me those very questions, they are probably betting the chances are low that I'll have much of value to relay. Anything more than vague generalities would indeed be surprising. Whatever they think they will hear, it is almost certainly not what I will tell them. The fact is, I know exactly where Wryan was the night before the race.

He was with me.

Chapter 3
Last Fall

At first, I don't say anything. I close my eyes and grab hold of a hunk of hair, squeezing it unconsciously. In a way, it's easy to explain, to show how it all makes sense, but of course none of it does, and the weirdest thing of all in this nightmarish chain of events isn't even the fact that Wryan Burley was murdered, which is shocking enough. No, the strangest thing is that we only met because of my involvement in that first murder investigation last fall.

Back then, I was on the tail end of recuperating from a years-long depression, the lasting result of a car accident in my sophomore year of college. At my lowest point, I'd reconnected with Tessa, who invited me to stay rent free in the converted pool house in her magnificent backyard, which encompassed the entirety of what was once the Mattaponi community pool. Watching her swim laps year-round, transfixed by the smooth quietude of her strokes, enticed me into trying it myself.

Swimming both calmed and revived me, and I started to venture back out into the world, landing at the Eye of Horus Yoga Studio one day almost by happenstance. Something about the combination of exercise, routine, and the peacefulness of my tiny but cozy abode helped me heal, and my depression began to lift. Instead of returning to college to finish my degree, I got my yoga certification and became an instructor. Things were falling into place nicely, but after dropping out of college, I'd ghosted everyone I used to know, and I was lonely. I was ready for excitement again, and desperately in need of friends.

On a sunny afternoon in October, I invited my yoga clients to sit in a circle for a cup of tea, which I do after every class. Its purpose is to provide a moment of peace and community before we all re-enter the mayhem of our lives. This time, though, instead of the usual remarks about the weather or upcoming holidays, Karen told us about a suspicious death at the hospital where she works. There were five of us at that tea circle, and we were instantly intrigued. We started seeking out and finding clues to try to help the police, and as morbid as it may sound, our collaborative venture solidified our friendship. Karen, Haisley Gilchrist, Miller Nguyen, Redd Thomas, and I: we were all in it together. What can I say? We didn't know the deceased person, and the more we learned, the more exciting it became. Dr. Ben was the medical examiner who'd performed the autopsy. Detective Dan Ridley was the investigator in charge of the case.

After the culprit was arrested, the five of us remained close. We continued to support each other by providing advice, encouragement, or a sympathetic ear. Even when everything is humming along, every few weeks, usually right after my last session of the day, we'll meet up for wine and conversation. That's what we were doing in June when we met Aspire for the first time.

Chapter 4
June

I distinctly remember the smell of rain in the air as I opened the door at five-thirty and made my way to the Iguana that evening. I spied Haisley as she walked over from her apartment building with her boyfriend, Simon. One year older than I am and a graduate student working on completing her PhD, Haisley is slender in a slouchy, non-athletic way, and pretty, with vivid green eyes and dark auburn hair. She has a brilliant mind that moves so fast that, depending on the day, she can come across as either a super geek or a total airhead. I walked over from the studio with Redd, who'd taken the class, and who is both the only male in our group and the oldest to boot at sixty-something. He's on the tall, skinny side, his ebony skin contrasting with his white-gray hair, with eyes that always emit kindness. Karen, in her mid-thirties and married with two kids, drove over from the hospital and parked next to Miller, who arrived at almost the same time. Miller was born in Vietnam and moved to the U.S. when she was in her teens, and she still has an accent that, to my mind, accentuates her sharp bossiness.

The Iguana, or rather, the Tijuana Iguana Bar and Grill, is your basic little local eatery. Its main attraction for us is its location in the same shopping center as the yoga studio, and early on we adopted it as our regular hangout. Star, eternally upbeat and energetic, is normally the one serving our table, and she is our favorite waitress. We are equally certain that we are Star's very favorite "regulars," although she's never actually said so. She's a year or two younger than I am, dark-skinned and rangy with hair that she has taken to wearing in a multitude of skinny braids, each one sporting a white bead at its end. On that day, she was busy taking orders from a big group but hurried over as soon as she saw us.

"Hi guys! I was hoping you'd come today! Guess what—there's another swim team here, and when I told them about you, they wanted to meet you." She added that this team was staying at the Castlevine Hotel down the street and had been in yesterday, too. Then she turned to look at the big group, who had apparently been watching, and pointed her finger at us exaggeratedly, mouthing, *it's them!* with a huge smile. They erupted in claps and cheers, called out "BEARS!" and waved wildly for us to come over. Of course, we joined them at once. That crazy table looked like fun.

I should mention that the swim team thing is a bit of an "in" joke, although Star doesn't know that. In a show of solidarity with me and to support my first open water swimming event, my friends ordered t-shirts modeled after the old mascot of the community pool that is now Frank and Tessa's backyard oasis. By unspoken agreement, we wear them when we know we're linking up for happy hour.

Even from the doorway we could see that everyone at Star's table was also wearing team attire, although not t-shirts—theirs was nice stuff, obviously sponsored: red track suit slacks with black polo shirts in high performance fabric, all with the Aspire logo. Their clothing brand was one I hadn't seen before—it looked like a stylized, encircled "T" leaning forward, with two artistic squiggles implying the wind at its back—and it was prominently displayed on everything.

As we walked toward them, a girl with frizzy red hair down to her shoulders scooched herself across the bench to make a space and said with a grin, "Hey shorty, sit next to me and make me look taller."

I laughed back as I squeezed myself into the space, instantly certain we would be friends. Short people "get" each other, for one thing, and there was something appealing in the way her entire demeanor exuded a wild-and-free-and-delighted-to-be-here aura. Pretending to size her up, I shook my head. "Thanks for the seat, but I think you might have that the wrong way around."

Her eyes opened wide in delight, and she grinned again as she sucked air in and stretched herself toward the ceiling. "I'm five three. Almost five three and a half."

At this depressing news, I slumped dramatically and groaned, "Damn. Five two here."

The guy to my left, sitting at the end of the table, gave an exaggerated "tsk" and remarked, "Uh oh. We've got the battle of the titans over here." Then, smiling, he held his hand out to me, introducing himself. "Duncan Wells. And pay no attention to Izzie. None of us ever do."

Woah, I remember thinking, because he was dazzling. Seriously, he must be the most handsome guy I've ever seen. I took his hand to shake it lightly, suddenly feeling so shy and inadequate next to this god that I was unable to speak, and barely managed an awkward smile back. Fortunately, I was saved from utter humiliation by Miller, who was trying to force order into the chaos by calling out introductions from her end. Pointing to each of us in turn, she'd gone around the table and finally gotten to me. "That's Lily. She's the only actual swimmer on our team!"

Not only did everyone laugh at this strange declaration, it also provided the perfect conversation starter. We Bears took turns telling the story of our t-shirts, and at the end of it Aspire cheered us, Izzie patted me on the back, and we all made a good-humored pact to keep our "secret" safe from Star.

They introduced themselves too, although it was something of a blur to me. I was distracted in part by my uncomfortable awareness of the proximity of Duncan Wells, who I noticed over the course of the evening the others were calling "Duke." I was fascinated by his glamor, but self-conscious to the point of feeling unworthy. Nevertheless, some of the others did make an impression. Certainly, Nahla Bowman was unmistakable and unmissable; everyone in the bar probably remembers her to this d ay.

Nahla is African American and tall, with the straight back and broad shoulders of a swimmer. Alone among her teammates, she forsook the team uniform and instead wore a sleeveless black and gold knit dress, which matched her shiny gold fingernails. To cap this off, her hair was dyed platinum blond and shaved close to her head, while large gold earrings dangled to her shoulders. The entire effect was stunning. In fact, if I wasn't already so dumbstruck by my neighbor to my left, it likely would have been Nahla who I'd have wanted to stare at all night, and for much the same reason: it boggled my mind that someone could go through life looking so good, while at the same time the insecure devil on my shoulder kept searching for some flaw, some reason not to feel the sharp bite of my own inadequacy. She was the quietest of the group and the most serious, and it was probably fortunate that she ended up next to Redd. While I wouldn't describe him as quiet, he comes across as the calm sage among our rabble.

As the evening wore on and the Iguana got louder, I ended up talking to the girl next to me, Izzie Walker, much of the time because it was difficult to hear anyone else. The ease I felt with Izzie was a relief because I never overcame my shyness enough to engage in any but the most basic conversation with Duncan / Duke.

As for the rest, I remember that Haisley and Simon sat on Izzie's other side, and the two of them were hamming it up with a guy named Carlo, who I pegged as the Aspire class clown. He was responsible for much of the noise emanating from our table, and while he came across to me as a bit juvenile, he was entertaining and unrestrained.

A woman named Gail Ghurani, who had wavy black hair and an intricate tattoo on the back of one hand, sat across from me on Duncan's other side, and she and Izzie took turns launching teasing zingers at his expense, which he adeptly fended off. I enjoyed listening to their breezy back and forth, as well as the opportunity it afforded me to observe him without being too obvious. It was like finding a Siberian tiger in a litter of tabby cats. I kept thinking I would get used to him and not find him quite so mesmerizing, but that didn't happen. Quite the contrary; the more I listened, the more I began to detect the faintest accent when he spoke. There was a tinge of *oi* when he would pronounce a long *i*, and an unusually distinctive *t* at the end of certain words. As the night wore on, the more convinced I became that my ears were not deceiving me, although I couldn't quite place it—sort of British-y, but not quite. Australian? No, not that either, but something. It was captivating. *Dang*, I remember thinking, and then castigating myself for sounding, even in my own internal dialogue, so very prosaically American.

Karen and Miller ended up at the far end of the table chatting with a short-haired woman named Celeste, who could be witty, but her comments came across to me as snarky. Next to them sat Wryan. The irony of the evening is that of everyone we met that day, Wryan made the least impression on me. I remembered his name, though, because Carlo told us they'd dubbed him "Wrong Way" long ago, when he had a habit of getting lost driving his truck to the more out-of-the-way competition venues with no cell service; that, and the fact that the moniker goes so irresistibly perfectly with the spelling of Wryan.

It turned out that Aspire wasn't technically a swim team, either. They were the preeminent core of a Pittsburgh aquatic club, trying to break into the echelons of top international competition. On this occasion, they were in town to compete in a sport I'd never heard of before: underwater rugby. If they did well, they'd be back in a few weeks for the finals.

"It works out that it's such great endurance training, because in July we're doing a three-day ultra triathlon," Nahla had smiled demurely at us. "The one down here by the Chesapeake is the biggest on the East Coast."

When we heard that, we toasted their success in both endeavors, hoping to see them again soon. Star had been right in guessing our two teams would hit it off. There was something about our collective personalities that seemed to work without us having to work at it. Each of us had magically landed next to the perfect set of partners for small talk, while the table as a whole seemed to laugh at anything and everything. It was such an enjoyable evening, loose and carefree. I had a sense that the blossoms of summer were opening up, full of bright and beautiful possibilities.

Chapter 5
Wryan

"He was with you? The whole evening? But... really?" Confusion, astonishment, dismay, and other equally nonplussed emotions vie for primacy in Karen's voice.

"Not all night," I tell her. "But we had dinner together and then he dropped me off at Tessa's, so I showed him the pool."

"Ah." Her inflection brought to that one syllable a myriad of questions and exclamations. On the one hand, it is understandable that Wryan would want to see Tessa's pool, which is as spectacular as it is unexpected. Frank's developer father had purchased a long-closed community swimming pool intending to erect townhouses in the highly desirable locale of Mattaponi, which sits right above the banks of the Potomac River. Instead, he fell in love with the spot himself and decided to build a home for his own family and renovate the pool to resemble a beautiful mountain lake, its surrounding hill of trees emphasizing the sense of seclusion. We'd talked about Tessa and the pool to Aspire before, perhaps in a vague hope of getting everyone together there one day. Nevertheless, from Karen's perspective, it's rather strange that Wryan and I would spend the evening before such a big event here in Bethesda, just the two of us, and stranger still that I didn't mention it. Karen and I get together often and tell each other everything, yet somehow I have left this part out. I take a deep breath and do my best to rectify the omission now.

"We were dating. I wish I could have told you before. Wryan and Izzie had split up, but they weren't going to tell the rest of the team until after the triathlon. They didn't want to start a lot of drama, everyone taking sides, or worse, trying to set them up with other people." I'm shrugging into the phone, remembering the sense of being helplessly constrained by so many secrets, secrets that up until now were not mine to disclose. "Wryan asked me not to mention it to any of the Bears yet, in case word got back. Hearing about it from one of us would have made it worse."

"Oh. Gosh." She's quiet for a beat, and then adds, "Did Izzie know?"

"She did. And you know what? I think she was relieved. She's the one who broke it off with Wryan, but she still wanted them to be friends."

"Oh. Gosh," she says again, and I can hear the wonder in her voice. "So how long were you guys…?"

"Honestly, almost right from the start. I've been dying to tell you, but I just couldn't. I had to wait until Wryan and Izzie told their own team," I blurt out, relieved despite myself, despite the horrible circumstances that have finally set me free from silence.

"I had absolutely no idea." She's quiet for another beat, and then tentatively adds, "But I really meant how long ..." she can't finish the sentence, and my heart starts racing as I realize what she's asking and why.

"You mean that night. Oh my God. You mean, how long were we together that night." Adrenalin kicks in, and my breath starts to come in short gasps. Did he die here in Bethesda? Was I the last person to see him alive? I think furiously, trying to remember. "It wasn't very late when he left; he needed to get to bed to rest up for the early start. Maybe seven-thirty. Eight at the latest."

"And you stayed overnight at Tessa's, right? So you could drive to the race together early in the morning?"

"Yeah. We were together when Wryan left for the Airbnb."

On Thursday, Aspire had decamped from the hotel in Bethesda to an Airbnb in Hillandale, about 20 minutes east. It was conveniently down the street from one of the race's headquarter hotels, and the team planned to pick up their packets and attend the pre-race meeting there early Friday morning. They would then drive to the state park for a test swim in the bay and to stage their bikes before the midday heat descended.

I picture Wryan, so full of life, smiling as he waved goodbye to Tessa and me from his truck. It was still light out, the warm evening feeling more like a late afternoon, giving us the sense of having all the time in the world left to enjoy. I was already looking forward to the next time we'd see each other. Was it love? No, not yet. But there was something there—a spark of potential.

This can't be happening.

Oblivious to my reminiscing, Karen exclaims, "Good. That's good!" and breathes out audibly. "Dr. Ben told me he estimates that the young man in the helicopter died eight to ten hours before race personnel found him. Definitely after he left you."

"Oh, okay." While "good" is not the word that immediately comes to mind for me, I know what she means, and I can't help the flash of relief that loosens my shoulders. That is indeed long enough after he'd left Tessa's for me to have an alibi. I am not heartless or overly self-centered, but this is new and terrifying ground for me. I am a person who needs an alibi.

The relief doesn't last long because another thought immediately enters my head. "Do they know where it happened? I mean, did he even make it back? If I was the last person to see him before he was killed..." My throat constricts, and my voice comes out in a croak. "I'll be a suspect."

"No! No, Lily, of course you won't be. Why would you kill him? That makes no sense. But you really might know something that could help. Think of it that way."

I feel like crying and wipe my nose with a tissue. "Do you think I should call Detective Ridley? Tell him I was with Wryan that evening?" I ask Karen, my voice wobbling at the thought.

She's not sure. On the one hand, this is information they probably want to know; on the other hand, we shouldn't even be aware that Wryan was murdered, never mind know who is investigating it. I agree, and besides, calling Ridley is too scary to contemplate right now. While our relationship is friendly, he's still a police officer, a homicide detective no less. He would see me as a person of interest; he'd have to. The thought makes me queasy.

Talking to Karen, though, calms me down. We discuss the other Aspire members and all that they must be going through. We remember with wonder the first time we all met, and what a riot it had been. In our memories, it seems simultaneously like only yesterday and a lifetime ago.

"You know what? We need to not be alone right now. We need to talk through everything we're learning and everything we're hearing," Karen says, voicing my own thoughts exactly. We agree to meet up later at the Iguana and to alert the rest of the Bears to come too. By then, it should be safe to talk about what's happened. We need friends and familiarity. We need cool, rational assurance. We need a drink. Our plan is elemental but sound, and somehow soothing just to know it's there.

Chapter 6
First Date

When Karen and I hang up, I sit still in my chair and stare into space, absorbing the news and thinking about Wryan. He'd bowled me over the day after that first happy hour by coming into the studio to ask if I'd consider having dinner with him. I'd had no inkling he'd noticed me at all, never mind taken an interest, and so said yes out of surprise, and because of my desperate need for a boost in self-esteem, and because seeing him on his own, without the team to distract me, he struck me as cute, and I liked his down-to-earth smile. We traded phone numbers, and he said he'd pick me up at six, and when he left, I was floating. I don't remember the rest of the day's classes, but I do remember that many of my clients remarked on my cheerfulness.

"You're in an awfully chipper mood today!"

"Nice to see you so peppy, Lily! You must be having a good day."

I had a great day. Wryan and I discovered that each of us, in our own way, was a new beginning for the other—a fresh face and a fresh start. Wryan and Izzie had been a couple since middle school, and while they were acting normally in front of the team, and both of them did want to remain friends, the breakup had been a body blow for Wryan from which he'd had a hard time recovering.

"Do you know the person she's seeing? I mean, is he a friend of yours?" I asked, thinking that losing two friends would literally double the pain.

"I doubt it, but no, I don't know who he is. Izzie's being really hush-hush about him, which is kind of unlike her now that I think about it," he frowned, and then sighed. "She's not a cruel person. She's probably trying to spare my feelings, but that's sort of like offering a band-aid to someone whose leg you just sawed off." He stopped and grinned sheepishly. "Well, not that bad. I've honestly reached the point where I think, hey, let her be happy with someone else. And let me be happy with someone else, too." He smiled gently, sweetly. It wasn't corny or suggestive; it was just... a person who was content, and I absorbed his centeredness enough to relax myself. When he asked me to tell him my story, it turned out to be easy to share, because at that moment the things that had been bothering me the most receded enough for me to consider them and describe them with some impassivity.

I told him that I was on a kind of rebound downturn from the depression I thought I'd beaten, because somehow, in the process of getting healthy and "normalizing" (for want of a better word), I completely lost my bearings. I described how I'd toss and turn at night wondering if everything I've been doing for the past few months has been a waste of time while my age cohort are all continuing apace with the business of life, maturity, and all the generally accepted measures of progress. Wryan, of course, laughed at my woeful assessment but took my dilemma seriously.

"I think you'd be surprised how adrift everyone around you feels, too. Despite appearances, most people are just kind of bumbling through the motions, grappling with the exact same things."

"You may be right about everyone else, but appearances sure are convincing. Most of my high school friends have graduated from college, have jobs with growth potential, and are either dating seriously or are married already. A few even have kids! Haisley's about to finish her PhD, and then she'll be on her way. It makes me wonder: what am I doing? I get paid by the hour, no upward mobility in sight, and I'm sitting here, flailing. Feels a lot like failing."

"Uh, huh. That sounds like head demons talking. Uncertainty about what exactly comes next can do that to you. For the record, you are NOT failing. You're young, smart, fit, doing a job you enjoy, with a circle of friends and family who love you. Some of us might call your current circumstances blissfully unencumbered."

His characterization did make me consider things in a different light, a much more positive one. There was something reassuring about being with Wryan. *Don't get too far ahead of yourself,* my wary side tried to warn me, knowing I was in danger of expecting too much out of a brief meeting with an out-of-town near-stranger. Nevertheless, it was undeniable that we clicked. He was smart and kind, and in stark contrast to his cousin Duke, he made me feel both comfortable and desirable whenever I was in his presence. We never ran out of things to talk about, and we laughed a lot. We hadn't discussed the future yet, but it was there, hovering, as an enticing possibility. There was no hurry. We had our whole lives still ahead of us.

***

I have to get out of here. I can't concentrate and don't trust myself to lead the rest of today's classes as if nothing has happened. I call Will, who gives the evening classes, to see if he can possibly come early today. He can tell immediately that something is up, both because I never do this and because I can't keep the quaver from my voice.

"Sure, no problem. It'll save me wasting time playing video games all afternoon. Be right over."

"Thanks, Will. I owe you big time," I reply, feeling myself tear up again. I must be in shock; anything and everything seems to set me off.

I'm sitting there, waiting for Will and staring into space, when I see Detectives Dan and Toni Ridley outside on the sidewalk. My stomach clenches, and I have an absurd urge to run out the back door. Instead, I watch through the window as they look for the studio. Dan is facing in the other direction, reading the signs above the shops, searching for Eye of Horus, but Toni sees me. She taps her husband lightly on the shoulder, and when he looks around, he sees me too. I wave casually at them. It's ridiculous, of course, given the circumstances, but I do know them, and I can't just watch them stroll toward me without acknowledging them in some way. So, like an idiot, I give the wave.

Chapter 7
The Ridleys

"Hi there, Lily," Dan Ridley greets me as he enters the studio, sounding friendly enough. "Long time no see, huh? You remember my wife, Toni?"

She smiles at me and says, "Hi Lily," as I nod and smile back, sitting up straighter.

"Of course. Hi. It's nice to see you. Sort of." I add this last with a wry expression, looking rapidly first at him, then at her, then back again. I'm on high alert because it doesn't matter who you are or what you have or haven't done; talking to the police is scary.

"Well put," replies Ridley with his own slight smile. "I take it you've heard the news about Wryan Burley."

It's strange having them here, visiting me on official business, because they're not strangers. It's not that we became friends last year, but I guess I got to know Dan Ridley better than I thought. Everything about him—the slight smile, the intonation of his voice, the way his shoulders set when he begins his questions—is familiar to me. It dawns on me that even though our interactions took place over a brief period of time, we still managed to have quite a few conversations, some of which mixed the personal in with the professional. I remember how he took me seriously back then, despite my relative youth, my naivete, and frankly, my recklessness in my search for clues, and that I'd appreciated it so much it had (inadvertently on his part, no doubt!) spurred me to want to do more, to impress him, to prove myself worthy of being taken seriously. I overstepped, and while everything turned out fine in the end, he's still leery of me and I'm still intimidated by him. But we're also kind of fond of each other. We have history together, occasionally thorny such as it was. All of this is playing out in the background, rendering our meeting both daunting and somehow companionable, almost nostalgic. I sit back more comfortably, no longer dreading this visit.

Toni seats herself on the only other chair, and after a brief look around at his options, Dan settles himself on the windowsill. They don't seem surprised that I know something already, probably assuming one of Wryan's teammates called and told me, and I say nothing to dispute that conclusion.

"I heard he died," I tell them, "And that it was his body that was airlifted from the beach the day of the triathlon. But he didn't drown? He died before the race even started?"

"I'm afraid so. Wryan's teammates mentioned they'd met you and your friends a few times at the bar and grill here. We were hoping you could tell us a little more about him and about the rest of the team."

"Okay, sure, but... what happened to him? I mean, if you're looking into it, does that mean you think someone killed him?" My voice rises to a squeak, as despite my conversation with Karen, I still can't quite believe such a thing could be true. The look on my face must be more than ordinarily stricken, because while the Ridleys don't actually look at each other, I sense some silent communication pass between them.

Toni leans toward me and replies very gently, "He was strangled, Lily. I'm sorry. Was there something going on between the two of you?"

If you're already emotional, kindness is the worst. It wrenches open the floodgates you are so desperately trying to keep shut, and there is no defense. I look into her worried eyes and feel my throat tighten, my nose clog, and my eyes begin to swell. I manage to choke out, "We'd been out a few times," and then just blubber. It's awful; I try to hide my eyes with my fists, but I can't stop this heaving, ugly crying. I shake my head in apology, but it's all I can do just to breathe without actually wailing. Dan Ridley grabs the box of tissues sitting on the windowsill next to him and passes it over to me. I probably go through half the box before the shuddering slows and I finally begin to come to myself.

"Sorry," I mumble.

The Ridleys are taken aback, no question about it, so surprised they actually do turn their heads to look at each other before zeroing in on me again.

"I'm so sorry," Toni repeats. "His teammates didn't mention it, and we had no idea the two of you were involved."

"It's okay. It was just starting… we hadn't told anyone else yet." I grab yet another tissue to blow my nose one more time, and then we all sit for a moment in silence.

"Strangled? You're really sure? Could it have been an accident?"

"No, this was no accident. He was strangled by a long strip of nylon, very possibly the zipper pull attached to his own wetsuit. But he didn't die in the water, so someone must have brought him down to the beach and put his body in the waves."

Hearing Ridley's account, the reality of it starts seeping in, and at this point all I can think is *why? Why? Why?*

I know that's a question no one can answer yet, so I ask, "Where was he when he died? Do you know?"

"We're not sure yet, which is why we're working this together for now," says Toni. "They were all staying at an Airbnb in Hillandale, which is on the Montgomery County border, so that's likely where he was. It's possible, though, that he went somewhere else, maybe even the state park."

They tell me he died sometime between 10 p.m. and midnight, and ask me if I'd talked to him that day. I'm ready for them, for this question, and relay the information about our early dinner with relative calm. "He dropped me off at Tessa's because he knew I planned to stay the night there. Tessa and I had to leave early the next day to get to the beach and into our kayaks."

Dan makes a note, and I look back and forth between the two of them, but neither says anything right away.

"That's awfully late," I charge in again. "Why would he go all the way to the state park, especially since it was dark? He wanted to get to bed early."

"It's baffling, but he was wearing his wetsuit, and it's almost impossible to get a dead body into one of those, so he must have put it on himself. Do you have any idea why he might have done that late at night? Do you think he may have intended to go for a swim?" Dan Ridley asks.

"I doubt he'd go for a swim, especially not all alone in the dark, but I'm not surprised he put the wetsuit on. That was part of his pre-race ritual." I explain that Wryan had told me he'd once arrived at the start of an important race only to realize he'd forgotten both his goggles and his bike shoes. He'd scrambled to borrow from other people, but the bike shoes he'd eventually scrounged wouldn't properly click into his pedals, and he'd had to drop out. He'd sworn never again, so the night before a race, he got into the habit of donning first all of his swimming gear, then changing into his full bike kit, and finally into his running apparel, before packing each piece into his race bag. "He told me it's become a good luck charm for him. He's never again forgotten to bring all his stuff, but he said going through the motions helps settle his nerves, especially if he can't get to sleep," I add.

"I see." In an aside to his wife, Ridley adds, "I told you she'd be helpful." Toni smiles briefly, but then her phone buzzes, and she glances at the screen.

"I'd better take this." She walks toward the door as she answers.

"So, after Wryan left, you stayed with Tessa for the rest of the night?" Ridley asks.

"Uh-huh."

Toni comes back inside and shakes her head at Dan, but doesn't say anything else. Ridley himself doesn't react to his wife other than to pause long enough for her to re-seat herself in the chair.

"Do you own a car, Lily? Any kind of vehicle?"

I shake my head no. "Just my e-bike."

"What about Frank and Tessa's vehicles? Did you have access to them?"

I shake my head again, no longer able to find my voice. Dan and Toni are both looking at me. Are they assessing me? Are they waiting for more? Are they imagining I could possibly be responsible for this? I freeze in terror.

"I mean, do you know where they keep the keys? Or do you have any of the spares, maybe left over from the time you were living there?" Ridley prompts, and I open my mouth, but no sound comes out.

Toni leans in again, encouraging me. "Take your time, Lily; we know this is difficult for you, but there's nothing to worry about. We just need to ask these questions now so they don't come up later. Are you okay?" She's being so gentle, an absurd thought pops into my mind: is this like on TV? Are Dan and Toni playing good cop, bad cop with me? A sudden urge to giggle comes upon me so suddenly I barely manage to quash it. *What is wrong with you? Jesus!* This is just who they are. Dan Ridley isn't being mean; he's naturally a down to business kind of guy. I don't know Toni very well, but she seems to be someone who is authentically more in touch with her softer side. Even if this weren't the case, they would not be playing hackneyed cop games with me. But at least my internal digression serves the purpose of mollifying my terror enough so that I can answer in a reasonably normal voice again.

"Yeah, I'm fine," I assure her. My mind is all over the place, and my emotions are out of control, but I do want to answer their questions. I want to help if I can, although that seems impossible right now. "I don't have any keys to their cars. As far as I know, Tessa keeps hers in her purse, and Frank usually has his in his pocket."

"Okay. And you didn't hear anything more from Wryan that night or the next morning?"

"He did text me once. I assumed he sent it right before he went to sleep." I pick up my phone and find our last text string, our messages so short it isn't even necessary to scroll to read them.

Wryan: Thanks for a great evening! [blowing-kiss]
Me: I had a nice time too! Good luck tomorrow! [smile + heart]

There's a tiny heart appended to that one, where Wryan had "loved" it.

I get a lump in my throat when I see them in all their light-hearted nothingness, feeling the full brunt of the reality that these are absolutely final, no further additions will come, and I swallow hard as I give the phone to Toni Ridley. She takes a look and shows it to her husband, who checks the timestamp and nods.

"What about Isla Walker? When was the last time you had any contact with her?" Ridley asks now as his wife hands me back my phone.

"Izzie? I don't know... We all had our last happy hour together at the Iguana on Wednesday evening. We wished them good luck, and to my knowledge, they all left Bethesda the next day for their Airbnb."

"You didn't see her on race day?"

I shake my head no. "I'd been hoping to see them all, but the way it worked out, I barely saw anyone." I explain the irony of having volunteered in part to get a close-up view of the race, but those of us in kayaks had our own safety meeting to attend in the morning, and then we had to paddle into the bay ahead of the first swimmers. Once in the water, the conditions made it nearly impossible to see much of anything.

I fall silent, watching Dan Ridley take notes. It takes a few moments before the oddity of his change in tack makes its way to the front of my brain.

"Why are you asking about Izzie? Is she okay?"

The Ridleys glance at one another, and Toni raises one shoulder the tiniest tad. Dan answers, "That remains to be seen. No one's heard from her, and no one seems to know where she is."

"Izzie's *missing?*" I ask, dumbfounded. This is getting even more bizarre.

"Well, we're having trouble getting in touch with her, and that's starting to get worrying. Do you have any idea where she might be?"

"No, none. If she's not with the others ..." I raise my shoulders and let them drop, completely flummoxed. She and Wryan had broken up, but they were still friends, and the rest of the team were practically family to her. There's no way she would just disappear if something happened to any one of them. The ramifications of this fact make me feel slightly ill.

Toni's phone buzzes again, and she glances at it. "Meet you in the car," she tells her husband. She raises the phone to her ear but still gives me a friendly nod before going out the door.

Dan remains on the windowsill, shaking his head and sighing at me.

"Lily, Lily, Lily. I know you want to help."

I open my mouth to leap in, but he holds up one hand to stop me.

"I absolutely do *not* want you to get involved in this investigation," he says sternly, staring directly at me.

I glue my lips together and don't make a sound, waiting for him to continue. He sighs again, but this time he smiles briefly before speaking again. "However, there is something I think you can do. It's likely that Wryan died either because he knew someone or because he was involved in something." He pauses, and it takes me every ounce of self-restraint I command not to jump in with more questions. He closes one eye and considers me intently with the other. Then he opens it again and continues. "I suspect that you know a lot more about Wryan—and the whole Aspire team—than you give yourself credit for, not only because you two were dating, but because I recall how naturally observant and interested in other people you are. If you take some time and think back, you might remember something that can help us." He reaches into his jacket pocket and withdraws a card, which he hands to me, saying, "That's what I'd like you to do. If something comes to mind that strikes you as unusual or important, give me a call, okay?"

He gave me his card last year, and I'm sure I still have it, although I'm not sure exactly where I put it. I take this new one and carefully place it in my pocket, promising Ridley I'll do whatever I can.

"Okay then. Let me know if you hear from Ms. Walker—your friend Izzie—too."

I promise I will, and with that, he gets up from the windowsill and stands looking at me. "Take care, Lily," he says. "And remember, don't go looking. All I want from you is what's already in here." He taps me lightly on the forehead and looks significantly at me, letting me know he's not kidding around when he says don't get involved. Then he goes through the door and joins his wife in the car. She looks over at me briefly, and this time it's Toni who gives a little wave before driving off.

I feel a well of emotion I can't quite describe. I'm blown away by Ridley's comment about me, and that he actually thinks I might know something useful. I stand up and pace to the window and back, too agitated to remain seated. Can it be true? If I can sort through my memories, I might find the key. It seems incredible, but I probably do know a lot more about Wryan and his team than I realize. I became embroiled with them in a significant way very quickly, first, because I was dating Wryan, and he talked a lot about his life, including Aspire; and second, because Izzie came to me for help with something so delicate she could not share it with the people she knew best.

I sit down again and swivel lightly in my chair, staring at the ceiling. Izzie. Where is she? Why has she disappeared at the same time Wryan was murdered? My heartrate quickens again, but this time it's from determination. I must not let my friends down. I *must* help the police figure this out.

Chapter 8
Lily

*B*ut *what if I can't? What if I can't remember anything important?* I think to myself, my heart pounding even faster, once again out of fear. I am afraid of failing. It's that feeling you get when everything is on the line, and you know you must give the performance of your life, but your body is suddenly weak and clumsy. It's as if everything that has been going on with me for months—the good and the bad—are coming together at this one, all-important juncture, and I'm not sure which will come out the winner.

The good was really, really good. My October high from the murder investigation that spawned the Bears stayed with me through November and I flew through the holidays. Things got even better with the start of the new year. I was "promoted" at work to a minimum of 32 hours per week, which meant not only a bigger paycheck but benefits, too. The world around me seemed to fall into place, lavishing me with turns of good fortune all of its own accord.

One of those happenstances was around MLK Day, when Haisley clomped through the snow and into the studio. We don't get a ton of snow in the DC area, so when we do, schools, churches, and government offices tend to shut down, and she had an unexpectedly free afternoon.

"Hey!" I greeted her with a surprised smile. "You do know our next class doesn't start for another 45 minutes, right?"

"I know, I know!" she laughed back, because Haisley has been a client here since before my time, and can recite our schedule in her sleep. "But it's gorgeous now with the sun shining off the snow, and I wanted to get out. Also … I wanted to ask you something. Do you have a minute?"

"Of course!" I waved her to the chair by the reception desk, my curiosity piqued. "What's up?"

Haisley explained that her roommate, Jen, won a poetry fellowship in England. They were both on the hunt to find someone to take over her share of the lease while she was away. "Am I totally cuckoo, or would you consider it?"

I opened my eyes wide, staring at her for a moment, the proposition having come so out of the blue as it did. The idea immediately grabbed me, even though it didn't make any sense. At the time, I had about the sweetest living arrangement anyone could imagine, living rent free in my very own petit but private house at Tessa's. And yet...

I've always loved the fun, funky vibe of Haisley and Jen's apartment building. A lot of the inhabitants are young, twenties and thirties, and the management holds all kinds of community events—I knew that, because Haisley has invited me to some of them. I felt the pull to get out there again, to start meeting new people. The serenity of Mattaponi was beginning to feel ever so slightly like isolation.

The apartment itself is bright and modern, with two matching master suites, perfect for the two of us. Also, I commute by e-bike as I don't own a car, and while I enjoy it most of the time, it's a whole different story when it's rainy or icy, and in the winter, it's dark when I ride to and from work. How nice it would be to live less than 10 minutes away on foot.

All of these thoughts were ping-ponging around my head as I sat staring in wonder at Haisley that afternoon. What I said was, "Jen writes poetry?"

"Aaaargh!" Haisley exclaimed, sinking low in her chair and burying her head in her hands. She groaned and sat back up, shifting her feet and causing melted snow to drip onto the floor. "If it's artsy and creative, she's great at it. I love her to death, but I swear, Lily, sometimes I really hate her too. She expects success to drop in her lap, and it always does. It is seriously enervating." She was joking as she said this, but she was wistful too, and I sympathized. Haisley was having a very hard time with her thesis and was starting to fear she'd never get her doctorate. "But you're stalling. It's okay to say no, but before you do, you should know that Jen's parents have offered to pay half of her half of the rent if you'll take care of her pets while she's away." At this, Haisley flashed a huge Cheshire cat grin, knowing this would make the deal irresistible.

I couldn't believe it. I would love to take care of Jen's pets. She has two cats in addition to little Otto, her mute teacup-sized dog, and a turtle named Putt Putt. For a luxury apartment in tony Bethesda, my quarter portion of rent would be laughably low, and while still a stretch for me, definitely doable, especially with my new work hours. I covered my mouth with my hands, merely nodding at her with shining eyes. Then we both leaped up, screaming, hugging and dancing around the room. It was a dream come true; one I didn't even know I had until that day. Moving to Haisley's felt like stepping out, like making a final break from the crumpled, woeful version of Lily that had lingered for far too long.

Alas, what goes up must come down, and as winter turned to spring, my big bounce began to subside and the shadows started to creep back in. It wasn't depression so much this time, but rather its malevolent sidekick, anxiety, that began to take hold. For months I've been lying awake nights telling myself I need to get a move on, but when I wake up, I'm totally lost and I just kind of go through the motions of living. During the day I'm fuzzy and scatterbrained, and the more anxious I become, the worse it gets. When people say things to me, all too often either I won't hear it or I instantly forget what they said.

It's only late at night that my mind finally engages, gnawing and scratching at every lost opportunity and every aborted plan, exhorting me to *DO SOMETHING!* But what? My nocturnal planning is a handful of sand that dribbles from my fingers, all but the dust gone by morning. Each day wasted only worsens my disquiet and my self-doubt.

Meeting Wryan should have been the final capstone, my shining knight appearing right on cue to sweep me off my feet, the two of us bound in eternal love and happiness. And possibly, ultimately, that would have happened—the worst thing about a curtailed future is that you can never know how that particular story would have ended. But I was in such a befuddled state over what was going on with me that I was almost oblivious to what was going on with us. With Wryan, as with everything else, all too often I was only half listening, half present.

My fear is that I've been so distracted, so absentminded, that I didn't pay attention when it counted. What if it's true that somewhere along the line, I came across a critical piece of information, a clue to the *why* and even the *who*—but it got lost in the ether of my own brain fog? This is the bad, and if the dual mysteries of Wryan and Izzie do not get solved, the bad will have won.

If I'm going to conquer that villain, my first task will be to figure out how to regain my focus and tap into my mind's eye. If a clue is in there, I must find my way to the key to unlock it.

Chapter 9

The Notebook

When Will walks in, I thank him profusely, and on a sudden whim grab a pen and notebook from the desk before quickly taking my leave. Since I don't trust my memory, my idea is to write down any thoughts that come to me before they disappear. Instead of heading home, I make for the dog park and the quietude of its myriad adjacent walking paths, because I need to think, but I'm much too jazzed to sit still. About twenty minutes later my phone rings, and while it's an unknown caller, the area code is the same as Wryan's, so I answer. Sure enough, it's one of his Aspire teammates.

"Lily? It's Gail. I'm sorry to surprise you like this. The waitress from the Iguana gave me your number; I told her it was an emergency."

"Gail! Hi! It's fine. I'm glad you called. Is it about Wryan?"

"So, you already know what happened?"

"The police were just here, asking questions about him and Izzie. Apparently, they can't locate her."

"That's why I'm calling. I'm at my wits' end, and it occurred to me that the two of you seemed to have become friends, so I was thinking maybe... hoping really... that she was with you and neither of you knew."

"Oh. I'm sorry. She's not here, and I don't know where she is either."

Gail puffs out air on the other end, frustrated and clearly worried.

"I've been racking my brains for any possible ordinary explanation, but I'm running out of ideas."

"Where else have you checked?"

"I spoke to her mom, and I also got in touch with one of Izzie's neighbors who also happens to swim at our club. They carpool occasionally, so I figured *maybe* she'd seen or heard something, but of course she hasn't. I know Izzie would have told someone on the team if she'd gone home for some reason, but I couldn't imagine anywhere else she'd be. Then I thought of you."

"I wish she was with me. I'm so sorry," I say again, because I too am at a loss.

"Let me know if she gets in touch, will you? You have my number now."

I promise I will, and ask her how long the team will be staying in town, as Wryan had mentioned going back to Pittsburgh right after the triathlon.

"We don't know yet. Duke, Nahla, and I were planning to stay the week in a short-term rental in Chevy Chase, anyway, because our main sponsor wanted us to participate in a trade fair downtown. Now we're all doubling up so that Celeste, Max and Carlo can stay too. The police haven't told us we can't leave, but no one wants to go until we know more."

Max, I should mention, is the eighth Aspire team member. He hadn't been there the first time we all met, but we'd gotten to know him in our subsequent happy hours. Shaggy blond hair, bright blue eyes, ripped body, Max is the quintessential California surfer dude, and he was the one Karen and Haisley giggled over when it was just us. To me, though, he doesn't hold a candle to Duke in the looks department, and by the time I met him, I was already falling for Wryan. He comes across as a gentle soul, though, and endearingly shy. Miller loves to tease him and make him blush.

"I get that. It's awful enough that Wryan is gone, but you all must be going mad wondering what happened and why. Is there anything I can do for you while you're here?"

"No, thank you, but I was going to try to contact you guys anyway," Gail says, "because Wryan really loved our joint happy hours. We were thinking of getting together one more time tomorrow to remember him. Do you think the others would be interested?"

"They definitely would. We loved our joint happy hours too, and I'm sure we'd like to see you all before you leave. It's a perfect way to commemorate Wryan," I burst out with heartfelt certainty. It wouldn't seem right for them to leave town without us all being able to say goodbye.

"Okay, then. I'll text you the time, if you could let the others know. I just hope we have news about Izzie before then."

"Thanks, Gail, me too. You guys take care."

We hang up, and I look down at the notebook I'm holding in my other hand, which now has a damp spot where my sweat has seeped through. I'd been galvanized earlier, my thoughts coming in rapid fire from all directions. Now, though, I feel sad and suddenly lethargic. It's swampy hot, and the sun is so bright I have to squint, which is giving me a headache. I'm not hungry, but even so, I'm craving the comfort of food and turn around to trudge back up the sidewalk. The news of Wryan and the disappearance of Izzie are almost too much to bear, and I can't get home fast enough to our cheery apartment. I'm in desperate need of a cool drink and the soothing aura of two sleeping cats and an adoring miniature dog.

I'm about to tuck my phone into my back pocket when I notice on the home screen that there are a bunch of new texts. I open the phone again to take a look and see that one is from Tessa, saying she'd heard the news and telling me to call or come by if I want to talk. The others are all from the Bears, everyone pinging about whether we've heard what happened. Toward the end, Karen and Redd both start asking me why I'm not responding, that they're worried about me. I feel a little bad and am about to text back when my ringtone goes off again, and this time it's Karen.

"Thank God you're okay!" she says as soon as I answer.

"What do you mean? Why?" Not only is it an odd way to start a phone call, the alarm in her voice has me spooked again. "Has something else happened?"

"No, but you didn't respond to the text string, and I thought you were at work, but when I tried the studio, Will said he was subbing for you today. I was starting to worry that maybe you got, I don't know, arrested." She ends with a titter, as if to acknowledge that saying this out loud makes her realize how ridiculous it is, but I'm touched by her concern.

"No, nothing so exciting. I couldn't concentrate on work, so I asked Will to take over early. But as a matter of fact, while I was waiting for him both Ridleys came to the studio to talk to me. Afterward, I needed a walk and some fresh air. I'm just seeing all the messages now."

"Ohh. Good. Good, good, good," she sighs in relief. "I guess that's good. Or did it feel like they were grilling you? Were they normal or ultra-official?" She asks, her tone of voice evolving from relieved back to tight and distraught.

"Just normal. Actually, they were both really nice. They could tell I was upset. No one read me my rights or pulled out handcuffs."

"Ha ha. Make fun if you must, but I really was starting to worry! I'm glad they were nice. Did they ask if you've talked to Izzie? Apparently, they can't get ahold of her, which is so weird right after Wryan... I mean, do *you* know where she is?"

"No. Ridley did ask, but I don't know, and I haven't heard from her. But I'm certain there's no way she'd just disappear and keep quiet all this time unless something serious had happened."

"Yeah. That's what's scaring everyone. Are you still coming to the Iguana later? Or does that seem insensitive? It's not a happy hour; it's that we all want to be together. We want reassurance, if that makes sense."

"It does, and I'll definitely be there. I want to be with you guys too, and I think that's normal. In fact, Gail just called to tell me they want us to come meet them there tomorrow, in memory of Wryan."

I give her the gist of the rest of my conversation with Gail, and when we hang up, I respond to the string to let everyone know I'm fine and that I'll see them later. As I'm walking, I call Tessa next and give her a quick rundown about my visit with the Ridleys, and she tells me Dan Ridley came to see her too.

"He was asking about the night before the race, and when Wryan left. I know that's just part of the routine, but it was a creepy feeling," she tells me.

"Definitely creepy," I agree. "I mean, there's no way I could be a suspect, right? Like, what if I thought Wryan and Izzie had gotten back together, and I was jealous? Maybe they think I took your car, drove over in a rage, and killed them both."

"But they hadn't gotten back together. He asked you out for the evening."

"Yeah, but sometimes it doesn't matter what really happened; people just assume things. What if the police suspect me because they think I thought they were together?" As soon as I hear myself say this out loud, I let out a slightly hysterical cackle. It's a release of tension, not from seeing any of this as funny, and I'm thankful that Tessa understands. She dampens the hysteria with reason.

"That's a lot of people thinking some pretty outlandish thoughts, Lily. I really can't believe that their investigation won't turn up more likely suspects than you."

"You're right. I'm sure that's true. Wryan never mentioned going anywhere else after he left us, did he? I don't remember him saying anything like that."

"No, and I got the same impression: that he wanted to get back and get to bed early. He was pretty focused on doing well the next day, so I can't imagine he had late-night plans."

I feel mildly better. If Wryan had said something important while he was with us, Tessa missed it too. I still feel guilty that I'd been so caught up in my own world not to be concerned when I hadn't heard from Wryan all weekend, but I tell myself there was no reason to be concerned. Wryan had been excited about the race, happy to be with me, and not in the least distracted—neither he nor I could have had an inkling that anything was amiss. *What changed?* I ask myself. *How could mortal danger spring up that suddenly, taking him so unawares?*

Chapter 10
Learning About Our New Friends

When I get home, Otto greets me at the door, jumping up and down, making his "Huff! Huff!" sound, which is as close as he ever gets to a bark. I pick him up and hold him close to my chest, feeling his happy wiggling. Then, I make myself a sandwich with extra mayo and add several handfuls of chips to my plate, not even bothering to look for a healthier option, and move over to one of the comfy chairs to sit down. Sure enough, Dee Dee, the white cat with black rings on her tail and ears, comes sniffing over and leaps into my lap. I give her some mayonnaise and a kiss, and she settles down, purring. It's not the most comfortable position for writing, but I manage to prop my notebook on the armrest because I'm ready to focus now and record my memories in some kind of order.

***

The evening of our first happy hour, it was raining hard when it was time to go, and Wryan ran out to pull the truck around to the door so all of them could squeeze in for the short trip down the street to their hotel. It had looked like a clown car, and we Bears stood in the doorway to wave them off, everybody laughing merrily. Wryan—showing the first hint of what I later discovered to be his trademark self-deprecating sense of humor—honked the horn and then drove the "wrong way," making an entire backwards circle (we could hear the girls inside shrieking, even with the windows up) and stopping for an instant exactly where he'd started before heading in the right direction out of the parking lot.

We then went back to collect our things and thank Star for getting us together, and the six of us ended up standing around the bar for a bit and going over our impressions of the evening.

"I knew you guys would hit it off!" Star grinned at us smugly. "The first time they came in, something about them reminded me of you."

"You flatter us," Karen smiled. "They were great, but I felt a little like a boring bumpkin next to them. They all seem so impressive, you know?"

"You got that right," Miller touched her fingers one by one and pretended to wrinkle her nose in disgust as she listed all their attributes: "good-looking, fit, successful, smart..."

"... and then that one guy with the accent? Oo la la la!" agreed Haisley in an absolutely horrible imitation of an accent of indeterminate origin. Cockney? Welsh? Pakistani? Impossible to tell, and the rest of us burst out laughing.

"I knew he had an accent! It's like I heard it and then I wasn't sure. I wonder what it is," I exclaimed, gratified not to have been wrong.

"I have no idea what *that* was," said Miller, indicating Haisley with her head, "but yeah, there was something about the way he talked. I've been wondering where it's from, too."

"Africa," said Redd, surprising us. "He grew up over there." We gaped at him.

"How do you know that?" I asked.

"I thought he was from Pittsburgh!" said Karen.

Redd chuckled and shook his head. "His mom is American, but he was born over there. His dad and his grandfather were big racehorse trainers. He moved to Pittsburgh to live with Wryan's family when he was eleven or twelve."

"How do you know all that?" I asked, agog.

"Nahla told me. She said Duke is one of the main reasons she joined the team, and she got to know that side of his family when they did a triathlon together in South Africa last year."

"Wow," said Karen.

"Yeah, wow," added Miller. "I didn't think Nahla could talk."

I had to laugh, because Nahla had indeed been very quiet the entire time, markedly different from the rest of her teammates. She didn't seem shy or unhappy, just very solemn in the way she interacted and carried herself. I admired her gravitas, but the flip side of that is that when she turned her staid gaze upon me, I instantly felt immature and a little foolish in her presence.

"Hey, now," Redd admonished gently. "I know she comes across as serious, and she doesn't say much, but Nahla's got a lot going on in that head of hers. She's ambitious as hell, and she thinks Aspire is a team that can catapult her where she wants to g o."

He told us Nahla not only wants to reach the pinnacle of her sport as an athlete; she also wants to become a model and a spokesperson to encourage more people of color to take up competitive swimming. She founded a charity to provide access to swimming pools, teachers, and coaches for underprivileged children. "She's got a GoFundMe page and everything, but Duke helped her take out a personal loan to get it all started."

I give a quick whistle at that. "Ambition *and* initiative. Impressive."

"Still waters run deep," said Karen, to which Redd nodded with a knowing "M'm h'm."

Star had to leave us at that point to work her other tables, and the interruption was enough to make us turn and check the window, noting that the rain had passed. We knew we weren't finished with the conversation, but it was later than we'd meant to stay, so we decided to hit pause until next time. It was the first of several such evenings in which we collectively learned so many interesting things about our new friends.

***

In my notebook, I make different pages for each Aspire member and start to fill in what I'd learned about their backgrounds, their families, and anything else that might become relevant. I'm hurrying, scribbling, because time might be running out. It's not just Wryan, who is already dead; there's also Izzie. Where is she? Is she alive? Is she in trouble? We need to find her. Fast.

Chapter 11
Third Eye

I'm writing and pondering when Haisley walks in.

"You're home!" she exclaims, doing a double take when she sees me.

"Yeah. I took the day off," I tell her.

She puts her things down on the bench in the entryway and comes closer, looking at me.

"What happened?" she asks. Haisley has spent the morning huddled with her professor, going over comments and corrections to the latest draft of her thesis. Buried in academia, she is probably the very last person to know.

"You didn't see our texts?" I ask, and she shakes her head, pulls out her phone, and starts scrolling.

"Oh, my God! Wryan? Wait! (she reads further) What? No way!"

She looks over at me, and then down at her phone again, rereading the string. Then she comes over and lowers herself onto a chair, staring at me. "I can't believe it."

"Me neither." I press both my hands into Dee Dee's fur, the better to feel the comforting hum of her motor.

For the past two months, Haisley has been distant, not on purpose but because she's had a lot on her plate. She'd met Simon, for one, and as the relationship grew more serious, its requirements grew too: time, emotional investment, head space. This coincided with her being in the thick of the grueling slog toward finishing her thesis. Her distance hasn't bothered me, as I knew these things were important to her, and I wished her well. Today, though, when I need her the most, she has reappeared.

It's like old times, the two of us kicking back in the living room talking, talking, talking. Our coterie of animals shows up as if to celebrate our reunion: Haisley's enormous flop-eared bunny Archie hops over and falls asleep on her lap, mimicking Dee Dee on mine; Otto settles on the floor between us; Putt Putt the turtle of course is always present in his terrarium on the bookshelf, but now even Dexter, Dee Dee's shy tuxedo brother, has tiptoed in, seating himself at the edge of the carpet, looking from one to the other of us. Here in our living room, all is comfortingly right with the world.

I tell Haisley everything that has happened, starting with Karen's call, filling her in about the fact that Wryan and I had started dating—including the night he died—as well as the fact that Izzie is missing, and end by showing her my notebook. I watch as she leans back against the couch pillows, skimming it pensively.

"I think you're onto something," she says.

"You do? Where?" It's not what I expected, and I stand up, cradling Dee Dee, and lean over her to see what she's reading.

"No, I mean, this is a good idea. You probably do know a lot, maybe even the motive behind all this. It's not here yet," Haisley taps my notebook, "because you're still processing everything. But you should keep this up."

I return to my chair, and Haisley studies me earnestly. "It's interesting that Ridley thinks what you remember could turn out to be the key to solving the case. It might be true."

No pressure. The murder of someone close to you is about as compelling a wake-up call as it gets. But is it too late? The fear from earlier rears its head again, and I swallow hard, then take a deep breath in and let it out slowly. Dee Dee settles back on my lap immediately and seems to sense that I'm stressing again. She doubles down on the purring.

"I'll write down everything I can think of, but I've been so out of it lately. What if I've forgotten all the important stuff?"

Haisley considers me earnestly before answering. "Yeah, I've noticed that." She frowns to herself, stroking Archie. "You've definitely been kind of out of it. Miller says your chakras are all out of whack." She looks up and grins. "But you're the Eye of Horus expert; you can get them realigned and bust your way through."

"Huh." I stare back at Haisley. She's not making fun of me; she's being serious, and, interestingly, she might have a point. I sit at the epicenter of all manner of avenues to refocus my brain, but I haven't even realized it because—duh—I'm not thinking clearly.

The Eye of Horus from which my studio takes its name is an ancient symbol of health and wellness. In particular, the eye is associated with the notion of rebirth and reawakening, and most closely equates to the concept of the third eye chakra of Eastern philosophies. The third eye is vital for self-knowledge, and if it is blocked, it can impair your self-awareness and your intuition (your "second sight"). The most common symptoms of a failing third eye chakra are a feeling of being lost and directionless, of general fogginess, and struggling to hear and heed your inner voice. Check, check, and check—these have been my issues all along. Could Haisley be right? Is this energy center out of balance? If it is, I need to address it now, because here's the kicker: the third eye is also instrumental to the brain's ability to store and recall information.

I consider my practice and the tenets of Eye of Horus teaching: body, mind, and spirit are all one, each contributing to a whole that is something more than the sum of its individual parts. Chakras fit with this perspective because they, too, can have physical, mental, and spiritual connotations. Why has none of this occurred to me before? If any of my clients had come to me asking for help with these symptoms, I would have been onto it immediately, but it's too late to worry about that now. One of the most effective remedies for problems with this particular chakra is a simple one: meditation. That is to say, simple but not easy. An anxious mind is one that is wild and jumpy, always in flight but rarely with direction . It is difficult to slow it down, to empty it of thoughts, or at least to watch them come and go without reacting emotionally, but that is what I must train myself to do.

"I'm glad you said that," I tell Haisley. She smiles and leans over to return my notebook to me, taking care not to disturb Archie. I stand up to leave, but then remember to ask her, "By the way, how did it go with your advisor?"

"Oh, jeez," she laughs. "It was awful. There were so many problems. But you know what? I feel kind of good. I know what I need to do now."

You and me both, Haisley. You and me both.

Chapter 12
Taking Steps

Haisley takes Archie with her back to her room, and I get changed and take the elevator up to the rooftop pool. This is yet another of the features of Haisley's apartment that really sold me on moving here. She invited me over one day to hang out for a while and gave me the tour, and I'd dreamed of testing its waters ever since. It is every bit as amazing as Tessa's, but in a completely different way. The surrounding patio is replete with lounge chairs and grills, and a hot tub that can fit a good ten people, while the pool itself is "L"-shaped. A beach style entrance into the water on the short side leads to concrete chairs for sunbathing and relaxation, but it's the long side of the "L" that provides the real wow factor, because it stretches out beyond the edge of the building and has a glass bottom. Swimming up and down the farthest lane, you can see people on the sidewalk far below. The first time you step from the roof area to the glass-bottomed area is terrifying, but once you get moving, it's as if you're flying.

At this time of day, the roof is empty. I drop my towel on a chair, don my swim cap and goggles, and wade in, making directly for that extraordinary overhanging lane. When I was living in Tessa's guest house, I'd often sit with a cup of coffee early in the morning and watch through the window as she glided up and back. It was so peaceful, Tessa's movements fluid and steady, that the scene always put me in a state of Zen. Now, the act of swimming myself does much the same thing. Unconsciously, I start counting my strokes, which has the effect of quietening my mind and keeping the worst of the errant thoughts at bay.

As I do each lap, I watch the people pass unwittingly below. It's such a different perspective, this bird's-eye view. Instead of individual piece parts, everyone and everything look like component elements of a system that is ticking along, with each constituent doing exactly what it needs to do, what it is supposed to do. I take this to heart, interpreting it as evidence of universal connectivity, and that each of us is playing the role we are supposed to play—including me. In this context, I see that my relationship with Wryan, Izzie, and team Aspire may well have happened for some cosmic reason, regardless of whether I succeed or fail in my quest. I speed up, completing my final twenty lengths as fast as I can. My goal is to tire myself out and make myself breathe hard, so that when I get out and relax on my chair, I can slowly empty my mind, paying attention only to the pace of my breath slowly returning to normal.

Meditation is not something I've done consistently before, so I decide to start very simply: count my breaths, in and out, up to one hundred. Will it work? I don't know, but I must try. At the moment, it is the only thing I can do, and Izzie is still out there, as is Wryan's murderer. Memory, clarity of thought, intuition — these are things I want, I *need*, to tap into now, and urgency lends diligence to my intention. I count my 100 breaths, and then remain in my chair, unmoving, my eyes closed against the sun. I breathe in and out, in and out.

Nothing happens.

No revelations materialize; no hidden truth emerges. I'm not surprised, but I can't help feeling disappointed and a little foolish. I wrap my towel around me and return to our apartment to continue writing in my notebook, but instead lie back on the bed and fall into a deep sleep.

Chapter 13
A Discovery

Around five o'clock, Haisley and I walk together over to the Iguana. Lately we've had Simon along more often than not, and while I like him well enough, today I'm happy for it to be just us again. Back when we first started meeting here, trying to help find the culprit behind the suspicious death at Karen's hospital, five heads proved better than one, as each of us went at the problem in our own unique way, contributing some piece that finally unveiled the mystery. Now we have another problem, one that is sickeningly close to home. This one isn't entertaining; it's a gut punch, and even though I don't know yet exactly how they can help, I know I need them. I've been looking forward to this unhappy happy hour for much of the day.

We're the first to arrive, and Star comes over to the table right away, apologizing to me about giving Gail my number. "I would never normally do that, but I know you guys are friends, and she seemed really desperate. I hope it was okay?"

"Yes, absolutely. I'm glad you did, and I'm glad she got in touch," I assure her.

"Oh good. Is everything all right?"

I exchange a look with Haisley, and then tell Star about Wryan, and about the fact that Izzie is missing, and ask if by any chance she's seen her.

"Oh my God," she gasps, bringing both hands up and laying them against her chest. "That is so awful. I had no idea." Shaking her head emphatically, she says, "No. Gail asked the same question, but she didn't say why." She drops her hands and stops shaking her head, as if a thought has struck her. "You know, though... I think she may have left her phone."

"Whose phone?" asks Miller. I didn't see her come in with Karen, but they're both here now, grabbing chairs and sitting down.

"Izzie's!" I whisper to Miller, and then turn back to Star. "Really? Someone left a phone? How do you know it's hers?"

"I'm not sure, but there's been one in the lost and found drawer for days. Usually, if someone forgets their phone, they either come back right away or call us. As far as I know, no one's asked about this one. It's pink, so probably a girl's phone, right?" She looks from one to the other of us.

"Is it still here?" asks Karen, with me chiming in simultaneously, "Can we see it?"

Star nods and hurries off, returning with a slightly beat-up phone in a salmon-pink cover. Was Izzie's phone pink? I can't remember, so I try calling her, but it goes immediately to voicemail. Star points out that this one's battery is dead.

"How long has this been here?" asks Karen.

"Awhile," Star says, frowning. "Someone found it and brought it to us on Friday or Saturday, but it could have been left even earlier. It's been here at least a few days, at any rate, which practically never happens. Like I said, people usually notice pretty quickly when their phone is missing."

I hand the phone back to Star slowly, because it's hard for me to bring myself to let it go. Izzie has been missing her phone for days, and that is not something she would ever not notice. My first thought is that it is proof that she, too, is dead along with Wryan, but I can't say it out loud. I don't want to let go of the phone, because I'm not ready to let go of Izzie herself.

Star puts the phone in the pocket of her apron, and no one bats an eye when she suddenly takes a seat at the table with us. She knows the significance of the unclaimed phone, too, and the news of both Wryan and Izzie is hitting her hard. Star always seemed to enjoy the hurly-burly of the Bears and Aspire crowded together around a space that was really too small for that size of a group. We were probably a pain in the neck as she hurried to fill orders and clear space to put them down, all while keeping tabs on who got what. Even so, I think she liked us, and for our part, she was always part of the fun. She definitely belongs here now.

Redd comes over and registers no surprise that Star is sitting with us; all he does is smile warmly and take the seat opposite. Miller tells him about the phone, and he closes his eyes for an instant and then opens them, shaking his head.

"Mm mm mm," he says, and we nod in agreement.

"I think you should tell the police," Karen says, and Redd agrees.

Star looks across at them, eyes frozen wide, shoulders hunched.

"I can let them know," I tell her. "I know the lead investigator, and I need to talk to him anyway. There's something else I want to tell him."

Karen looks over at me curiously. "I know where he is," she says, "if you want to see him now."

"Really? Where? And how do you know?"

"Dr. Ben was moaning at lunch today that Ridley roped him into coming to the public service careers expo at the rec center." She grins and adds, "He said he'd agreed in a moment of weakness, and that Ridley only wanted him to come to be his excuse to have a beer after."

That gets a chuckle out of all of us, and I look at my watch. Karen notices, and says, "I can drive us. It's from four to six, so if we go now, we should catch them just as they're finishing."

The thought of immediate action gives me cold feet, and I look over at the others. "What do you guys think? Should we?"

"Yes! Get out of here," Miller orders us, while Redd gives a more muted nod in agreement.

"Let's go," says Karen. "We all want to help, and the sooner we tell the police about the phone, the better." This time it's Star who nods in agreement and passes me the phone.

"Okay. You're right."

We gather our things to go; I tell Haisley I'll see her later; and the rest of the gang wishes us luck. Karen and I climb into her SUV, quiet at first, as she pulls out of the parking lot.

"Do you think Ridley really invited Dr. Ben because he thinks he's lonely?" I ask as she makes her way slowly through the rush-hour traffic. Karen confided to me over the winter that Dr. Ben's wife left him, and that they are now in the throes of a divorce. They have one daughter, but she is in college in Massachusetts. He's been leaning on his friends and colleagues to fill the void, and Karen eats lunch with him now almost every day.

"Probably. They're really good friends, and he must know how hard Dr. Ben is taking his separation."

We glance at each other and have to laugh, because we've both made identical frowny faces. Even so, I feel bad for Dr. Ben, because he's such a kind soul and I like him a lot myself.

"I think it's a good thing that he's there, regardless of why. He might have something to add that he wouldn't normally tell us," Karen says, and I nod in agreement. I was thinking the same thing.

Chapter 14
Izzie's Secret

"Their ears must have been burning," Dr. Ben says as we approach the booth. It's a few minutes to six, and almost empty. Most of the exhibitors are already breaking down their tables, but the row of police / firefighters / EMTs is staying the course until the very end. Dan Ridley and a young uniformed officer are standing desultorily by their display, Dr. Ben having commandeered the only chair.

"We were hoping you'd still be here," Karen greets them brightly. "You weren't talking about us, were you?"

"Ladies. Good evening," Ridley says. As usual, he doesn't quite smile, but his tone is welcoming enough. Neither he nor Dr. Ben answers her question.

"We might have found Izzie's phone," I blurt out without preamble, holding it out to show them. I explain about Star and the Iguana, the timing of when it was found, and watch as Ridley takes the phone gingerly with two fingers.

"You're sure this is hers?" he asks.

"No, we're not sure," I shrug, "but we thought it made sense because she hasn't been answering calls or texts. Her number goes straight to voicemail, and this one's battery is dead."

"I see. Thank you for bringing it. If it really is Izzie's, it could be very helpful and save us some time." He grabs one of the free bags meant for prospective recruits and places the phone first in the bag, and then in his jacket pocket.

Someone has unfolded another chair for Karen, and now she sits side by side with Dr. Ben, the two of them watching us expectantly, as if they're settled on the lawn at Wolf Trap waiting for the show to start. The young policeman is packing brochures and trinkets into boxes, leaving Ridley and me alone to talk.

"Actually, there's something else," I pipe up, trying not to stutter. "I'm not sure anyone else knows this, but Izzie had a boyfriend. I don't know who it was, but she was keeping him a secret from the rest of the team." I shrug. I'm shrugging a lot, probably out of nerves, but I need to stop. It must come across to Ridley as adolescent. "I don't know if he has anything to do with her disappearing, or Wryan, or anything, but I thought you should know about him."

Ridley looks over at Dr. Ben, and then back to me. "The only boyfriend of Izzie's anyone's mentioned, including her parents, was Wryan. You're absolutely certain?"

"I'm sure. Wryan told me Izzie left him for someone else, and then Izzie told me herself."

"She confided in you? That's interesting. Why do you think she did that?"

"I think she was at her wits' end. She needed a friend, but everyone she knew was connected to everyone else. And I was here." This is true: it was as if I had dropped out of the sky at the moment of her greatest need, an instant friend with no strings attached, and thus someone who could be trusted completely. Izzie was in desperate need of a friend she could trust.

***

Aspire returned to Bethesda on the Monday before the triathlon. They were in town early to do some promotional interviews, and I suspect they chose the Castlevine so we could congregate together in the Iguana. We'd become accustomed to sitting in the same seats every time, and I was once again next to Izzie. At one point she lowered her voice so that only I could hear and asked if we could get together, just the two of us, in the morning. I was surprised, but I could tell from the way she asked that this was important, so I told her to meet me at the studio at 7:30.

She was waiting for me when I arrived at 7:25, and looked tired, as if she hadn't slept, her eyes slightly puffy, but she smiled when she saw me.

"Thank you," she said as I unlocked the door and ushered her into our reception area. "I feel like if I don't talk to someone, I'll explode. You're the only person I know I can trust."

I was flattered but also incredulous at this declaration, and my curiosity mounted, but I didn't want to put her off her stride, so all I said was, "Of course, no problem. What's wrong?" and then just listened.

Izzie raked her fingers down her face and then opened her eyes to look back at me in despair. I felt so sorry for her, whatever her predicament. She was used to being surrounded by teammates, admirers, Wryan, and, presumably, her family. What could have happened? Whatever it was, she landed here, all alone and in need of advice because, for what may have been the first time in her life, she did not know what to do.

"I think I'm pregnant. I'm almost sure I am. It's not Wryan's; it's someone else," she added quickly, seeing my face. "It's such a mess, not at all part of my plan for this year. I took precautions; I'm not an idiot, but somehow, I guess..." She looked at me, chagrin chasing perplexity across her face, and raised one shoulder in defeat. "Now I just... I don't want to face this. I don't know how to do this."

She grabbed a tissue from the box on the windowsill, but she didn't start crying. She dabbed her eyes anyway, as if expecting tears, but maybe she was all cried out. I looked over at her wan face, incongruously paired now with that exuberant, springy red hair, and felt myself awash in sympathy.

"Almost sure or absolutely sure? You tested?" I prompted.

She rocked her head from one shoulder to the other in a way that suggested not exactly.

"I started gaining weight, like, for no reason. I felt like I was ballooning up, and nothing worked to lose it again. Then I started feeling nauseous almost all the time. That made me suspicious, so I bought an at-home pregnancy test."

"And you took it? It was positive?"

"As a matter of fact, it was negative, but I probably did it wrong or something. The nausea won't go away, and I feel so tired, like I have no energy at all. I'm totally out of it, as if even my brain is tired. I took another test yesterday, and it said negative, too, but they're all the classic symptoms, Lily," she said miserably.

"Have you missed a period?"

Izzie lifted one shoulder and let it drop. "I think. Maybe. I'm not sure. I don't get a period very often; they're really sporadic, so it's hard to say. But what else can it be? I've been traveling for a few weeks now and haven't been able to see my doctor. I've actually taken three home tests since I started suspecting, and they're all negative, but maybe it's too early. Or maybe I'm just one of those people who get erroneous test results. I mean, it has to be that I'm pregnant, doesn't it?" She looked at me, desperate for a reason to hope that the negative results were correct, but not daring to allow herself to go there. She needed affirmation from someone else that there could be another reason for her symptoms.

The gears in my head started to turn. Izzie said she took precautions, and those tests are pretty good. Something else might really be going on, and I had an idea what that might be.

"Look, I know you know this, but you really should go see your doctor and get a blood test when you get home. For what it's worth, from what you've told me, I don't think you're pregnant. I think your symptoms might be caused by something else."

"You do?" She looked at me but shook her head, still afraid of hope. "Like what? I've never felt like this before, and everyone knows these are the signs," she said miserably.

"Maybe, but they're also pretty generic. They could mean a lot of different things. Here's an example: I've noticed that last time and this time, you only drank iced tea at happy hour. And last night some of the guys teased you about it—like you're suddenly drinking a lot of tea all the time. Is that true?"

Izzie gave a snort and nodded. "It's supposed to help you lose weight, so yeah, I've been drinking it a lot. It's not helping, though."

"Have you always been a tea drinker?"

"No, almost never. Up 'til now I've always been a coffee person. Why?"

"Because tea, especially black tea, which has the most tannins, can cause nausea in some people. If you aren't normally a tea drinker, you may never have noticed how it affects you, and now it's hitting you hard. Try backing off, or stick to just herbal teas like ginger or peppermint, and see if you feel better. That could be all it is."

"Really? No way. You think that's it?"

Now it's my turn to lift my shoulder and let it drop. "I don't know, but it might be."

"But what about my other symptoms? What else would cause them?" Izzie looked down at herself and prodded her stomach with her finger. I certainly couldn't see anything remotely like a bulge, but I didn't discount her concern. Elite athletes are usually aware of very minor changes in their body weight and composition that are not obvious to the rest of us. I had a theory, though, based loosely on my own change in habits as a result of living with Haisley.

"Didn't you say you hosted an endurance runner from overseas for a few months? I remember you telling us about her, that she's vegan and she doesn't use gels or powders, but instead takes her own homemade fuel when she goes running."

Izzie nodded her head, but she was giving me a baffled look, as if she wasn't quite following why this was relevant.

I was thinking about Haisley, how she lets go when she's out on the town, but at home she is extremely careful about what she eats, which includes a lot of organic vegetables, some fish or occasionally white meat chicken, and virtually nothing processed or sugary. I'd been pleased with myself for having made a lot of healthy changes in my own diet in the past few years, but next to Haisley I felt like a big galumph. I found myself imitating more of her eating habits and making the same recipes she did. The shift has been good for me, but I wondered about Izzie.

"The thing is," I explained, "if you haphazardly stop eating animal proteins but don't make other changes, you can miss some key nutrients. Unconsciously changing your diet to something more like your guest's, but maybe not as complete, while still doing the kind of workouts you do could end up stressing your whole system and running you down."

"Yeah, maybe... I don't know..." Izzie responded skeptically, but I could tell she was considering it.

"You might be taking in more carbohydrates than you're used to without realizing it, which could cause weight gain; or if your vitamin D levels drop really low, it can affect your appetite and metabolism, including making you gain weight and feel lethargic. Then there are things that might be happening with you that have nothing to do with your diet—maybe something's up with your hormones, or iron... really, Iz, there are a lot of possibilities."

"Huh." She looked at me with interest. "Maybe."

"Either way, if you felt like you were 'ballooning' and then went into restriction mode to counteract it, it could all just spiral. If you're not eating enough of the right things, it would be surprising if you *didn't* feel tired all the time. The tests could definitely be accurate, and you're not pregnant."

"Jesus," Izzie looked at me, shaking her head, her eyes wide. "Je-*sus*. Maybe that is it. Not pregnant, just stupid." She let out a deep breath, her shoulders loosened, and I could see relief all over her face. "You really think that's all it is? I've been tearing myself to pieces about this; being pregnant right now would ruin everything." At that, her eyes welled up and her lips started to shake, but she took another deep breath in and let it out, and managed to smile.

"Do a real check!" I laughed. "Get tested by a doctor! Not knowing for certain is only making you feel worse. And whatever the result, take it step by step. Don't get overwhelmed by trying to figure everything out all at once."

I'm not sure if she heard me about not getting overwhelmed too soon, but she went to the restroom to clean up, and when she came out, she looked a little less worn, a little more spunky. As she was gathering her things, I noticed a ring on her hand that I hadn't seen the night before.

"That's a pretty ring!" I exclaimed, because it was, and because I wanted our conversation to end on something positive.

She held it up for both of us to admire, and said, "It was my grandmother's. She gave it to me to wear for good luck, although I'm so afraid to lose it that I almost never do. I put it on this morning because I really needed some luck, and because it reminds me of her, which is comforting. And you know what? It worked!" she added with a huge smile.

"I like it—it's simple but unique."

"Thanks."

Izzie gave me a big hug and left the studio with a bounce in her step. Later that evening she sent me a text:

Couldn't wait! I went right to urgent care. Negative!! vitamin D & iron both low and thyroid may be underactive—need to see doc when I'm home. You're amazing!!

The rest of the line was filled with heart emojis.

***

"My goodness," says Dr. Ben. "Quite a deduction, Lily. Perhaps I should be trying to recruit you to the medical field."

I grin awkwardly and hope I'm not blushing, not sure what to say, but glowing with his praise. Karen slowly lowers her hand from covering her mouth and says, "Seriously! Lily, you're incredible," which is nice of her, but now I'm definitely blushing.

"So, she wasn't pregnant," says Ridley.

I shake my head no. "She wasn't, but the whole thing bonded us, you know? If she'd been home in Pittsburgh, I don't know if she would have come to me, but down here she did. So, if she had run into trouble while she was here, I really do think she'd have called." I stop myself from shrugging and add, "But she hasn't."

"No. Well. This is certainly useful information. And thank you for bringing the phone—I'll have it checked out. You have absolutely no idea who this new boyfriend was?"

I shake my head. "I should have asked. I wish I'd asked. But I didn't want to pry."

Ridley looks at me and then gives his slight smile. "You're a good friend, Lily. You were right not to pry. And you were right to bring this to my attention. It's exactly the type of information I was hoping you might have gleaned. Don't beat yourself up for doing the right thing."

His praise makes me want to cry, so all I do is nod back and look over at Karen. As usual, she reads my mind and hops up from her chair. Taking over, she tells them she's my ride and she needs to get home, and then steers me gently out to the car.

"Poor Izzie. She was always so bubbly; I had no idea."

"You weren't supposed to know; that's sort of the point of a secret."

We smile mirthlessly at each other.

"Do you want to go back to the Iguana, or just straight home?"

"Home, James. They've probably left by now. We can catch everyone up together when we see Aspire tomorrow."

"You're right. Okey doke, but please, call me Jim."

The rest of the way home, we discuss the boyfriend, because another thought has occurred to both of us. Maybe finding that phone is a reason for hope. What if Izzie truly is alive but unable to make contact? Was she involved with someone who turned out to be dangerous? She might be a kind of prisoner, too afraid of him to dare reach out.

"What if he and Wryan had a fight?" I turn and look at Karen. "Wryan got killed..." I stop.

"What?" Karen glances over at me, noticing I've gone pale.

I don't answer right away, unwilling to put to voice the last part of my thought: what if Izzie witnessed her new boyfriend kill Wryan, and that's what scared her? What if he forced her to help him move Wryan's body into the water, and they are both in hiding from the police? In a certain state of mind, could Izzie possibly act in that way?

Finally, I say, "What if her new boyfriend killed Wryan and then forced Izzie to go with him somewhere?"

Karen stares grimly ahead and makes a careful turn before she responds. "If that's what happened, she could still be alive. That's the main thing. If she's alive, Ridley will find her," she assures me. "You're helping him find her by telling him what you know, even if it doesn't seem like enough to you."

Karen is right, of course. There's still a chance that Izzie can be saved. I know I know more; I just have to remember.

Chapter 15
At a Standstill

It's slow through the center of Bethesda, where there are lots of stores and restaurants all crammed together, and thus lots of cars, lights, and pedestrians. At one point I look over and see the little international market, which reminds me of my tea lessons. Going to these wacky but fascinating sessions had been a first step in my attempt to regain my sense of who I was and what I should be doing. It was Karen who'd suggested I give them a try one day when I described how stressed and unsettled I was feeling. Instead of going over my conversations and impressions from today, I find myself pondering our discussion from months ago.

***

"I really don't mean to complain," I sighed, "because it's not that anything is bad right now. It's more like I'm at a standstill when I need to be on the move—but I don't know what to do." I paused, collecting my thoughts and trying to decide how to explain what I was feeling more clearly. "A normal, full life requires growing, and I'm not growing," I concluded.

"I'm not sure I agree with that, but I see how much it's bothering you." Karen leaned back in her chair and knitted her brows together in concentration. "I think you should follow what you love and let things develop from there. Don't worry about where it will go, just focus on getting better at that."

"Um... okay..." I'd been hoping for something a bit more specific, and squinted skeptically at her.

"I mean it. For example, you like tea. You always talk about whatever mix you've picked for the day at the studio, and you tell us why—sometimes it's a taste, sometimes it's because it's calming or rejuvenating or whatever. It's a huge interest of yours, so why not follow that?"

"Tea?" I stared back. "Follow my interest in tea? But that's not... I mean... where could that lead?" I gave a laugh and added, "You got me, though. I was expecting the usual 'go back to class and finish your degree' line, so you definitely get points for originality!"

Karen blew on the fingernails of her right hand and shined them on her shirt in mock pride. "Why, thank you. But seriously, from my perspective, I don't see passion for that in you right now. I do know you love your teas. We all see that." She leaned back in her chair again, smiling at me knowingly.

I'd swear sometimes Karen can read my mind. Her suggestion came as a complete surprise, and my first reaction was truly, *What? That's crazy talk*. But there was something else, too. I felt a spark. And from the way she was looking at me, I could tell Karen saw it. For an instant, my heart leaped, and the primitive part of my brain squealed with glee—*Yes! Cool! That'd be awesome!*—before reason sprang up and took back the reins. I mean... tea?

"Didn't you tell me there's some Russian woman who gives lessons about tea in the upstairs room of that store near the metro?"

Good memory; I'd mentioned this some time ago.

"Ye-e-es... but it's forty dollars a class."

"And this is what, once a month?"

"Every three weeks."

"Uh huh. And how much does it cost for classes to finish your degree?"

At that, I grinned a little sheepishly. "A lot more. But for a degree, I could get a student loan."

"For forty dollars every three weeks, you wouldn't need a student loan. You doth protest an awful lot. How about this? Take one class. If it's not worth it, then don't take any more." Karen shrugged and threw up her hands. "No harm, no foul, no big deal."

As usual, she'd gotten me thinking. The reason I had mentioned the unusual notice about the tea lessons was that it had intrigued me on the spot. I had convinced myself it was foolish and a waste of money, but Karen didn't see it that way, and my initial excitement at the idea flared again. I wanted to take a leap, to do something, and this was something. I decided to go to the next session, if nothing else for the relief of taking at least some kind of action.

It turned out to be one of the weirdest classes I've ever attended. Madame Klimenkova is the woman who gives them, and I soon learned quite a bit about her: she is, in fact, ethnically Russian, but she grew up in Ukraine. Later, she lived in France for a long time with her husband, who was also Russian but a French citizen. He was offered a teaching position at George Washington University, which is how they ended up in the States. She speaks five languages, but her accent is so heavy I could barely understand a word she said, made worse by the fact that she never seemed to stay on topic. My first class was supposed to be about what makes the main types of tea different—black, green, white, etcetera, and it sort of was, but she kept getting sidetracked, talking about history, and her own past, and literature, and philosophy. For the first half hour or so, I sat there dazed, trying to figure out what was going o n.

After a while, though, I started to get used to the accent, and then it was almost hypnotic. The more I listened, the more impressed I was with her wealth of knowledge about tea, and the more interested I became. It was a wild ride, but I learned a lot. For example, it was from one of these classes that I'd learned tea tannins can cause nausea. Perhaps tea lessons are not such a waste of time after all.

***

"What are you smiling about over there?" Karen breaks into my reverie.

I glance at her, slightly abashed. "Nothing really. Just thinking."

"Aargh! Quit with the wandering daydreams and get with it!" I castigate myself, furious; but then I realize something. I wasn't daydreaming. I mean, I was, but not in a bad way. I'd just had exactly the kind of memory jolt I've been aiming for, because as we'd passed the store, and I'd thought about Madame Klimenkova, I'd had a feeling that this was important, and not just to me in general. It was important to me *now*, to what I'm doing *now*. How can that be? It's impossible, ridiculous. But I know I'm right.

Chapter 16

Madame

We're almost at my apartment, but I close my eyes and think back to my last lesson. I arrived a few minutes late, and came racing up the stairs, but when I saw the door was already closed and they'd started, I stood there stock still, too afraid to go in but not wanting to miss it. Madame is very strict, and I am terrified of her. She's old-world conservative, where manners and etiquette reign supreme, while I'm comparatively a bit of a hot mess and always tongue-tied in her presence. Nevertheless, her stern exterior hides a soft heart, and for some inexplicable reason, she seems to like me.

She could see me through the window in the door and beckoned me to enter. I kept apologizing and took my seat as fast as I could, certain she must be terribly annoyed, but she wasn't.

"Lily, come in!" I heard her greet me in her heavy accent. "Is no problem. Sit, sit. I understand, you get here as soon as possible. Of course, you have your job; you must bring bacon to your house."

Karen pulls over to drop me off, and I realize I'm grinning like a moron again, but she doesn't seem to notice. We wave to each other as she drives off, and as I turn to go through the front doors, I stop for a second before very slowly pushing them open and walking through. I've suddenly had the strangest feeling—something I can't articulate. It's so light, it's not even a niggle; it's a hint of a niggle. Intuition? Insight? A memory on the brink of surfacing? I can't begin to put my finger on what it means, but as soon as I'm back in the apartment, I take out my notebook and write, *bacon?*

Chapter 17
Last Date

I lie in bed very late the next morning. I told Will yesterday that I need to take the week off. In his own way, Will is a kind person, and while we don't ever see each other outside of work, we've been the two key partners at our studio for years now, and we take care of each other. He understood immediately and told me not to worry, to take whatever time I needed, and that he would call the corporate office to organize a substitute.

Haisley poked her head in briefly to make sure I was okay and offered to take Otto out for his morning walk. I heard him huffing when they came back, but since then all has been quiet. She is either in her room or at the library revising her thesis. Eventually, I decide I want some tea and toast, and get up very carefully (so as not to disturb Dee Dee, still fast asleep, stretched out languidly across her two-thirds of the bed) and go into the kitchen. I'm not thinking straight, and I immediately forget my original intent and instead help myself to the remains of the coffee Haisley made earlier and a big bowl of Captain Crunch. The sugar hit is scrumptious, and I go back for a second bowl. I'm debating going back for thirds, but I stop myself and decide a little fresh air would be a better choice.

Without a true destination in mind, I take my e-bike out along the Capital Crescent Trail to the C&O Canal towpath. This beautiful tree-lined route is my old commute to Tessa's, and since I'm going that way, I decide to stop by and see if anyone is home. To my surprise, I arrive to find a full house. Instead of going directly around to the back as I used to do when I lived there, I ring the front bell and Frank opens the door.

"Lily! Perfect timing! Now the gang's all here," he greets me and leads me through to the kitchen. I see that he is working from home, his laptop and papers spread across the kitchen island.

"They're all in the pool. Did you bring your suit?" he asks.

Unfortunately, I hadn't had the forethought to bring my bathing suit, but I go through the French doors out to the pool deck, anyway. Not only are all four kids playing in the water, but they each seem to have a friend, so there's quite a crew. Tessa, lounging on a recliner float, calls out, "Lily!" when she sees me. This gets the kids' attention, and they jump up and down in the water, waving and echoing her with their own shouts of "Hi Lily!"

I wave back and sit on the edge of the pool, having removed my shoes to dangle my feet over the side.

Tessa paddles with her hands to guide her raft over to me. "Did you bring your suit?" She asks.

"Nope. I didn't know I was coming here when I started out this morning. Hey, is that Phyllis?"

There is a big rock grotto with a sliding board in the middle of the pool, and when I first sat down, I spied an older lady taking turns with the kids going down the slide. I've just now recognized her as the second wife of Emil Corbin, Frank's father. She moved back to Florida to be closer to her daughter after Emil died, and I'd only met her a few times, years ago, but I'd always liked her—she has a quick sense of humor and an appealing sparkle to her.

"Sure is! She's staying in the guesthouse until the end of September. She's doing a half ironman and asked if we could train together. How could I resist? In fact, I've signed up for the race to do it with her," Tessa says, her face alight with anticipation.

"Hurray!" I exclaim with a huge smile, because I know that Tessa must be overjoyed. She's told me in the past that she feels torn when she takes on a big race, because the training is so time-consuming that she always feels like she's shortchanging everyone else in her life. But in this case, she is prioritizing Phyllis, so the time spent is an act of love, which appeases her inner conflict.

"Wait a minute," I say when the whole of this news has seeped into my non-optimally working brain. "Phyllis is doing a *half ironman*? How old is she?" I ask.

"Seventy-three," Tessa laughs, used to this reaction. "She's done a ton of triathlons in her life, but told me she really wants to do seventy-point-three at seventy-three."

"Whoa! Phyllis is a badass!" I say, sincerely impressed.

"That she is," agrees Tessa.

We both look over at the island where, just at that moment, Phyllis races across the top of the rock and leaps, flipping backward before entering the water. I can't believe it. The whole pool—all the kids, me and Tessa, and even Frank, who has been standing watching through the French doors—erupts in cheers. Phyllis looks surprised when she pops her head up, but takes it in stride, laughing and blowing kisses back at all of us.

I always thought I wanted to be Tessa "when I grow up," and I still do, but now I want to be Phyllis when I'm a grandmother. I watch as she goes back up the slide to continue playing with the kids, so full of life, and energy, and joy. How did she end up like that? What is her secret? I wonder again at my own inability to get on with my life. Did Phyllis become who she is by her own design or by chance? She looks so carefree, as if everything has come easily, and I have to remind myself that she's been through her share of hard times.

"Hellooo!" Tessa calls and splashes me. I've spaced out again.

"Sorry. I was lost in thought."

"No kidding. Do you want to talk, or shall I leave you in peace?" Tessa looks over her shoulder at the noisy pool. "Not that this is peaceful."

I give a laugh. "Honestly, I'm not sure what I need. I was on my bike and suddenly here I was." I lift my hands, palms up, in a "who knew?" gesture. I tell her about having the week off, and that I'm trying to concentrate on remembering everything I can about Wryan and Izzie, in case there's something buried in my subconscious that will help the police.

"Interesting, but why not? Since you're here, let's do a deep dive into something, like, tell me about your last date. What did you guys talk about over dinner?"

Looking around at the pool and the hill of trees, I remember that this was the last place I saw Wryan. It had been a surprise ending to a surprise get-together, and it had unfolded so perfectly. It was just a few days ago, so I remember it well.

Wryan and I had already said goodbye just before the team left for their Airbnb, and I'd wished him success, believing I wouldn't see him again beforehand. But then on Friday he'd called me in the afternoon, saying he was back in downtown Bethesda and asked if I was up for an early dinner somewhere simple. I was surprised, but had no other plans in mind and so said "yes" right away. He picked me up in his truck, and we decided to go to Guardado's for tapas. Since it was early, it wasn't crowded, and we had a quiet corner in which to relax and chat.

"He was in a really good mood," I tell Tessa. "He was so pumped about the upcoming race." I lapse into silence, thinking back, because I've just remembered something that gives me a chill: we'd actually talked about murder. We'd been laughing because I'd been describing my ill-fated attempt at a doing a podcast a few months ago. My vision had been convoluted: take old screenplays of whodunits and do a "true crime" style review of the "evidence" to determine if the wrong person was "convicted." It was fictional, but it was still murder.

The podcast had been Miller's idea, which should have been my warning to beware. The end result, which had included recorded "interviews" with "witnesses" and "experts" (played by the Bears, naturally) had had the five of us doubled over laughing when we listened to the final playback. We'd botched our roles horribly, and I abandoned the project forthwith. At the time, I was frustrated at having wasted so much time on an effort that was doomed from the start. What comes to mind now, though, is Miller's striking observation when she'd first brought it up. "The light comes on when you're hell-bent on solving a crime, and you're good at it too." It had sounded comical when she said it, but she was right. I'd never felt so invigorated, so on point, and so resolute as I had when we were looking into Karen's suspicious death case. At least, not until now.

Despite my shock and my grief, I can feel my focus starting to sharpen, my brain grinding into gear, and my senses waking up. I'm hell-bent on solving another murder, *Wryan's* murder, and that in itself is revitalizing me and giving me purpose. There's something momentous about this realization.

"You there, Lily? Or have I lost you again?" Tessa waves her hand in front of my face. So maybe my spaciness isn't cured, but self-awareness is evidence of progress. *Three steps forward, two steps back.*

"Sorry," I grin and kick my feet to splash Tessa. "I was just reliving the evening. We confessed our esoteric hobbies to each other."

"Cute! Let me guess: yours was tea. What was Wryan's?"

"Pinball! Or, more specifically, fixing their broken circuit boards."

Tessa was correct — I had described my fascination with all things tea-related to Wryan, but I don't think he was nearly as surprised by this as I was when he'd said his secret passion was pinball.

***

"You mean like video games? Or the real thing, where you shoot the ball and use those little paddles to keep it in play?"

"Playing real pinball, sure, but mostly I fix old machines. It's totally absorbing, and kind of cathartic when I get them going again."

"Your living room must look like an arcade!"

"Oh, no, nothing like that, I promise you!" Wryan shook his head, smiling broadly. "My workshop, such as it is, is in the garage, but in any case, I mostly just buy broken circuit boards, because that's the cause of the problem most of the time. I fix them and sell them back to grateful machine owners."

"That's alright, then," I say with an exaggeratedly serious look.

"You laugh, but it's big! Did you know there's a whole pinball museum down in Roanoke? It's on my bucket list to go one of these days."

"Bucket list? Why don't you just fly down one weekend? You could go Saturday and come back Sunday."

"I know, but it's easier said than done right now, partly because our competitions are on weekends, and I don't want to travel more than I have to just yet."

"Because of your mom?"

"Yeah."

"I'm sorry."

***

The mention of Wryan's mom had sobered us instantly, but in a good way. As much as I always enjoyed our lighthearted jokiness, I appreciated our heart-to-heart conversations more. He had told me previously that his mother is fighting metastatic bone cancer, and that she is now very near the end. He has taken the year off between medical school and starting residency so that he can spend time with her and help take care of her.

The evening followed the old refrain: we laughed, we... well, we didn't exactly cry, but our conversation ran the gamut of emotions for both of us, and it drew us closer. There was so much to talk about, so many things we discovered we'd like to do together, things each of us wanted to introduce to the other. It was as if we'd subconsciously made plans without having to say it—plans for more dates, more activities, more life spent together.

I relay some of this to Tessa and ask her plaintively, "Who took that away from us? And why?"

She gives me a long look. "Whoever it was won't get away with it."

Frank comes out with iced teas for both of us, and we change topics to the Corbin family: next week the twins, Julie and Christopher, are going to an away camp for a week, and then they're all going to the beach before school starts. At one point Phyllis drifts over and tells me how nice it is to see me again, sounding like she means it. It's nice catching up, but I decide I'd better be on my way and let them all get on with the rest of their day.

When I get back home, I write down the details I'd just remembered about our last date into my notebook. It's a lot, and it's organized, and this small success energizes me. I go up to the roof to swim some laps, and when I get out, there's a nice breeze on the patio, and there's no one else around, so I decide to take a dip in the hot tub.

It's a perfect summer afternoon as I relax in the heat of the spa, my head leaning lightly against the edge. I take deep breaths, close my eyes, and begin counting slowly as I take air in, and again as I let it out. It may not yet be true meditation, but I am doing my best to quiet my mind. *Give it time*, I tell myself, *at least it can't do any harm*. Had I only known.

I concentrate on my breath and on refocusing my attention every time it wanders. I am warm and comfortable and light in the water, and I begin to feel a deep sense of calm. Time stops, and my mind goes truly blank. *It's working! I'm doing it!* I think, just as it all collapses, and once again thoughts—random and nebulous—flood my brain. I sputter and gasp but can't get any air, and start to panic. I thrash my arms and open my eyes in sudden realization. I fell asleep. Fully awake now, I lift my head above the water, coughing and gasping, my heart pounding. Only a few minutes have passed. The sun still shines, and nothing has changed; everything is fine. But I am deeply unsettled. I have never fallen asleep in the hot tub before, never felt so utterly disoriented coming out of a dream. I try to shake the feeling of prescience, of peril that I know isn't real, but I can't.

Chapter 18
A Real Duke

I hear my phone ding and practically leap out of the hot tub to check it, hoping against hope that it's Izzie getting in touch at last. Of course it's not. It's a text from Miller.

Head's up. His highness has invited Aspire's corporate sponsor to the gathering tonight

I "like" it, and pretty soon the phone buzzes as the others do too. At some point, Aspire told us that Tau Activewear is their main sponsor, and that is the logo we see on all their gear. I assume that Miller means Nathaniel Tau, founder and owner of Tau Activewear, will be at the memorial. While his presence will probably make the evening feel more formal, I'm curious to meet him. Wryan has talked quite a bit about Tau, who was very instrumental in the team's trajectory really taking off.

The "his highness" allusion is typical Miller—she's not a big fan of Duke, usually referring to him as "smarmy" and "oh-so-smooth." When I'd excitedly informed the Bears that he didn't just have a cool nickname, he's an actual duke, she'd rolled her eyes and said, "Well, of course he is, because there are so many dukedoms in Pennsylvania." The others had had a hard time believing it too, Redd suggesting that someone might be playing a joke on me. But it was true. Wryan had given me the incredible, fascinating story one day as we chatted on FaceTime.

***

"Do you guys call him 'Duke' because he's your team captain, but 'Duke' starts with a 'D' like Duncan?"

On the screen, I watched Wryan shake his head with a grin. "Actually, it started a long time ago, when we were kids." He took a swig of Diet Coke and continued. "When he first came to stay with us, my friends and I thought the name Duncan was hilarious. Don't ask me why; we just did, and we teased him mercilessly. Not mean, just constant. One day my mom told us, 'You shouldn't make fun of him, you know. He's going to be a duke one day!'" Wryan smiled at the memory. "We thought that was even funnier. We started calling him 'Duke' as a joke, but then it stuck."

"But your mom was kidding, right?"

"Oh no, she wasn't kidding. It didn't mean anything to us, but it's true."

"Wait a minute, back up. You don't mean he really is a duke?" I stared wide-eyed at Wryan.

He laughed, probably used to this reaction. "He will be one day. It's kind of a long story. Have you ever heard of St. Sava?"

I shook my head no. "It sounds like an island in the Caribbean."

Wryan applauded me for a good guess, because, he conceded, it's similar in a way, but it's not in the Caribbean. St. Sava, he explained, is a British Overseas Territory in Africa ("it's like a nibble out of Botswana right on the border of South Africa"), and that is the Wells family seat.

***

I gather my things and go down to the apartment to get dressed, pondering the story of the Wells lineage. I'd noted the main things on the "Duke" page of my notebook, but there were a lot of details that Wryan had given me over time, when our conversations looped back to his family, and Duke in particular, that I think I should write down now, while I'm thinking about it.

The duchy was established when one of their ancestors was commissioned the first governor of St. Sava, and he owned an enormous estate there called Hilander. He became engaged to a woman who was either a princess or a countess (Wryan wasn't sure), and upon their marriage he was knighted the Duke of Hilander.

When their grandfather, George Wells, inherited the estate, he turned it into a highly successful training center for racehorses, feeding the popular racing scene in nearby Gaborone and becoming well known not only locally but among the racing community in Great Britain and beyond. His training methods were not only effective but famously humane, and he became a favorite of Queen Elizabeth. Their relationship, such as it was, helped re-solidify a royal connection that was otherwise tenuous. Upon George's death, his oldest son Alistair—Wryan and Duncan's uncle and the current Duke of Hilander—took over the training center. Duncan's own father, Callum, worked there, too, until he died in a riding accident when Duncan was eleven. (Thus precipitating Duncan's move to Pittsburgh. His mother was American, and she brought him home after her husband died, but her job as a racing journalist required her to travel constantly. Wryan's mother offered to have Duncan stay with them over his first summer vacation in the U.S., and he never left.)

"Uncle Alistair has no sons, so Duncan is next in line to inherit the title. My mom wasn't kidding. When Uncle Alistair passes away, Duncan will become the next duke," Wryan had shrugged.

I'm absent-mindedly chewing on my pen, a bad habit I've picked up recently, and I stop myself abruptly. The idea of a real duke had hijacked my attention and my imagination, but writing down the family history brings up other pieces that might prove more important. For one thing, any whiff of aristocracy imparts an equal assumption of money. A huge inheritance is certainly a good motivation for murder, but in that case, Duke should have been the victim, not his cousin. So, why wasn't he? I sit still, covering my eyes with my fists, thinking hard.

When I'd asked Wryan if Duke would go back to run the training center after his uncle died, he had shaken his head "no" definitively, explaining that Uncle Alistair had made his girlfriend Manou joint owner of the estate, so that upon his death, Manou would own it outright. The full story comes back to me. Uncle Alistair divorced his first wife a long time ago. Manou was his manager's younger sister, and Alistair fell madly in love with her from the day they met. They never married, but they've been together ever since and have a teenage daughter.

"How does Duke feel about that? I mean..." I'd started to ask and then found myself blushing and stopped. "Never mind, sorry. It's none of my business."

Wryan, however, had laughed. "You mean, is he missing out on a big fortune? Nah. What he's mostly missing out on is a big headache, and he couldn't be more delighted. He's inheriting exactly what he wants."

I'd laughed at that, thinking it an odd comment. Why would anyone care about a title if he didn't get the land or the money?

"Duke has realized the extraordinary value having a title can be if you only know how to use it," Wryan had said in explanation, and I write that down. It has given me an idea.

Chapter 19

In Memoriam

It's getting late, so I put away my notebook and hurry to get ready for the gathering with Aspire. Miller, Redd, Gail, and Celeste are already seated at "our" table when I arrive. We greet each other with muted hellos, and I scoot onto a bench, unconsciously taking my usual seat that should have been next to Izzie. Star is serving one of the far tables and catches my eye. I wave a greeting to her, but she frowns and shrugs her shoulders. I'm not sure what that means exactly, and our communication, such as it was, ends there as she concentrates on laying the food and drinks down at the other table. Oh, well.

I turn back to ask Gail how she's doing, and she swirls her half-finished glass and sighs. "Honestly, we're all in complete shock. It's incomprehensible, and we're so worried it's not just Wryan. There's no word about Izzie, and we've all realized that no one has seen her since the night before the race."

"You didn't all go to the start together?" I ask, wondering how it could be that they hadn't noticed Izzie wasn't there.

"No. Wryan wanted to change his bike, so he was going to go early across the bridge to the bike start and then come back and meet us for the swim. We all assumed Izzie went with him when they were both gone in the morning."

Gail takes a sip as we watch and wait for more.

"What do you mean by 'change his bike'?" asks Redd finally.

"Oh! Sorry. He was going to use his TT bike—his time trial bike—and that's what he put in the staging area on Friday. He was worried about it, though, because his hamstrings tend to cramp up, especially in the heat, so at the last minute he decided to switch to his regular triathlon bike. It's a gentler ride. That morning was his last chance to make the change."

Celeste takes over. "Actually, the morning was pretty chaotic because a lot of our pre-planning had gone to shit. As usual. Max and Gail were slated to do the relay, but during practices, Gail was having a really hard time with the heat. She kept getting dehydrated, and the last time we ended up calling an ambulance, and they had to put an IV into her."

We all look at Gail in surprise and sympathy—we'd had no idea. She turns red at the sudden attention and takes another sip from her glass to compose herself. "There was nothing I could do. I tried to drink more, but then I'd throw up. The fiasco with the IV was the final straw, because it was kind of scary and it was obvious

I wasn't going to do well in the race, if I managed to finish at all. We all agreed that the smart thing to do at that point was for me to drop out."

"Probably should have done some heat-specific training," Celeste gives Gail a look, but Gail doesn't react other than to give me a *this is what I deal with all the time* look of her own. "Anyway, not only did Wryan decide to change his bike the evening before, but now we had to figure out what to do about losing Gail," Celeste continues.

"Nahla was going to do the individual race, but she agreed to partner with Max instead and do the bike leg of the relay," Gail says.

"Yeah, which was disappointing for her, since swimming is her biggest strength, but it gave the team the best chance for a good placement. And since Nahla would be starting off on the bike, we all assumed Wryan took her across the bridge, too, but I guess that would have made too much sense because we found out later that he didn't," Celeste looks up at the ceiling in disgust and picks up her glass.

"Why later? She didn't go with the rest of you? Then, how did she get there?" asks Miller.

"She said she took the participant shuttle from the hotel down the street," Celeste sighs, implying what? I wonder. Did she think Nahla should have told the others her plans ahead of time? Or that she should have ridden with the others in the car? This last makes sense to me, but before I can ask the question, Gail is already answering it.

"The shuttle dropped the swimmers at the beach and then took the bike-leg-only competitors across the bridge to the bike start. It really did make more sense for Nahla to do that rather than ride with us, so we wouldn't have to hurry to get back."

Celeste is on the brink of a rejoinder but breaks off, seeing Karen enter the restaurant closely followed by Haisley. They come to the table together, and we all get caught up in greetings. Haisley is on her own again today, no Simon. Interesting. Or is that interesting? Maybe it's just normal. The thought gives me a start. I've just noticed an inconsequential detail and intuited something about it. No big deal under normal circumstances, but that hasn't happened in a long time. Is it working? Are the clouds dissipating and my third eye beginning to open after all? I look around the restaurant with a renewed sense of focus.

A new server, not Star, comes over to take our order, and Gail says, "Get anything you want. It's on our tab. Nathaniel said he'd come by too, and that he'd pay for everything."

"Have we mentioned Nathaniel Tau to you guys before? He owns the company that sponsors us," Celeste adds.

We nod in reply, as all of us do indeed know the name Nathaniel Tau by now. Early on, Miller had taken it upon herself to look into the Botswana-based company Tau Activewear and its purportedly charismatic founder. She reported back to us, and by this point we were all interested to meet the man in person.

"Did he fly over when he heard what happened?" asks Redd.

Gail shakes her head. "He was already here. He's in DC for an international trade show given by the Commerce Department." Once again, Celeste breaks in to add that since he was going to be in town, Tau had told the team he'd take them out to celebrate after the big race. When disaster struck, he wanted to lend support. Gail speaks up again, saying, "I don't think he knew exactly what he could do, but when Duke told him about us coming here tonight with you guys, he thought it was a nice gesture and wanted to contribute."

"He sounds like a really good person," says Karen. "I'm glad it works out that we'll get to meet him, although I hate the reason why. We're still in shock about what's happened, too."

The rest of us nod and murmur general assent. We fall quiet, and at that moment, Duke comes in accompanied by Carlo and a large, slightly pot-bellied black man, who I take to be Nathaniel Tau.

Nathaniel turns out to be eminently likeable; his personality expansive and preternaturally optimistic. Today he is avuncular and sympathetic, clearly troubled as we all are by the news of both Wryan and Izzie, but his natural effervescence shines through. Even in tragedy, he is positive and upbeat. "Hello, hello" he greets each one of us as we introduce ourselves, and beckons to the server as he reiterates Gail's offer. "Please, what would you like? A refill for you, Redd? Anyone? How about some food?" He orders a slew of appetizers because we're all suddenly too shy to answer.

Duke, in the meantime, has walked up behind me and given me a kind of shoulder hug, saying in a soft voice, "Hey Lily. I heard you were on the beach and saw it all. I'm so sorry." He sits down next to me and squeezes my hand. It all happens in the blink of an eye, but I'm touched to the core. Warmth and compassion rush over me, and I am transported—simultaneously happy and immeasurably sad. It was such a Wryan move. In the midst of his own unspeakable loss, grief, and confusion, Duke still thought about my feelings and reached out to comfort me. It's exactly what Wryan would have done, and I feel both his presence and his absence more intensely than I have since we learned that he had died.

I squeeze Duke's hand back and murmur how sorry I am for his loss. It's a private, sweet moment for the two of us; for the first time, my insecurity in his presence is overcome by my profound sympathy, but it's quickly interrupted by Gail filling in the newcomers on our conversation to date. She finishes by looking over at me and picking up where she'd started. "We didn't know anything was really wrong. When it was clear they weren't going to make the start of the race, we were mostly kind of mad about it. Duke was livid (she nods her head toward Duke, who closes his eyes and bows his head in abject remorse), but there was nothing we could do at that point. Everyone just had to go."

Duke covers his eyes with his fists and breathes out deeply. Then he looks around at us and says very quietly, "We didn't know they'd found a body, or anything like that, and after they did, the organizers didn't know it was Wryan until later, so for a long time we had no idea."

"I mean, yeah, it was really strange, but none of us thought anything had actually happened to them," Carlo pipes up for the first time.

"Why not? Have people just not shown up for a race like this before?" asks Redd, reasonably. I was thinking the same thing.

Carlo lifts his shoulders and lets them fall morosely. "No, never. But Celeste told us Izzie was pregnant. We figured she decided it would be bad for her to race, and the two of them ran off together to get married."

My eyes lock with Karen's, but the rest of the Bears swivel theirs to Celeste.

"When we're traveling, we room together a lot." She stares everyone down defensively. "You share a bathroom, you see things. There were test indicators in the trash. It's not like I don't know what those are, and the lines were positive..."

"Love can make you do some crazy things; that's for sure. But Wryan? Abandon you all without a word?" Redd shakes his head dubiously.

Aspire is quiet until Gail says, "Once he knew she was pregnant, Wryan wouldn't have wanted her to do the race. It's really grueling and takes a big toll on the body. Izzie would probably insist she could do it, so maybe Wryan was the one who pushed for them to leave right away. It would be like him to be the bad guy who makes the decision not to race, and do it so they're both out, not just Izzie."

My throat closes up at this wholly accurate description of Wryan. The others don't know he and Izzie had broken up. With the knowledge they had, their assumption makes perfect sense to me. He'd never ask Izzie not to race while he did, but he wouldn't want to risk any kind of complication with the baby. Around the table, all of Aspire are nodding their heads.

Carlo takes back the conversation. "Izzie could be pretty impulsive. And Wryan always did whatever she asked. We all knew he wanted to marry her, and she was balking—maybe he figured he'd better jump on this while she needed him. Something like that." He looks down at the table, no longer able to hold our gaze, and takes a big gulp of his drink.

"I had a bad feeling," Duke's voice is still barely above a whisper. "Wryan would have told me, or texted, or something. I knew something bad had happened, but I didn't want to believe it." He takes a shaky breath, his expression so stricken that my heart contracts, a stranglehold that renders me speechless and immobile.

I wish Wryan could see and hear him and know the depth of his feeling. Did he already know? I fervently hope so.

Gail turns to Redd. "When Izzie didn't answer our calls or texts, we were worried sick but thought maybe, maybe, *maybe* she's in Atlantic City or wherever in a big Izzie fuck-everybody huff thinking Wryan stood her up, so she turned her phone off. Like if he was supposed to meet her there later or something. Even now, it's still possible that she just doesn't know, isn't it? Do you think it's possible that that could be all it is?"

It's a false hope, and they probably know it, but it's cruel to keep them in the dark. I take a deep breath and try to keep my voice calm as I tell them Izzie's secret.

"Izzie wasn't pregnant. Home pregnancy tests have to be read within a specific time period because the reading can change and default to positive. And she and Wryan had broken up. They wouldn't have eloped—not that night, or any other. She did have another boyfriend, though."

Of course, I knew what would happen, and I wasn't wrong. There is a huge clamor. How do I know this, what exactly do I know about Izzie and Wryan, who told me, how can I be sure, etc., etc., etc. I don't even try to answer at first, waiting for the hullabaloo to die down. I feel Duke stiffen beside me, and when the table finally goes quiet, it's Redd who speaks first, directly to me, unassuming but spot on as always.

"Mm hm. By the looks of it, you're the only one who knew about these things, Lily."

They're all riveted on me, and I'm blushing up a storm, but I don't back down. When I blurted this out, I was hoping to see their reactions, to identify anyone who seemed off. It backfires, though, because I'm so discomfited by all the attention, I can't even look at their faces and meet their eyes. Nevertheless, it's too late to take it back, so I forge ahead. "Wryan told me he and Izzie had broken up, but that they'd both agreed not to mention it to you guys until after the triathlon. They didn't want everyone to have to deal with a lot of weirdness and drama in addition to the stress of the race."

"Why would he tell you?" Celeste asks skeptically.

"Because he asked me out. I was confused, since the first time we all met, you all acted like they were a couple. I asked him if that was true, and that's when he told me."

The table erupts again with questions. Gail is the last to weigh in, and hers is the most on point.

"Izzie had another boyfriend? What was his name?"

It is at that moment that Max and Nahla arrive, and we go through the entire conversation all over again. I'm more ready this time, and more comfortable because the attention has shifted slightly away from me and onto those two, the last ones to know. Max lets out a quick giggle, but I think it was out of shock. Nahla makes no comment, but looks as if she finds this anything but funny. Duke still hasn't said anything, and I turn my head to look at him, only to find that he is looking at Nathaniel. The two of them seem to be having a silent conversation. Nathaniel's look is wide-eyed, questioning, *did you know about this?* Duke's response an almost imperceptible head movement, *I had no idea.* I have the definite impression that this is true for all of them: no one knew about Wryan and Izzie; no one knew about Wryan and me; and no one knew about Izzie and her new beau. Remarkable, really. Secrets so rarely stay secret in close-knit groups.

I tell them the whole story, how Wryan came to ask me out the very next day after our first happy hour, why Izzie thought she was pregnant, why she came to me rather than any of them, and how determined she was to keep the fact of her new boyfriend very much on the down low. There's no uproar this time. Something in their faces registers that they had suspected something was up. Given an answer to a question that had hovered just out of view, they knew in their bones that what I'd told them was true.

The table is completely quiet, and Duke stands up. First, he speaks of Izzie, and how much they want her to come home, whatever the odds against may be. Then he gives a touching toast to Wryan and closes saying, "My cousin, my brother, my best friend, our teammate. I wish, I wish, I wish you were here now to tell me to shut up and get on with it. Cheers, mate."

It's beautifully understated, and we all have tears in our eyes. Duke himself had to choke out those last two words. A few people add their own subdued "cheers" as we raise our glasses.

I look around the table, first at Redd, who has chosen just that moment to peek over at me too. He shakes his head sadly, and I nod in agreement. Then I take in Karen, who puts her hand lightly on Celeste's shoulder for a moment in sympathy. Haisley looks sad but distracted. For no good reason, I'm suddenly certain that something is amiss between her and Simon. My intuition is definitely waking from its slumber, and I feel a flash of excitement but quell it quickly because it doesn't fit the solemnity of the occasion. Continuing around the table, I note that Max and Carlo both look troubled, understandably, although of course no one dares mention...

"Well, we're all thinking it, why not say it," Celeste says. "Whoever killed Wryan probably killed Izzie. Izzie's body must have floated further away, so no one found her. Don't look at me like that! Of course it's not what I want, but it's the most likely possibility."

"Jesus, Celeste," Carlo mutters.

"But she could be right," Miller says, herself never one to shy away from hard truths. "I know no one wants to imagine it, but what if this boyfriend was jealous and afraid Izzie would go back to Wryan? He could have killed them." She stops, probably realizing too late that it's not really her place to talk about their close teammates like this, but she's only saying what the others are surely now considering. Who else would want to kill Wryan? And why? We may hate the idea, but once it's said out loud, it's as if everyone is now at liberty to deal with it.

"Yeah, the police need to find that boyfriend. Seriously, none of you knows anything about him? Not even any guesses?" pipes up Haisley, back with us again.

Carlo shrugs, "We all thought Wryan was her boyfriend."

There is no good rejoinder to that, and Nathaniel has to leave. He stands up and says his goodbyes, adding, "My tab stays open. Please, keep ordering. Make this evening a memory of friendship and family." He pats Duke on the shoulder, saying, "Call me later, chom, yeah?" and then he's gone. We shift around the table a bit to close the empty space, not sure what to do.

"Come on, let's eat," says Duke. "You guys want dinner or more appetizers?"

"YES! We do. And everybody, order from the top shelf tonight! No bill is too high for Uncle Tau and the bank of Hilander," Carlo calls out, getting grins from Gail, Max, and Celeste.

Duke sweeps both hands around the table and says, "That's right! Tonight, for Wryan, we go all out!"

I feel a tap on my shoulder and turn around to see Star. I give her a big smile, glad to see she's still here, but her return smile is more guarded. She gestures for me to follow her, and we move together toward the hallway that leads to the restrooms.

"The phone wasn't Izzie's," she says tightly when we're more or less alone.

"What? How? What do you mean?" I'm stunned.

"It turned out to belong to a sixth-grade girl who was too afraid to tell her parents she'd lost it. Your detective friend knows—he called here to let us know they've given it back to its rightful owner."

"Oh. Damn. Thanks for telling me." I'd been so sure it was Izzie's, and had clung to the hope that not having her phone was the reason Izzie wasn't in contact with anyone. Emotionally, I'm not ready to let that go, but I force myself to be rational. False hope doesn't help anyone; all it can do is lead us down ratholes and waste time. If Izzie still has her phone, even if it's turned off, it might lead us to her. There's still hope.

"I'm so sorry about the confusion. I really did think it was hers."

Poor Star. She'd been trying to help, and now she thinks she's just messed everything up. I give her a quick hug and say, "It's okay. Everything worked out because I needed to see Detective Ridley anyway, to give him information that might help solve all this. And hey, now even that little girl got her phone back!"

Star smiles at that, her shoulders loosen, and we walk together back into the dining area, where I find our table crammed with plates of food and glasses and pitchers of drinks. Everyone is talking quietly, in stark contrast to our boisterous gatherings of the past, but it's nice in its way. We share memories of Wryan, many of them funny, and affirm our collective belief that Izzie will be found soon. In the end, the evening felt like a needed pause, a deep restorative breath, and it did indeed lend us all a warm sense of kinship.

Chapter 20

Where is Izzie?

Back at our apartment, Haisley makes hot chocolate—a ridiculous drink in summer, but we both want some. We settle ourselves comfortably in the living room, and soon Haisley's bunny Archie is asleep in her lap while Dee Dee is asleep in mine. The two of us are wide awake, and in the mood for talking.

"Where is Izzie?" Haisley asks.

"I don't know. I wish I did," I answer, my face a question mark. I know Haisley well now, and this is how she thinks. She's not asking the same redundant question everyone has been asking all day; she's about to make a point, and I'm keen to know what it is.

"No, I know you don't. I mean, *where is Izzie?* That's the question we need to follow if we're going to figure this out."

"Huh. Well, she's either alive somewhere, or she's... not. The answer has to be one of those."

"Exactly," Haisley nods emphatically. "If she's dead, she and Wryan were both murdered together. They can't have coincidentally died the same night, right?"

I nod at her and sip my chocolate.

"Right. And if she's alive somewhere, what is keeping her from contacting anyone?"

"I see what you mean. To figure out the whole thing, we have to figure out why one or the other of two things happened: why would they be murdered, or why would Wryan be murdered and Izzie disappear with no word."

"You got it."

I sit perfectly still, hovering my mug above my armrest, and things start to click. Haisley has found a way to focus our mental efforts into a few specific avenues, and I go instantly from overwhelmed and mentally frazzled to energized and mentally "on." We can do this. We really might be able to do this.

"Let's start with both murdered, as that seems the most likely," Haisley knits her brows and then suddenly looks up, chastened. "Are you going to be okay?"

"Yes. I mean, I'm ready. This is exactly the conversation we need to have. Let's do it."

"They were both involved with Aspire. I know it seems obvious, but is that the connection that matters? And if so, is anyone else on the team in danger?"

"I was just thinking about that this afternoon, and there was something big Aspire was doing—something on the line between insanity and genius, and they were hoping it would launch them into the stratosphere." I squeeze my eyes shut and take a deep breath to release the tension in my jaw and neck. "I hadn't thought about anyone else being in danger, but it's possible. They were all part of it."

"Woah, Lily. This sounds serious. They were all part of what?"

"They call it the 'master plan.'"

Chapter 21
The Master Plan

One evening when Aspire was in town, Wryan picked me up after work and drove us into downtown Bethesda. We parked in the main public garage and then spent a comical fifteen minutes trying to decipher from the little blue dot on his maps app in which direction we needed to go to find the tiny Thai restaurant that was our destination. We eventually found its entrance below street level in the basement of a much larger establishment and were seated almost immediately. This was fortunate; by the time we left, the crowd of people waiting for a table was spilling out the door, up the steps, and onto the sidewalk.

On the way he confessed that he'd steered the conversation at his end of the table at our last happy hour with the express purpose of finding out my favorite food (and he'd had to learn everyone else's to carry off the ruse), and that he'd spent the morning looking up the best Thai place in town. I was touched, and also amused: I do like Thai food, but it's not necessarily my favorite. This had to have come from Miller, getting in a dig about the time I'd ended up the deciding vote against her favorite Indian buffet in favor of Thai.

Once we were seated, we flitted lightly from one subject to the next. At one point I broached the situation with Izzie, and why it was so imperative not to tell the rest of the team until after the triathlon. It must have made things exponentially more difficult for both of them. I don't see the Bears nearly as much as Aspire is together, with all their training and traveling, but I was still near to bursting trying to keep myself from mentioning my dates and calls with Wryan by accident.

"Why is that race so important? And how does it fit in with underwater rugby, by the way? I thought top level athletes had to be totally locked in to one primary sport."

"Ah, yes! You would wonder that and think that. Most people would anyway. But not Duke. Duke has a very unique perspective on these things, and he has a master plan." Wryan wiggled his eyebrows up and down and smiled enigmatically. I imitated him, and we both started laughing.

"Ooh. I have a feeling this is going to be good. Do tell!"

"My problem is, I don't know how to explain this without sounding like a crazy person. But when I think about it when I'm alone, I'm positive it's mind-bogglingly brilliant, and I get super excited!"

He explains that everything started in his freshman year of college, when the team that became Aspire was four friends—Duke, Wryan, Izzie, and Celeste—going scuba diving over spring break. That turned into an introduction to freediving, which they all found enthralling and which took over most of the vacation. They continued in the sport of freediving after they returned home, and from there got connected to other underwater sports, namely rugby. Separately, Wryan was getting serious about triathlon, and Izzie was quickly improving her ranking as a collegiate cross-country runner. Duke and Celeste were stars on their respective college swim teams. After college, they continued with both freediving and underwater rugby at their aquatic center and decided to train together as a team to continue pursuing their individual sports—which eventually morphed into all four gravitating toward triathlon.

"That sounds reasonable enough. But then, I'm thinking something happened? Something propelled you to where you are now?"

"I see you are an astute listener. You are correct. Duke happened. He is an inveterate mover and shaker." Wryan paused for a few bites and shook his head, chuckling to himself. "His degree is in marketing, and I won't be surprised if he becomes a multi-millionaire promoter by the time he's thirty. He networks, he sells, he influences—he can't help himself. He's always figuring out ways to make small things big."

The food was delicious, and our table felt cozy and private despite the increasing bustle of the restaurant. Wryan seemed to be enjoying himself, and I was too. I didn't feel self-conscious; my anxieties about our future had disappeared, and I was genuinely interested to hear more about the evolution of Aspire. I relaxed, ate, and waited for Wryan to tell me more.

"The rest of us were driven by the things you'd think would drive athletes who want to compete at the top level: we wanted to get faster, we wanted bigger and better events, we wanted podiums, we wanted gold. But not Duke."

"Duke doesn't want gold?"

"Oh, he does. He certainly does. What I meant was, Duke had, and has, a *much* bigger picture in mind."

Wryan and the others were focused on improving and mastering for the sake of the sport. Duke, however, thought about everything from the standpoint of potential for future return, for future gain.

"One day he up and announces he thinks we have a shot at making ourselves famous, and thus marketable, if we can just get to the Olympics."

I let out a muted guffaw. "Oh, just that? Very nice idea. Um... in what sport exactly?"

"That's the beauty of it. A *new* sport, because the easiest path you'll ever have to make it to the Olympics is in a sport that's on the docket for the first time." Wryan paused here for effect.

"Underwater. Freediving has a lot of buzz, but the pressure of competition can make it very dangerous, and that's holding it back. Ever since Duke discovered underwater rugby, he's been plugging it hard."

Duke knew that it was so little known, its chance of being added to the Olympic roster was slim to none, but if that did happen, the fact that Aspire was already doing it at an internationally competitive level meant that some if not all of them would have a good shot at being selected for the team. "Also, doing anything underwater is an incredible workout that translates into gains in almost any endurance sport," he added with a wink, "and it's really fun."

"Kapow!" I put my fists to my head and spread my hands as I pull them away to show him he's blowing my mind. "But then... this big triathlon? How does that fit?"

"We were already into triathlon by this point anyway, and it's a much better-known sport—more followers, and a much larger pool from which to recruit top-ranked athletes."

"But it's already an Olympic sport—won't that make it harder?"

Wryan shakes his head sadly. "Grasshopper, grasshopper," he tutted. "You showed such promise," which made me laugh and toss the crumpled paper from my straw at him.

He grinned. "The current Olympic-distance triathlon is relatively short, if you compare it to an ironman tri, and Ironman the company essentially has a lock on that name, which is too closely associated with that distance; but Duke thinks that the *ultra* triathlon—super long racing—might be in with a chance at being added as a separate event."

"Oh! Like the Great Eastern."

"Now you're getting it. The Great Eastern is one of the biggest and best-known ultra triathlons in the world, and will probably get a fair share of press, which is what we want. This is our first time racing it, and we need to have good showings both in the individual race and the relay, because either format could be the one that makes it through." He tilted his head and shrugged, checking my reaction to see what I would make of this.

"Fascinating. It's devious and audacious, but still seems like a long shot. There are lots of other new sports they could put in the Olympics."

Wryan grins but doesn't say anything yet. I lean back in my chair. It sounded like an awfully big gamble on a small probability, and Duke didn't strike me as the gambler type. He was more of a wangler, someone who knew how to manipulate the status quo to make it be exactly what suited him. And what was this about a much bigger picture?

"There's more to it than that, isn't there? You said Duke was thinking much bigger, and I can't believe he'd leave whatever that is up to chance... Ah. I get it. The master plan?"

"Give the lady the prize! The master plan. And you better believe there's much more to it."

The plan included Duke himself working behind the scenes to make things come together on schedule, including capitalizing on a unique "in" that he'd realized he had and quickly learned to exploit. The mutual interest in horse racing shared by his grandfather and the late queen laid the foundation for a kind of friendship, and the Wells family is still part of the outer perimeter of that sphere. The Duke of Hilander is often included on the invitation list for royal events—events also attended by influential personalities with the means to make things happen, or "all the people who are People," as Wryan put it. Uncle Alistair was rarely inclined to travel anymore, so Duke, the heir apparent, would willingly go in his stead. He leveraged his connections to make more connections, eventually wheedling his way onto the committees he needed to sway.

"If it were me, I'd stand around like a chump who doesn't have a clue, and even if someone took pity on me and said hello, as soon as I opened my mouth I'd be pegged as the proverbial dorky American. Without question, that person would pretend to need to talk to someone across the room, and I'd trip over my own feet to get out of his way."

I grinned, chuckling to myself, because I could indeed imagine Wryan uncomfortable in such company.

"Not Duke." Wryan looked to the heavens in wonder for a moment, smiling, and told me how his cousin knew the goldmine that his title offered within this circle, and he not only didn't waste it—he relished the challenge of milking it to the hilt.

"He'd make nice with maybe the one person there that he knew, and that person would be so charmed he'd be inspired to introduce him to someone else. Like, 'Have you met Lord Duncan, Hilander's nephew? He's making quite the splash in sports promotion. Duncan, this is so-and-so. I feel sure the two of you will hit it off.' And of course, So-and-so's interest would be piqued enough to talk to him."

"And they'd hit it off."

"Always. Duke is irresistible, while I'm..." He raised his hands and gave me a helpless look.

"You're not a dork!"

"Ha! Then how did you know what I was going to say!"

We laughed, knowing it both is and isn't true. Wryan was comfortable with himself; he knew his own strengths and weaknesses, and he was no slouch. Nevertheless, Duke stepped forth into the world as if sprinkled with fairy dust. In comparison, almost anyone would come across as a little bit of a dork.

"Seriously, though, Duke is the best there is at spinning whatever he has to his advantage to get what he wants," Wryan told me. "He's very subtle, but he never lets go. He landed his first job out of college by meeting someone at a major league "do" that led to an interview with one of the biggest sports promotion firms in the world. That's all he needed to get himself involved with SportAccord."

SportAccord, Wryan explained, is a global event organization that, among other things, manages the process for sport associations around the world to apply for inclusion in the Olympics. "Through SportAccord he was able to meet and make an impression on some key people in the ARISF." (He couldn't remember offhand exactly what the letters ARISF stood for, but I Googled it later: Association of International Olympic Committee Recognized International Sports Federations.)

"Getting to the ARISF is a first step in the process of inducting a new sport into the Olympics. It normally takes forever, but Duke always finds a way to speed things along."

"That's amazing. He's done all that already?"

Wryan laughed. "Give Duke time for an elevator speech, and he'll move the world!"

***

It is an intricate, multi-faceted plan, and as I recount all I know to Haisley, I marvel again at its intricacy and its moxie. Duke had thought about everything from achieving the necessary competitive level, to selling his team's sports to the Olympic committee, to how any degree of fame or success could be exploited and maximized. Haisley takes it in, asking only a few questions, her face puckered in concentration.

"Woah. That's pretty sick," she says in admiration when I finally finish.

"It is, isn't it? A master plan from a mastermind."

We nod wide-eyed at each other.

"Is it worth killing for?" I ask.

She looks grimly back at me. "It could be for someone. If knowingly or unknowingly Wryan and Izzie got in the way somehow, they might have been expendable in someone's pursuit of a huge payola."

The air conditioning is making me feel chilly suddenly, and I grab the folded blanket from the back of the couch and wrap myself in it. When I settle back down, I remember we've only discussed one part of our two-part problem.

"What if Izzie is still alive? What might explain her silence?"

"That's an easy one—the boyfriend. There's something up with all the secrecy there. But it could be so many things."

Of course she's right. We're back to the two foundational crime motives: love or money.

"In that case, we're going to need some reinforcements. Boyfriends and secrets mean gossip..."

"We're going to need Miller," we say in unison.

Chapter 22
Developments

Miller must have heard us invoke her name. I'm eating breakfast at our kitchen counter the next morning when she sends out a text with a link to an article about Aspire. It's not very long, and the only athlete it mentions whose name we know is Nahla. They've given her a special call-out box, and I'm fascinated to learn that her mother is from Botswana, and that Nahla competed for Botswana in both the last Olympic and Commonwealth Games. A male diver also had a call-out box highlighting his story, and several others were noted within the body of the article for their post-collegiate achievements. Aspire's coach is quoted as being blown away by the incredible scope of the team's sport repertoire, the talent of the athletes it was attracting, and its enormous competitive potential. There's a photo that looks like Izzie from the back checking the practice schedule next to a group picture of people laughing, and I recognize Carlo in the middle, but the caption only says something about a typical day in the life. It's an interesting article, which is why I add my own "like" to Redd and Haisley's "likes" of Karen's comment:

Interesting

I'm deciding whether to text or call Miller for her help in continuing our theorizing from last night when I hear a ding and pick up my phone again. It's Miller, this time with an eye-roll emoji. To that, she adds the following:

Guys! I think it's him

I wait a few minutes for further elucidation, but there's nothing, so I add my own follow-up:

?

This is immediately "liked" by Karen, Redd, and Haisley in quick succession, but apparently Miller has no time for us. She texts:

I gotta go. Fill you in later

The wind goes out of my sails at that, both because my own plans of getting together with Miller must now be put aside for the moment, and because her cryptic message is going to drive me nuts until she gets back to us. I'm momentarily at a loss how to proceed when another text dings, this one from Gail.

The police found $10K in cash in Wryan's bag. They're asking all of us if we have any idea what it's for??!! Do you know???

I don't even try to text back. I call her, nearly knocking my coffee cup off the counter in my agitation.

"What? What the hell? Sorry. Is this an okay time to talk?"

"Hi Lily. Yes, it is. I wanted to call, but wasn't sure if you were busy. It's crazy, isn't it? But apparently there was a whole wad of money in one of the pockets, and it amounted to something like ten thousand dollars. I was hoping there was a simple explanation, and he'd told you about it."

"No, he never mentioned anything like that. But whatever it's for, I'm sure it must be on the up and up. Wryan would never be mixed up in anything bad, right? It's impossible."

"That was all of our reaction, too. Still, no one has any idea what it could be, not even Duke."

We go on in this incredulous vein for a few minutes, and I ask if she knows what the police are thinking. Gail sounds disconsolate when she answers that they seem to be going down the tried-and-true paths: drugs, performance-enhancing drugs, gambling. She blows air out of her nose when she finishes, and we both fall quiet.

"Do they think it's why he was murdered?"

"Maybe. Probably. It's weird that the money's still there, though. You'd think the person would have taken it."

We're quiet again.

"Do they think he brought it with him from Pittsburgh, or that he got it while he was down here?"

"Oh, good one. I don't know. They're not telling us much, only asking questions."

We agree to let each other know if either of us hears anything more before hanging up. I remain standing in the kitchen, trying to make head or tail of this new development. Why would Wryan have so much money in cash with him? I change the question to: What legitimate reason could *anyone* have for needing so much cash in hand? But I can't answer that either. Moving in a daze, I get dressed and gather Otto into the Bogg bag we use to smuggle him out of the apartment when we take him for walks. Haisley insists that the building's "no pets" rule is more of a guideline, but she also insists on the subterfuge of the Bogg bag.

I walk to the corner before taking him out and attaching his leash, and decide on a whim to turn not in the direction of the dog park, but toward the shopping center and my yoga studio. I had it in my mind to get a green tea lemonade at Starbucks, but halfway there had argued myself out of spending the money. It's busy and I regret my decision to walk in this direction, but I'm already here, so it's too late to change. I'm watching Otto pee on the grassy area between the sidewalk and the tarmac when I hear my name.

"Lily! I wasn't expecting to see you here today."

I look around and see Redd carrying a bag and smiling over at me. I give him a big smile back and walk toward him, Otto jogging slightly ahead.

"Well, hey! Did you go to the morning class?"

"Not today. I came for a bakery run — they have babkas on Wednesdays." He proffers me the bag to take a sniff, and when I inhale the delicious aroma of fresh-from-the-oven babka, I loll my head back rapturously. "Mm hm," Redd grins. "Best in the county right here."

I'm so happy to see him that I launch directly into the news of the ten thousand dollars, adding that I can't believe Wryan would be involved in anything criminal, but that I can't think of a reason why he would have had so much cash. Redd listens patiently while I go through my few postulations, and then explain why each one doesn't sound right. Finally, I give a big sigh and look at him woefully.

"Can *you* think of anything?"

Redd shakes his head slowly. "It's a strange one, no doubt about that. But you were dating, right? Maybe he was gonna buy you a ring."

I actually feel the blush rise from my stomach to my neck and hit my cheeks. I'm gobsmacked by his suggestion.

"Oh, uh, no. No way. I don't... We weren't anywhere near... no really, I, um, nuh uh."

He chuckles and stands there grinning ear to ear, his eyes shining at my extreme discomfiture. "Okay, okay. Maybe not, then. I was just trying to think of something. Some people buy diamonds in cash."

Now I'm blushing out of embarrassment for my embarrassment. Is that even possible? I thank him for the idea, still shaken by it but able to chuckle back at him a little myself.

"I appreciate the creative leap, but I don't think that was it. It's a nice thought, though."

He tells me he'll have to think about it some more to see if he can come up with anything else and tosses a wave as he heads down the sidewalk toward his car. It's already hot out, and Otto is panting, so I put him in his bag to carry him home. I'm distracted the entire way, wondering about Redd's off-the-cuff guess. I decide I really am sure he wasn't going to buy a ring for me at this point in our relationship; and while I get it that a lot of people go directly to diamond dealers, I didn't think Wryan was the type. It was more likely he'd go to a jewelry store at the mall. But Redd's suggestion might not be completely off the mark: is there something else like that, legal but out of the ordinary, for which a person might need a lot of hard cash? The thought is like a marble rattling in my brain; I can't catch it, but it keeps circling and won't disappear.

Back in the apartment, I text Miller that when she has a moment, I need her help with something. Feeling antsy, I then text Karen to see if I can swing by for a quick coffee. She answers almost immediately that she has a meeting first, but she'd love to chat if I can come to the cafeteria at 11:30 for an early lunch. Don't ask me twice—in a flash, I'm out the door and on my e-bike. There's plenty of time to get there, but anything is better than sitting at home. It's so hot I use the throttle for most of the way, preferring not to be drenched in sweat sitting in the air conditioning of the hospital.

After locking my bike in the parking garage, I'm delighted to spy Dr. Ben walking along the covered sidewalk that connects the new wing to the old. It's rare that I ever get a chance to talk to him on my own, and I enjoy it immensely when I do. He and I both find the symbolism of my studio's Eye of Horus logo fascinating, and surprisingly germane to our modern lives. We've had some deep and wonderful discussions on this topic, and there aren't a lot of people who will do that.

"Ah, Lily! Are you going to the main building? Walk with me!" he greets me cheerily. I quicken my steps to cover the last few yards between us, and when we're side by side, he continues. "Tell me, have you been pondering any quandaries of existence during your yoga practice lately?" There was a time when I would have thought he was teasing me, but now I know he means his question seriously, and I answer him in kind.

"As a matter of fact, yes. I've been thinking a lot about the parallels between the Egyptian Eye of Horus and the Hindu third eye chakra."

"Oh? And why this facet in particular? What's special about the third eye?"

I tell him about what I've been feeling lately—the fogginess, the forgetfulness, and the general rootlessness of wondering what my path in life is meant to be. "The third eye is like a bridge between our thinking brain and our inner being. We all have a lot of innate knowledge, including self-knowledge, that our conscious minds can't always access. The third eye helps us see it."

"Very interesting. And you think there's something amiss with yours?"

"Maybe. At least, I think if I could jump start it, things would become more clear for me, but more than that, I think I might recall something that will help figure out what happened to Wryan Burley and Izzie Walker."

"Oh, my!" He looks at me in surprise. "Now, that's not what I was expecting you to say! I'd love to hear what you think is the connection."

He's smiling, but I can tell he really is interested, and once we're inside the blissful cool of the building, we stop walking but continue our conversation standing in the middle of the lobby. I explain that the literal sense of the word "eye" for both Horus and the chakra incorporates all types of sight, not just what's directly in front of us, including hindsight, second sight, insight, and the mind's eye (aka, memory).

"I learned so much about Wryan and Izzie without even realizing it. Somewhere locked in here (I knock my fist on the top of my head) might be some piece of knowledge that only I have and that the police need, but I can't remember it. Maybe I zoned out right at the most important moment." I look up at Dr. Ben to gauge his reaction to this, and am gratified by his look of rapt attention.

"Wouldn't that be something?" He muses wonderingly. He cocks his head and asks whether I have any tricks up my yoga sleeve that can help, and I tell him about beginning a meditation practice, as well as doing yoga flows focused on opening the third eye.

"And do you believe it's working?"

I wiggle my hand side to side. "Sometimes yes, sometimes no. It's hard to tell."

"Ah. Perhaps what you need to do is change how you're looking at the problem?"

I flash him a quizzical look.

"Let's look at your first problem. You say you are struggling to find your path and purpose. Rather than ask yourself what you are supposed to do, or even what you like to do, maybe you should ask yourself why you've ended up where you already are?"

"Well, I had that accident, and I dropped out of college and…" I sputter to a stop, because Dr. Ben knows my history. I can see from his expression that that's not what he means.

"Things happened to you, yes, of course, that's all part of life. But what happened when you picked up the pieces? Why a yoga instructor? And how is it that you are in sleuth mode for the second time around in as many years, regarding a homicide investigation no less? You must admit that really is too extraordinary not to mean something."

My scalp tingles. Dr. Ben watches me intently, smiling as he sees the gears start to spin. He looks at me with his usual warmth and intensity, but in his bright eyes I also see encouragement. In a low voice he says, "Don't think, Lily. Say the first thing that comes to mind: what is it about you that brings these things together?"

I start to shrug but stop halfway and knit my brows instead. I feel my heart beat and a bead of sweat tickles the back of my neck, but I don't dare break from this moment. "I need to befriend people and... help them. Help them find peace and well-being. It's like a compulsion for me." I feel myself nodding unconsciously. "I gravitated to yoga to do that, but also... when I hear about a crime like murder, I have to make sure the light gets shed on who did it and why it happened. People who knew and loved the victims need that, and I want to help them. I *have* to help them get to the truth. So they can find peace."

"Like Wryan's friends and his parents; Izzie's too. You feel compelled to help them, and that compels you to help yourself. Makes sense to me."

Time stops, and something inside me releases, as if my whole body is saying, "Aaaaah." Dr. Ben's smile remains in place, and he gives me a kind of bow before heading toward the elevators to get back to work. Watching him, something else occurs to me: I was completely engaged in our conversation—no spacing out, no half-hearing, no half-anything. Then I had that moment when I *knew;* I could put into words exactly what is at my core. Clarity and insight, literally. It was ephemeral; even now I can't recapture it precisely, but I remember it was there. I am simultaneously exultant and despondent, because as transcendent as that moment was, Wryan is still dead, Izzie is still missing, and I don't have any idea why.

Chapter 23

Lunch

Needing to move but not knowing where to go because it's still too early to meet Karen, I wander aimlessly down the hall. I'm still contemplating my conversation with Dr. Ben as I drift toward the Nook to check out the line, and notice another familiar silhouette stirring creamer into a cup. He senses me watching and looks up, and I nearly catch him break into a smile.

"Ms. Piper," he hails me. "What brings you here today?"

"Detective Ridley! Small world. I just bumped into Dr. Ben outside, and now you in here. I'm supposed to have lunch with Karen, but I'm a little early."

"Ah, that explains that. I was looking for Ben myself, but he wasn't in his office. I guess I'd better go back now and try him again. Are you and Karen planning to eat in the cafeteria?" At my nod, he adds, "Good. I'd like to swing by for a few minutes, if that's okay with you?"

"Sure, of course. We're usually over by the windows."

Ridley places the cap carefully back onto his cup. Then he lifts it at me like a toast, and says, "I'll find you," before moving toward the elevators.

This is unexpected, and now I'm much too hyped for coffee, so I go into the gift shop and waste time reading through greeting cards. When it's finally 11:30, I jog up the stairs to find Karen waiting for me.

When we're seated at a table with our food, I immediately blurt out that the police found ten thousand dollars in Wryan's bag. Her reaction is much the same as both mine and Redd's—her eyes open wide and she gapes for a second before shaking her head.

"Never saw that coming. It must have something to do with why he died, doesn't it? It's the only thing that sticks out."

"I thought so too at first, but now I'm not so sure. The money's still there, so the murderer didn't take it. Wryan may have brought it to DC to purchase something unique that he couldn't get in Pittsburgh." I feel my face redden remembering Redd's suggestion about what that might be, but Karen doesn't say anything and I continue with the rest of my thought. "Haisley and I were talking last night about the big master plan behind all of Aspire's competitions. It occurred to us that there's potentially a *lot* of money at stake, and since both Wryan and Izzie were involved in it, they both might have been in the way, or something."

I'm in the middle of recapping last night's discussion when she suddenly looks up. I turn my head to look around and see Ridley and Dr. Ben coming toward us. They're each carrying a tray of food, although Dr. Ben's is laden with fried chicken, coleslaw, and a slice of pie, while Ridley has satisfied himself with only a bowl of gazpacho.

"Hi Lily, Karen," Ridley nods at each of us, adding, "Sorry about this," indicating Dr. Ben with his head. "I couldn't keep him away."

Dr. Ben pretends to look put out, saying, "And here I got you my doctor's discount."

"You're right. I do appreciate the seventeen-cent savings."

"Hmph," Dr. Ben mutters, but his eyes are twinkling.

"May we join you?"

"Of course!" Karen and I answer at the same time, unnecessarily shifting our chairs as a way of inviting them to sit down.

"Gail told me about the money you found in Wryan's bag," I tell Ridley. "Is that what you wanted to talk about?"

"I figured you'd hear about that. Since you mention it, I would be interested to hear your thoughts on it. Any idea what the money was for or where it came from?"

We both shake our heads no. "I think it must be related to why he was murdered, but Lily doesn't," Karen bursts out.

Ridley doesn't answer, but raises his eyebrows and looks over at me as he eats a spoonful of soup. I explain about the master plan, and how much everyone was banking on each piece of the puzzle working to future advantage. "Duke's dreams didn't end with a gold medal; they started there," I say, adding that while many athletes have to figure out what to do once they retire from the sport, according to Wryan, Duke was fairly salivating to get to that point in the game. He was calculating Q-factor, and promo opps, and all the ways to turn a moment of glory into a lifetime o f affluence. He had a detailed business plan that made it seem like he could really make it happen, and everyone bought into it: Max turned down a highly desirable job offer in Boston so that he could continue to train with Aspire in Pittsburgh; Carlo quit his second serious sport (golf) to go all-in with Aspire; and Gail switched her major from International Relations to Sports Management and Promotion.

It was coming together, too. For example, Nahla was the first high-viz athlete Aspire had recruited specifically as a result of the plan, and she is perfect for the part: she is a deep thinker and planner who wants to know there's always a next step, never a plateau. Then there is Nathaniel Tau, who has big ambitions for his Tau brand, which is already one of the biggest in Africa, but he wants it to go global, and his dream market is the U.S. His activewear is good quality, but it needs to be seen, to be showcased.

What better way than to be the uniform of choice for famous American athletes?

Duke knew about Tau from St. Sava, where the brand is very popular. He sought out and won Tau sponsorship for Aspire not just by convincing Nathaniel of the team's potential, but also with the implied potential to connect and promote Tau to the global sport industry heavyweights.

"Ten thousand dollars is a lot of cash, but even though I can't imagine why he had it, I'm sure it's something legal. Wryan was one hundred percent a straight arrow. The master plan was a big deal and involved big players. I don't know how it would lead to murder either, but Wryan was a piece of it all, and so was Izzie. The money doesn't seem to me to connect both of them, but this does."

The others continue to eat as they watch me, hanging on my story. The more I talk, the more things come back to me. I fiddle absently with an unopened packet of ketchup as I recount a FaceTime conversation from a few weeks ago.

"You know WhereGear?" Wryan had said. "Well, Duke connected with them through ARISF, because they sponsor several sports teams already, and pitched Tau Activewear to them."

Dr. Ben gives a low whistle, and Karen whispers, "Holy moly." Ridley has finished his soup and is regarding me with interest.

"It certainly is extraordinary, and very clever. He lures in one big sponsor by dangling a coveted partnership, and if it takes off, through that very partnership they get a much bigger, much better- known sponsor." Ridley makes a clicking sound with his tongue. "Impressive."

"Isn't it? And with each step, the pressure and the money involved keep getting bigger."

"WhereGear is big, I take it?" asks Dr. Ben, and we all stare at him.

"You don't know WhereGear?" I ask. "They sell sporting goods. You know, like REI, or Dick's." We all continue to stare at Dr. Ben because WhereGear really is one of the biggest retailers on the east coast, although it caters to the more niche events—think sport climbing, fencing, kayaking, or skateboarding.

"I've seen Dick's," acknowledges Dr. Ben.

Ridley shakes his head sadly into his empty soup bowl and mutters, "You really need to get some exercise, Ben."

At this, Dr. Ben shoots Karen and me one of those frowny moues, but Ridley sees it too. It makes us laugh and breaks the spell.

"Okay, okay. Please continue, Lily. We're all ears," Ridley says, and I cast my mind back again, but there isn't much more to tell.

"Wryan did say that WhereGear was interested in meeting with Nathaniel at the Commerce Department trade show. Apparently, they like the Tau clothing design and quality, but what they really love is the idea of getting in on either underwater sports or ultra tris as the newest thing. If the Olympics add any one of them and it suddenly gets popular, WhereGear wants to be the 'it' brand for it."

Now Ridley and Dr. Ben look at each other. "That's a fascinating bit of background," Ridley says, "and it tracks with what others have told us, although I must say your version is particularly well laid out." My heart swells at his praise, and I look down at my ketchup packet to hide my shining eyes.

"That's another reason why I wanted to see you and Karen today. If there's anything to this hypothesis, it suggests that inadvertently getting in the way can be very dangerous. Until we know more, we have to assume others on the team—or their associates (he looks very pointedly at me)—could find themselves in the same boat."

I look up quickly at Ridley and then over at Karen. We stare at him, wide-eyed. Somehow Ridley saying it makes it seem more real, more possible that Wryan's murderer might not be finished. Until we know why he died and what happened to Izzie, that danger is still out there, lurking.

"Remember what I said, Lily. Memories are good; taking action of any kind is not, and that includes asking your friends a lot of questions. You could accidentally poke a very angry hornet's nest," Ridley continues somberly. Karen and I nod back, indicating that we understand and that we would never dream of poking nests of any kind.

Ridley and Dr. Ben have to leave then, so Karen and I accompany them out to the hall, where they go down the elevators and we walk slowly toward the stairs. Neither of us says anything; we don't have to, because we're both absorbing Ridley's words. I'm about to say a quick goodbye when she breaks the silence first.

"You know what? You should come with me to Miller's tonight. I'm going over after dinner to drop off my kid — Miller's husband is taking their daughter and my son to the movies."

I form an "o" with my mouth and pretend to look shocked. "Ooh la la! Young love!" My heart isn't really into humor, but I do think it's cute and I want to glom onto anything that offers relief from the heaviness of our conversation.

Karen, I know, feels the same, and manages to give a laugh and say, "Who knows? But it'll give us a chance to talk. What do you say?"

I agree immediately because I want to find out what Miller meant by her text this morning, as well as hear whatever other gossip she may have gleaned. I haven't forgotten the importance of the "love" half of the "love or money" murder motive equation. The master plan might be big, but nothing trumps the primal emotions: love, jealousy, anger, hate. Getting to the root of these is Miller's forte.

Chapter 24
Caught in a Storm

It's still hot when I go outside to get my bike, but there's a crackle to the air, like a thunderstorm is brewing. Where I'm standing is bright sunlight, but I can see dark clouds off to my left. I select the fastest setting on my bike and pedal hard to get home before the rain hits. I'm concentrating on my route, trying to time lights and crossings so that I don't have to stop too often, but I can't quite get Ridley out of my head. My nerves are on edge, and I wonder if I've already said too much, whether someone out there thinks I'm getting too close.

The rumble of a big truck right behind me makes me start, and I glance over my shoulder to see how close it is. I have to slow down anyway because I'm now biking on the sidewalk and need to watch out for pedestrians. The truck is a gray putty color, just like Wryan's. It's the same make, too. I make a turn and almost forget about it when I hear the rumble again. Sure enough, when I glance back, the truck is still there. Now I'm certain: it *is* Wryan's!

Someone from the team has taken it and has come looking for me. It's darkening and the rain will be here any minute, but I slow way down, waiting for the truck to pass. It doesn't. The sweat on my back freezes; there's no one on the sidewalk but me, and I hear that deep, malevolent rumble coming slowly up behind me. I panic.

I gasp for breath but can't get any air, and I have to stop my bike and get off. When I do, the bike falls over and I almost trip over it. Leaning low with my head almost to my knees, I force myself to take long, deep breaths. Raindrops hit my neck and helmet.

"Lily? Lily! Are you all right?"

Star's voice emanates from the lowered window of the truck. It isn't Wryan's; it's Star. I remain leaning over with my hands on my knees, but I lift my head to watch as she pulls over and parks. She leaps out of the truck and helps me pick up my bike.

"Are you all right?" She says again, "I thought that was you on the bike, but I wasn't sure. It looked pretty stormy, though, so I figured if it *was* you I'd offer you a ride."

The rain has picked up and I calm down enough to stand up straight and flash her a sheepish grin. "Hi! You scared me at first! Thanks, though, I wouldn't mind a lift."

Together we get my bike into the bed of her truck, and I hop into the passenger seat just as it begins to pour. When we get to my apartment building, I guide her to the guest area of our parking garage, and when she pulls in, we both start laughing, watching the rain come down in sheets from the dry safety of the car park.

Star apologizes for scaring me, and I assure her it was my own head seeing shadows.

"Your truck looks just like Wryan's and I guess I… I thought someone was following me," I look sideways at her, abashed at my stupidity.

"You're right—it does look like Wryan's! It's not mine, actually. I usually take the Ride On to get to work, but I just bought a new couch. My manager let me borrow his truck to drop off the old one at Goodwill."

I let out a deep breath. "Well, your timing was perfect, so thanks again. I'm such an idiot."

"You're definitely not an idiot. I'm freaked out by this murder myself, and he was your *boyfriend*. It's spooky. Also, you're not the only one to make that mistake about the truck. Did you hear what happened last night?"

It turned out that Nathaniel also mistook the truck for Wryan's. When he left the memorial gathering, he saw Star's manager loading something into the back. He went over, demanding to know what the guy thought he was doing.

"Apparently, he went ballistic and made some nasty threats. My manager is pretty chill, but he said it really threw him—the way the guy's eyes were staring, and the expression on his face."

"Nathaniel? I can't believe! What happened?"

Star smiles. The manager kept his cool, calmly letting Nathaniel know he'd made a mistake; the truck wasn't Wryan's.

Nathaniel had calmed down immediately and was extremely contrite. He'd apologized over and over, and the two of them had laughed it off, shaking hands at the end.

"He'd just been with you guys, so he was probably really emotional, you know? Protective. He didn't want anything of Wryan's mauled by some car thief."

"That sounds like Nathaniel," I smile back at Star.

The rain has nearly stopped, so she helps me get my bike out and beeps her horn on her way out. I lock the bike and go inside, telling myself to get a grip. I haven't been asking a lot of questions, and while I'd dropped a bombshell last night, it wasn't news that would make me appear dangerous to anyone. It would make no sense for someone to come after me now. I overreacted horribly, but then, so had Nathaniel. I take this as another reminder to watch my step. We're all traumatized, at least to some extent; we might think we're okay, but we're not, and the tiniest thing can set us off. That can make anyone dangerous. I should definitely step back and leave this all alone, but I know I won't be able to do that. No, I will be doing quite the opposite.

Chapter 25
Miller's House

Early in the evening, I arrive at Miller's to find Karen already there amidst the commotion of all the kids milling around the hallway while the two teenagers and Miller's husband prepare to depart. I say hello, and they greet me politely, but their minds are elsewhere. Hair up or hair down? A quick change of shoes, and where is my green purse? Then it's glasses, phones, money, car keys—there's a lot that needs to happen in a short period. Eventually, though, they're off, and Miller's younger kids drift away to their rooms. Karen, Miller, and I seat ourselves at the dining table, each with a glass of chilled white wine, and lean in like a cabal, ready to get down to business.

Karen has already managed to give Miller the news about the ten thousand dollars, as well as some of the details of the master plan from our discussion this afternoon, so I'm mercifully spared going through it all again. I take the opportunity to start us off on a different tack, asking Miller what she meant by "I think it's him."

"Remember at our last happy hour, when Carlo made that aside about how their coach can't possibly leave the babies on their own for a weekend?"

"I do now you mention it," says Karen. "Celeste was sitting next to me, and snorted softly, like in sarcastic agreement. When I asked what that meant, she said he'd told them he needed to be at a run-of-the-mill 18U meet instead of with them for the big ultra. She said it as if she was disgusted, but I actually thought she was mostly disappointed."

"Yeah, well," says Miller, "at the memorial I heard Max ask Carlo if Romin was coming, and Carlo was surprised. He said something like, 'It's a long drive. He'll probably go to the funeral at home.' Then Max said he thought he saw him in Hillandale."

Karen and I look at each other and then back at Miller, who complacently sips her wine while we work out the rest. Now, Karen and I get into a telepathic debate over which of us is going to 'fess up that we are not up to the task.

"Who's Romin?" I ask at the same time Karen pipes up, "Where's Hillandale?"

Miller groans, closing her eyes and letting her head drop back for a moment. She's only pretending to be frustrated; secretly, Miller is ecstatic to be the one in the know. "Guys. Didn't you read the article? Romin Anjani is their coach." She turns to Karen. "Hillandale, Maryland, is where the team had their Airbnb. One of the event hotels is there, and it was running a shuttle to the start line for participants. The one Nahla took." With this, she sits back and takes another sip of her drink.

Karen and I flick our eyes at each other for another quick instant of telepathy. Neither of us had remembered the coach's name, and how does Miller know so much about the Airbnb? Aligned in our thinking, we each take a sip of our own wine.

"Got it. This all means...?" I wade in carefully.

"They weren't expecting him to be at the race, but he was there. So, why would he come down and not tell the team? I think maybe to see Izzie."

Mic drop. Silence.

"Wait a minute. Do you mean you think Romin Anjani was Izzie's secret boyfriend?" I ask, askance at first, but something in my stomach lurches. How could we have missed this? Coach-athlete illicit romance—it's practically a cliché. He was right there with the team every day; he was someone Izzie would have admired, and their liaison would be something both she and he would absolutely have wanted to keep quiet. It fits.

"Ding ding ding!" crows Miller. "I'd bet money on it, at any rate. I don't buy it that she just wanted to avoid drama. She wanted to keep people from prying and finding out she's dating her coach."

"Ho-ly moly! You could be right," Karen exclaims. "And now you mention it, I remember someone else mentioned that hotel, because Nathaniel Tau was staying there. He drove up from DC after work to give them new gear to wear at the race."

"Whatever. Tau was supposed to be there, but Anjani wasn't." Miller sets her glass on the table.

"Okay, let's consider the Anjani-as-Izzie's-boyfriend angle," says Karen. "What if Wryan was trying to bribe him to leave Izzie alone? Maybe that's why he had the money. And something went sour...?"

Miller replies, "Oh, yeah, that could have been what happened."

I turn my thoughts to Izzie with a new sense of hope. "I was convinced Izzie and Wryan were murdered together, and it was a fluke that only his body washed ashore," I ponder out loud. "But if there was some kind of fight like that, she might have fled. With Anjani or without him. Do you think she might have fled when it started and didn't see Wryan get killed? And since she's not in touch with anyone, she still hasn't heard the news?"

"It's possible if she panicked, but if that's all that happened, she'd have gotten in touch with someone by now," Miller says. "But what if there was a fight, and Izzie witnessed Anjani kill Wryan, and that's what scared her? She might still be terrified and in hiding from him."

"That's definitely possible." I pause, thinking about Izzie. Fiery, intense, capricious, spontaneous. If she fell in love with someone, it would be all-consuming. I imagine her being overcome by the emotion of a moment, acting with passion, and then utterly, abjectly regretting it later. "Or, it could be even worse. What if Anjani forced her to help him move Wryan's body into the water, and they're both in hiding from the police?"

"Oh no! No, no, no! Back up a minute. Have the police talked to Anjani? I mean, if he's missing too, I'm sure we'd have heard about it by now," Karen says reasonably.

"True," I agree, feeling somewhat better until another, worse thought occurs to me.

"You guys don't think Izzie... on her own... that she's hiding from the police because *she*..." I can't finish it. We look at each other, but no one speaks. Could Izzie have killed Wryan? No way. Impossible. Forget it.

"No, we don't," Karen says adamantly. "She'd have absolutely no reason to, especially right before the race, and no matter what, she never would."

"Karen's right, Lily. There's no way. Hey, do you guys want some ice cream? I want dessert." Without waiting for an answer, Miller gets up, crosses to the fridge, grabs a box of Good Humor bars out of the freezer, and waves it at us. It's a clumsy attempt at pulling us out of the horror of our musings and the despondency that has descended upon us. I don't feel like eating, but I appreciate her intent.

"Sure," I say, and Karen holds up her hands as if to suggest she toss one to her. Instead, Miller takes out three bars, puts the box back in the freezer, and passes the bars to us as she re-seats herself.

"Izzie and her coach. Nice catch, Miller!" Karen shakes her ice cream at her, and I nod.

"You guys," Miller scoffs, but I could tell she was pleased.

"What do we do now? Do we tell the police?" I ask.

"Nah. All we have is speculation right now. But haven't you been texting Gail? Maybe we could get together with her while she's still in town. Ask her if *she* thinks we might be onto something first. We could be totally off base, and she might be able to tell us why."

"That's a good idea. I'll see what I can do," I agree, completely forgetting for the moment Ridley's caution. Outside the kitchen window, I notice that it's starting to get dark, and while I have a light on my bike, I didn't come fully equipped for night riding this evening, so I tell them I'd better get going. They both hug me, and then I'm off, pedaling through quiet neighborhoods back to the apartment.

Maybe the ice cream worked, or maybe it's the fresh air, but as I move along, the bleakness of our conversation dissipates and I'm left with a buoyant sense of possibility. I can't imagine Izzie helping, much less *being*, Wryan's murderer—but I can imagine her fighting someone off, even if it was her new lover, to protect Wryan, who was her friend and teammate. Izzie could be on the run from the murderer, or she could be his captive, but either way, she could still be alive. No one can bring Wryan back, but I'm now elated at the possibility that there is a chance for Izzie. I pedal easily, enjoying the light breeze and the relief from the oppressive humidity that has been lifted by the afternoon's storm. Fireflies flicker here and there in people's yards as I pass, and there's something about the evening that is so peaceful and yet so invigorating; right at this moment, I'm as optimistic and relaxed as I've been in days. Somehow, everything will be all right. *Things have a way of working out for the best*, I think to myself, *even if you can't see how yet.*

No one has a crystal ball, of course, and that's too bad. It would be useful to know sometimes how completely and catastrophically wrong you are going to turn out to be.

Chapter 26
Izzie

I wake up the next morning feeling calm and content, and my mind is clear, neither numb nor swirling. I go for an early morning swim, but forgo the hot tub afterward, opting instead to stretch out on my towel on one of the lounge chairs to count my 100 breaths. Every move is mindful, neither done in a hurry nor taking too long. I go downstairs and get dressed, thinking I would make the short trip to Starbucks for coffee, but just as I'm about to leave, I convince myself I don't need to spend the money. I'm standing in the lobby of the apartment building and have the sensation that everything is bold and bright, as if I can sense every detail of my surroundings: the vibrant colors of the seats and carpets, the piano music playing softly over the speakers, the ebb and flow of chatter as people come in or depart. I'm completely tuned in to the entire scene, but not thrown off by it. Here and now, I'm ready to think.

I cross the lobby to the library alcove and sit down, pulling my notebook and pen out of my bag. The alcove is a semi-private common area with a few chairs surrounded by shelves, where people are free to either take or leave a book. Some committee organizes the books more or less by category, and it's a rather cozy spot, but today I just want a quiet place to start writing my thoughts down before they fade away.

I start with Izzie. She had a boyfriend—someone serious, and someone she kept secret from the rest of the team. The most likely candidate is her coach, Romin Anjani. Could she have run off with him? Deciding that that would be easier than facing everyone, or maybe swept up in the romanticism of it all? It's strange that she would abandon the team before the big race, but maybe it was their only opportunity. Despite the timing, it's a possibility; Izzie had a wild streak to her. It's the simplest solution to her disappearance, and even if Romin is not missing, it can still make sense. Maybe he came home to, I don't know, clear up loose ends or something while Izzie waits for him. She wouldn't contact anyone because she wouldn't want anyone to try to dissuade her. I chew on this, liking the idea but still not sure...

I don't know what made me look up, but I do and see Toni Ridley open the double doors of the apartment building and walk toward the front desk. She's looking around the lobby as she does so, taking it all in, and stops when she notices me. She keeps eye contact with me as she changes course to come over to the alcove and sit down.

"Hey there," she says as I watch her and wait. "How've you been doing?"

"Good," I tell her, suddenly feeling anything but. "Were you coming to see me?"

"Mm hm," she murmurs gently, so gently, her head slowly moving up and down while her dark brown eyes stare solemnly at me. She doesn't have to say any more than that; I know why she's here, but I ask anyway.

"What happened?"

"They found your friend Izzie, Lily. I came here to tell you myself. I'm sorry."

Tears well up, but then subside. My curiosity, at least for now, quells the worst of my grief.

"Where was she? How did you find her?" For a second I lose my voice, but then manage a tremulous, "She's dead, isn't she?"

"Yes, she is. She appears to have sneaked into the yard next door to the team's Airbnb house to use the neighbor's hot tub. The owners of the hot tub found her yesterday and called the local police, but it took a while for everyone to put the pieces together that that body was the young woman we've been looking for."

"A hot tub? So... not the same as Wryan? Wait... why do you say she snuck in herself? Was it an accident? She wasn't murdered?" The news was confusing, too bizarre to have considered.

"It is very strange. She wasn't strangled, and her body wasn't moved, so no, not like Wryan."

"But if they weren't killed together, then why didn't she... I mean, when did she die?"

"The ME's report is pending, but as of now it's a good bet she died the same night he did."

"By *accident?* No way. That's impossible. It's too much of a coincidence!"

"It certainly is very strange," she repeats. "I don't have any other information for you, but it's Montgomery County's case, and they're still investigating. The officers on the scene didn't see any obvious signs of struggle, though, so their original assessment was accidental death. That's not confirmed, of course. Now that everyone knows it's Isla Walker, they're reviewing everything."

She tells me that Dan is talking to Izzie's Aspire teammates, and that he's requested Dr. Ben be consulted, because Dr. Ben did the autopsy on Wryan. Her voice is soft but definitive. Izzie is dead. It looks like an accident, but they will investigate thoroughly to be sure, because it would indeed be a coincidence for the ages.

"All this time? No one saw her in there?"

Toni explains that the hot tub is surrounded by plantings to make it private, so it is hidden from the street and not even visible through the windows of the owners' single-story house. The husband didn't notice anything was wrong until he went to cut the grass.

"You can see it partially from one of the upstairs bedrooms of the Airbnb, which is how Isla might have known it was there. But it was still dark when everyone left to get to the race. They probably wouldn't have seen her even if they'd looked."

I rock back and forth on my chair a few times, taking it in and barely holding myself together. When she pauses, I say, "Can I help? Somehow? Thank you for telling me. I wish I weren't so useless."

"You're not useless," she gives a sorrowful smile. Pointing at the notebook, she says, "Keep that up. If you come up with something that seems relevant, call Dan. Or call me." She places her card on the table next to me.

"I thought you said this was a county case now?"

She smiles. "It is, but I know the lead investigator. And I know Lily Piper."

Now it's my turn to smile, appreciating her kindness. "Actually, there is something. We think Izzie's boyfriend might have been the Aspire coach, Romin Anjani," I tell her.

"What makes you say that? Did she or the coach say something to someone?"

"No, it's just that it makes sense it might be him. And Max thought he saw him near the Airbnb the night before the race, even though he was supposed to be in Pittsburgh for a junior meet."

"I see. Thank you—I'll make sure the investigators are aware of your suspicions. Is there anything else you think they should know?"

What does that mean? Is this news? Is Anjani a suspect? Did they clear him? Is there someone else? Toni conveys no inkling. In her way, she is even better at keeping mum than her husband.

She doesn't move, and I realize her question was a real one. Is there anything else? I shake my head slowly, sadly. I'd been wound-up, determined to find Izzie, to extricate her from whatever nightmare had enveloped her. I'd convinced myself she was alive and in trouble. The fact that she is dead, and has been for days, knocks the air out of me. I feel lifeless and slow, both physically and mentally.

"Okay, then. Take care of yourself; you've had a shock. And if you want or need to (she indicates her card on the table), you can always call."

"I will. Thanks again for coming to tell me."

I watch Toni depart and then I text the others. It's not my preferred method of communication for something like this, but I know that if it were me, I would want to know as soon as possible, by whatever medium.

T Ridley told me they found Izzie's body

I add a broken heart and a flowers emoji because it is too stark without something to show emotion.

Karen: Oh NO! How?
Miller: Seriously? When?
Haisley: Damn. Who?
Redd: I'm so sorry. Where?

I can't begin to answer their questions via text; I'm not absolutely certain I even know what they're asking. Presumably Karen wants to know how Izzie died, but perhaps she is wondering how they found her. Miller's question, too, has multiple possibilities—when did they find her? When did she die? When did Toni Ridley tell me? Ditto for Haisley—I'm assuming she wants to know who found Izzie, but is she assuming murder and wants to know who the police suspect? Redd wants to know where she was found, but I know more info will only beg more questions. I text back:

idk

It's all I can say at the moment that covers everything.

Everybody "hearts" that one, but I know that what they really mean is that they're sending me their love. Our text strings are generally mass confusion, but some things come through loud and clear.

I'm still sitting in the chair in the alcove, and I look down at the notebook in my lap. *Useless! This is useless!* is the first thing that comes to mind, so forcefully I have an overwhelming urge to hurl the notebook across the lobby. Instead, I use it as a shield to hide my face as I cry tears of fury, grief, and frustration.

When I stop and calm down, I actually do feel a little better, but I'm a mess. I go back to the apartment and check on Otto and the cats, plug my phone in to recharge, and force myself to regroup. We've learned something. It's terrible knowledge, but it's crucial. Izzie isn't missing anymore. Two members of Aspire died the same night, in the same place. We are well ahead of where we were yesterday, which means we are making progress. Now is not the time for grief; it is the time for action.

The problem is I don't know exactly what action, so I call my mom.

Chapter 27
Mom

She sounds upbeat when she picks up, which is encouraging. After my dad had a stroke, they had to move together to a nursing home that could provide nearly full-time care for him. It has been a particularly stressful change for Mom, as she is nearly 30 years younger than Dad and only in her fifties, and she is still so full of energy and vivacity. The good news is that the array of physical, occupational, and cognitive therapies provided to my dad has helped him dramatically improve his ability to move and to talk, and this in turn has been a great relief to my mom. In fact, all the additional care has afforded her more freedom than she ever imagined, not only to continue working but to follow her own pursuits. I'm having second thoughts about my original plan, which was to tell her all about Wryan and Izzie and ask her what she thinks. She sounds so chirpy that I don't want to lay anything on her that might disturb this very welcome frame of mind.

I barely get a word in anyway before she tells me excitedly that the girls' trip she and her two best friends from college have been planning is taking shape. They're going to Belize in November, and she's already received a bunch of travel information in her email.

"How do I keep track of all this? They've already changed the flight time from when we first booked it. I don't want to mix everything up."

I'm immediately sucked into "help" mode, because organizing a trip to Belize is infinitely more appealing than contemplating the murder of two friends. "They usually send a link or something you can click on to add it directly to your wallet, and it'll default to the latest update. Did you do that?"

"No," she says, and I can tell from her voice she's looking through her email. "I was trying to keep all the messages in a folder, but I may have missed some."

"Your tickets should go straight to your wallet, and your hotels and flights should go to your calendar."

There's silence, and then she says, "It wants to know which calendar."

"You still have an iPhone, right? Select the Apple calendar."

"Oh! There it is! Now I just add it, right? Nice!" she says, talking to herself as I grin down the phone.

"All good?"

"Yes! It's all here, and the calendar has the flights, the hotel, the address, everything. Technology is amazing."

"Yes, it is! When it works, that is," I caveat, and she laughs.

I crave the joy I imagine on her face, and ask her to tell me more about her trip.

"Oh, Lily, it's going to be amazing, and I think of you all the time because you'd probably love it too. We're starting out on a three-day yoga retreat, and then we're staying for the rest of the week to do our own thing. Thursday there's a boat that's going to take us all snorkeling, and on Friday we're going..." She chatters on happily, describing the itinerary and what the various day trips entail, and although I love hearing her so animated, I'm only half listening.

When we were going through the calendar steps, she said something that got my brain ticking. *It's all here, and the calendar has the flights, the hotel, the address, everything.* Call me obsessive, but I'm locked into anything that feels like intuition now. What is it about my mom's comment that seems important? I don't know, but I'm paying attention. It may be late in the game, but I'm wide awake now. I write *calendar?* in my notebook as we finish our phone call. Then I focus my mind on Aspire, allowing any memories to drift where they will, confident that if I wait patiently enough, these whispers will find their way into my consciousness.

***

"Is this it?" Asked Wryan, veering toward a ramp with so many numbers indicated, I didn't have time to read half of them.

"I think so," I said, having no clue.

After our last dinner together, Wryan offered to take me home to grab my things and then give me a lift to Tessa's, where I was going to stay the night. We were both delighted with the plan, as I'd talked about her magnificent pool many times and this would be his chance to see it. He'd headed toward the river, knowing Tessa's house is right by the canal, but we ended up going in the wrong direction, east toward DC instead of west. Unable to get to an exit to turn around, we found ourselves barreling across the Potomac, realizing all too late that we were en route to Virginia. Traffic momentarily kept us at a crawl, and we both started giggling at our predicament.

"It's very pretty," commented Wryan, looking on the bright side.

"Sure is! I'm glad we decided on the scenic route!"

We continued on; traffic sped up again, and road signs, arrow directions, and merge information flashed at us confusingly. Wryan spotted another bridge, and we crossed the river again.

"Is this DC? Or Maryland?"

"Um... pretty sure it's DC. Take that left!"

We drove along, me mortified at being so lost in the place where I supposedly grew up, Wryan utterly amused.

"I think we passed that."

"Really? I don't recognize it."

"I don't want to be insulting, but you do look adorable when you're concentrating."

I glowered at him for an instant, and we both laughed.

"This one?"

"Yes! Take it!"

Damn, we were crossing the river again, back to Virginia, which sent us into conniptions.

"I think we must concede defeat and use the navigator."

I covered my face in shame, but nodded and reached toward the navigation screen, where Wryan's phone was connected to the car's display. I was about to press the top Castlevine, when Wryan stopped me.

"Not that one! We need the second one."

There were indeed two Castlevines in the "recents" list, and it was the second one that was located near my apartment. At the time, I didn't think twice about it and pressed the button for the quickest way home. But what if...?

***

"Lily? You here?" Haisley calls. Mom and I finished our conversation twenty minutes ago, but I haven't moved.

"In here!" I call back, and she pokes her head in the door.

"You okay?"

"Yeah. I mean, you know."

"I know." Haisley comes over and gives me a hug. I tell her the little information Toni Ridley gave me, and she screws up her face and looks at me through one eye. "That is so strange. There's definitely more to the story. I hope they can find out what it is."

I tell her about talking to my mom and getting that funny feeling that I'm onto something.

"Wryan had two Castlevines in his nav list. I'd just assumed it was a case of entering the wrong address for a hotel chain that had two Bethesda locations. Wrong Way Wryan, remember? But now it seems more likely that he would have received an email like the ones my mom just did, where all that information is provided for you, no possibility of error. If it wasn't a mistake, then what was it? Why would he have had two close but different locations for the same hotel name?"

"Beats me, but trust your gut. Did you look up the top one? That would have been the most recent place he went, too. Maybe it was why he came back to Bethesda."

I nod. I'd thought the same thing and checked the website. It's bigger than the one near us, and advertises space and amenities for conventions and other large gatherings. "I checked the listing of events, thinking that might be where Nathaniel Tau's trade show was taking place, but I didn't see anything like that."

"Good idea, though," Haisley acknowledges.

I tell her I'm meeting Tessa and Phyllis in the morning to accompany them on a training run on the Capital Crescent Trail, and that I've decided to take a detour on my way back to check out this second Castlevine.

"I don't know precisely what I'm looking for, but I'm convinced it wasn't a mistake—Wryan went there for some reason."

"It can't hurt, right? Hey, you said you'd been talking to your mom when you got that feeling. Could Wryan have gone there for his mom? Like, if there was some alternative medicine conference going on?" muses Haisley. "Maybe there's some non-FDA approved cancer treatment that required cash."

"Yeah! Now that is something I can imagine him doing." I make a note. "Thanks, Haze. Good idea."

Chapter 28
Families

After Haisley leaves, I lie back on my bed thinking about Wryan's mom. We'd discussed our families at length over the course of our dates together, and his mom's cancer and my dad's stroke had been something of a bond between us. Before I know it, I'm fast asleep. I dream weird dreams, and start to wake up in the middle of one, ending up half-thinking, half-dreaming. Dee Dee jumps onto the bed and turns in slow circles, finally settling herself against my back. It's a comforting feeling, and I continue to lie still, even though I'm wide awake now. My half-thinking turns into reviewing a real memory of one of our phone calls.

***

"Your parents must love flowers," Wryan remarked when I told him my middle name is Rose.

"You'd think so, but not really. My mom's maiden name is Rose." We were on a video call, and I rested the phone against a pillow and pulled the strap of my tank top aside to show him my shoulder tattoo of two little roses nestled together. "We went to do this when I graduated from high school. She got the same one on her wrist."

"I love it! Your mom sounds awesome."

I smiled at that, thinking he was right; but the truth is, from what he's said about his mom, she sounds awesome, too, and I turned the conversation to his parents.

"Duncan is a Wells, but your name is Burley; your mom must be Uncle Alistair's sister?" I asked at one point.

Wryan shook his head, finished the diet soda he was drinking, and tossed it somewhere off-camera, presumably into a trash can. "Nope. My dad's name is, or was, Barrett Wells. He left us when I was still a baby, so I have no memories of him, and my mom doesn't talk about him much. I don't think it was a happy marriage, and then one day he was just gone. No contact ever, no divorce, no not hing."

"That's horrible."

"I'm sure it was for my mom, but then she met Fred Burley. They never married because my mom believed that she was still technically married to Barrett. But she changed her name legally to Burley after they'd been together for a few years, and I did the same when I turned eighteen. To me, he's my dad, and I've always thought of us as the Burleys," he grinned. "Makes perfect sense, right?"

"It totally does! I know you're all close from the way you talk about them. It's kind of sad, though. You never tried to find out what happened to Barrett?"

"No, and honestly, I've barely ever thought about him at all. We did learn a few years ago that he committed suicide while in a rehab facility in California—someone informed Uncle Alistair, and he contacted my mom. By that time, it was all water under the bridge for us, but you're right. It's a sad ending."

"Yeah." We were both quiet for a moment, and then another thought occurred to me. "Wait a minute—if you're a Wells by birth, do *you* have a title?"

Wryan burst out laughing. "Oh no, we're out for the count, disinherited from all that. I'm not sure what I would do with one, anyway; the only title I really want is 'Doctor!'"

I smiled understanding, and then he added more soberly, "I've never even been to St. Sava. I keep thinking I should go one day, but the timing is never right."

"Not even visiting together with Duke?"

"Not so far, but maybe one day. It's funny. Even though we have no real ties to it, except for Duke of course, there are still a few things that have stuck from 'the old country' (he pronounced the phrase in an accent very like Duke's, only more distinctive). Little traditions, you know? Like, we celebrate Boxing Day, and I always keep a St. Sava coin in my glove box for safe travels."

***

I sit up in bed and lean over to open the drawer of my bedside table. From inside, I pull out the one thing Wryan ever gave me, a jokey-sincere reminder of our discussion. It's a postcard—a postcard!—he'd sent me not long after. It's from St. Sava, and very old. On the front is a photograph of a rose intricately carved in wood. Smiling to myself, I turn it over to read his note.

Hahaha! Don't laugh—I found this cleaning out my desk and immediately thought of you! Have a wonderful day, Lily Rose!

(PS: If you've never seen one before, this is called a postcard. It's not supposed to have an envelope!)

It was signed "W" and he'd added "xxx" below his initial.

I swallow hard and put the card back in my drawer. Then I get up to make myself a cup of tea.

Chapter 29
Tea

I'm sitting at our kitchen counter waiting for the water to boil, idly flipping through the previous pages of my notebook, when I stop at the *"bacon?"* notation. I remember that frisson of recognition that something here might be important, but, seriously, bacon? That can't be it. So, what then? And what made me stop at this particular spot? Was it my memory of Wryan and the postcard? Is there some connection to Madame? I think back to the lesson topic the day I was late, which had to do with mushroom infusions.

Click.

Have you ever noticed how, once you hear a strange new word or learn some piece of wacky trivia, you suddenly bump into it everywhere? I found this to be true of many of the things we learned from Aspire. I came across an underwater rugby match surfing TV channels late one night, a sport I'd never heard of before meeting Wryan. Redd mentioned that a horse in this year's

Belmont Stakes was foaled at Hilander and trained there before being sold to a stable in America. Then, only a day or so after the mushroom class, I was in the international grocery store and noticed a small placard on a shelf with teas from *South Africa, Botswana, and St. Sava*. I couldn't believe my eyes because Wryan had just told me about St. Sava. I took a box at random to study it when I heard Madame Klimenkova's voice beside me.

"Lily! I see you remember talk about *mukhomor*—the teas of the Amanita mushroom! Very good! Very beneficial. I think you will like." She picked up a box from the shelf herself and started reading.

"St. Sava! Yes! Is British now, but you know it was originally Serbian?"

I always feel shy around Madame, never quite sure what she thinks of me, so it flusters me when she pays attention to me. All I could do was shake my head.

"Is true! There's still big monastery there. You know, women in St. Sava wear their wedding ring on right hand? It is Slavic way; in Russia is the same." She shows me her wedding ring, and I smile at her stupidly, still too shy to speak, although I do find it interesting that she still wears the ring; her husband died years ago.

Madame returns to her study of the box, tsking. "I don't know this brand. Here, I show you good one you can trust."

Not wanting to insult her, I quickly replaced the box I was holding and followed her over to the shelf of teas from Russia and Ukraine.

"Here is one. This is company I know. You take this with honey, very tasty, very relaxing. Help you sleep and give you good mood. You try, you tell me what you think." She hands me a box of tea bags, along with a bottle of capsules.

"Try as tea, I think you like best, but for sleep maybe better to take pill. Only one! More is not better with the *mukhomor*, you understand? And no alcohol!"

She smiled encouragingly, and I smiled back, wanting her approbation, wanting to be a good student, despite the fact that the entirety of our conversation had been one-sided. I never said a word, but, too embarrassed not to take her recommendation, I'd bought both the box of tea and the bottle of capsules at what was—to me—horrendous expense. I wasn't unhappy, though. Madame's rambling, entrancing, highly entertaining class on mushroom tisanes, powders, and tinctures had been fascinating, and while I hadn't intended to try any of them just yet, the lore and benefits associated with them had indeed been intriguing. The fact that she was smiling at me in the shop as if I were her pet pupil didn't hurt either.

As instructed, I'd tried both of my purchases, but quickly abandoned them. Tasty is not the word that came to mind for the tea. Or perhaps it was the rather earthy aroma that struck me first, spoiling any chance for my taste buds. As for the capsules, while they definitely put me to sleep, my dreams were wild, the colors overly bright and disturbing. I almost couldn't tell if I was asleep or awake; my visions seemed so real. I woke up unsettled, just for a moment not even sure where I was. The other thing that turned me off was the warning label, the breadth and severity of potential consequences of ingesting Amanita muscaria not being something I could put out of my head. I didn't want to hurt Madame's feelings, so I told her they made me sleep like a baby, and the way her face lit up and she smiled proudly back at me certainly did do wonders for my mood.

Listen to your gut.

I sit still, not racking my brains but letting thought come to me. Something about this tea is bothering me, calling to me, so I go to the cabinet to find my own box. This one is from Ukraine, not St. Sava, but it's the same mushroom. I go back to my chair and start searching on my phone for warnings and side effects, of which there are plenty. The coincidence of its provenance from St. Sava strikes me as significant. Did Izzie drink this tea and experience these side effects? It seems far-fetched, and anyway, if she did, any complications would be an accident. I don't believe her death was an accident. Nevertheless, I write down "muscimol," the English name for Madame Klimenkova's "mukhomor," the mushroom's active substance, in my notebook.

I stare off into space, a thought forming. Are we looking at this the wrong way around? Maybe we need to consider...

My phone dings loudly, the third time in as many minutes. This might be important.

Chapter 30
Relationships

When I pick it up, I see a slew of new text messages.

Miller: He's married!
Redd: Fiancee
Haisley: Broke up
Karen: ???

I'm with Karen on this one, but rather than piling onto the bedlam, I text back asking if any of them are planning to come to class this afternoon, figuring we could meet at the studio and talk sensibly in person. Miller and Redd both say yes, so I give a thumbs up and mentally plan to walk over to Eye of Horus near the end of the session. I'm about to put the phone down again when another text appears from Gail:

Have you heard? Call me when you can

"Gail! Oh my God. I'm so sorry." She picks up at the first ring, and I tell her I did hear that they'd found Izzie, and we take turns commiserating and scratching our heads at how strange it is. Two expert swimmers drown at the same time, one by murder, the other by accident. It simply does not compute.

"Maybe Wryan saw something or thought Izzie was in trouble and went out to help, and that's when whoever it was killed him," Gail says.

"Is that what you all think?"

"Kind of, I guess. It's the only remotely feasible explanation that any of us can think of, but it leaves an awful lot of questions unexplained," she says, her voice tight and frustrated. In the background, I hear faint noise and music.

"Are you at home? Or out somewhere?"

"Actually, that's another reason why I texted you. I couldn't take it sitting in our rental anymore. Are you around by any chance? I'm at that pizza place you told us about."

"Sure," I tell her, surprised but pleased. "I was going to try to meet up with Redd and Miller when they finish their yoga class. Would you mind if I text them and ask if they can drop by too?"

"Yes, of course! Just as long as they're Bears and not... ugh. I'll tell you when you get here."

I'm mindful of Ridley's warning, but beside myself with curiosity. I convince myself this doesn't count as asking questions; after all, it was Gail who invited me. It's broad daylight, in a popular pizza place not far away, so hardly dangerous. In less than 10 minutes I'm there, and immediately spy Gail sitting by herself at a corner table, a plate with a submarine sandwich and chips in front of her. She signals to me, but I'm already on my way over.

"Hi." Her eyes are puffy, but she smiles briefly at me. "Glad you could make it. You want anything?"

A server has arrived, and I order a Coke to keep Gail company.

"Tell me, what did you mean by 'as long as they're Bears' they can come?"

"Oh, God, Lily. It's all bad enough; the police came to tell us about Izzie and ask more questions, and then on top of that, SHE has arrived. The B-I-T-C-H," Gail groans and picks up one of her sandwich halves but puts it down again without taking a bite. I realize this is because Redd and Miller have shown up, and she is waiting for them to grab some chairs and join us.

"We got your text and decided to skip class today and come right over. How you doin', Gail? You okay?" Redd says as they sit down.

Gail nods, but her eyes fill at his concern, and she's unable to answer right away. To give her time to collect herself, I catch them both up on our conversation. When the waiter comes over, Miller also gets a Coke and Redd orders a beer.

"Ah," nods Redd perceptively when I finish by quoting Gail about the B-I-T-C-H. "The fiancée? Thought they'd broken up."

"Who on Earth are you guys talking about?" I ask, wondering how and what I'd missed.

"Anele," Gail groans again, pronouncing it *AH-na-lee*. "Duke's girlfriend."

"Oh!" I'm surprised, because as much as Wryan had talked about Duke, he'd never mentioned Anele.

Gail sticks out her palm and rotates her wrist up and then down and says to Redd, "They're on again, off again. As of an hour ago, they were on again. Who knows? If we wait long enough, she may storm off. She's such a diva."

Gail has picked up her phone and flicked through it, and is now holding up a picture of possibly the most beautiful woman I've ever seen in my life.

"Oh!" I repeat.

"Wow," says Miller.

Redd whistles softly in appreciative agreement, but looks questioningly at Gail. "I figured you all would be leaving pretty soon. How come this Anele came down now?"

"*Excellent* question. No one wants to leave without answers, but we have to get home and get on with... I don't know, our lives, I guess. So, yeah, we're all planning to leave Saturday, but she probably couldn't stand it that so much excitement is happening without her and came down, anyway. Of course, she says she's here f or *Duncan*." Gail rolls her eyes and stresses Duke's real name in a way that suggests that is the one Anele alone uses.

"And she's staying with you guys?" Miller asks.

"Oh, yes," Gail moans. "I don't know how she can be comforting, because those two go at it constantly, and when they do, everyone and everything sets her off. I finally escaped here because she screamed at me for doing the laundry loud."

Miller snorts and asks what that means.

"I don't know. There's a washer-dryer next to the kitchen. I was using it." Gail harrumphs.

"How about the others? How are they taking everything?" I ask.

Gail had been eating potato chips, but she stops, dropping the one in her hand back onto the plate. Her eyes suddenly glisten, and she has to pause before she can speak. "Badly. Maybe it's a relief for Duke to fight with Anele, because anything is better than thinking about what's happening. First Wryan, now Izzie. And then there's Wryan's mom, who's practically Duke's second mom, in hospice care from cancer. She could go any day now." Gail covers her mouth with her hand and looks away for a moment before continuing. "It's even more unbelievable because almost exactly a year ago another cousin of his in St. Sava died in a horrible accident."

"What? No way," says Miller.

"Oh my," Redd frowns and shakes his head. "What a lot of tragedy for one family! Mm mm mm. What happened?"

Gail tells us that Duke and Nahla had gone to Africa to compete in a triathlon in Durban, and had decided to spend some time with Duke's uncle in St. Sava. Nahla had been enthralled—despite her family ties, she'd never been to Botswana, or anywhere else on the African continent, so this was a chance of a lifetime. On a day trip to Gaborone, Duke introduced her to Nathaniel Tau, and they toured the Tau Activewear headquarters. "She told me it was the best two weeks of her life, and then the barn caught fire."

We can't help ourselves: we're glued to Gail, horror-stricken. She explains that Duke and Wryan's uncle, Alistair Wells (the current Duke of Hilander), had a daughter by his first wife named Faye who was visiting. Alistair and his longtime girlfriend Manou also have a teenage daughter, Chloe, who was staying in one of the barns overnight because her horse was about to give birth and she wanted to be there for it. Faye went out to keep her company and found the entire structure on fire. She didn't see Chloe and ran into the barn to get her, not knowing that, in fact, Chloe had escaped the fire and gone running after her terrified horse (which had bolted) to bring it back before something happened to it.

"And Faye is the one who died?" I whisper.

Gayle nods. "Nahla came home right away, but Duke ended up staying another month to help them through it."

We sit frozen by the enormity of it all, the litany of woe that has befallen the Wells family in such a short period of time. It's only when our server comes by to ask if we'd like anything else that we start to move again, forcing ourselves to speak in normal voices for his benefit. Since we're occupying the table, I can tell Redd feels like we need to order food. He asks for wings and fried zucchini, and when the waiter leaves, we look at each other, unsure where to start. I ask Miller about her last text, wondering if perhaps she'd heard Duke and Anele had eloped, and that's why Anele is here no w.

"Oh, yeah, no, I didn't mean Duke. I meant the coach. Romin. He's married."

"No way!" I gasp.

"Why? What's going on? What about Romin?" asks Gail. Miller explains her theory that he and Izzie were secret lovers, and asks Gail if she thinks that's possible.

Gail frowns. "Maybe," she says slowly. "Could be. I wouldn't have guessed, but... thinking back, there were times when Izzie seemed to be the first one of us to arrive at practice. I'd come in and they'd be sitting in the office chatting. It seemed pretty normal, but you know..." she looks around at us, "I've never once sat in th e office alone with Romin just chatting."

"Did you all know he was married?" asks Miller.

"Of course. His wife came by sometimes, or we'd see her at competitions."

"How did they seem? Happy?" I ask, at which Gail stretches both arms wide, raises her shoulders and looks up to the ceiling.

"I never thought about it."

Redd's order comes, and he invites us all to dig in. We fall quiet, each of us thinking our own thoughts and munching distractedly, when he suddenly stops.

"Hey wait a minute. If Romin is married, and Duke is still engaged, who broke up?"

I raise my hand as I finish eating and swallow, and they all look at me. "I think Haisley was talking about herself. I'm pretty sure she broke up with Simon."

Redd and Miller both make "oh" sounds, Redd adding that that's a shame, while Gail looks on in puzzlement. I explain about the convoluted text string, and it feels good to have something to laugh about. I tell them I'd had a feeling that something was wrong, and Miller says she thought the same. We avoid the topic of murder for the rest of the meal, and in the end we all leave the Iguana feeling a little bit better.

When I get home, I find Haisley sitting on the couch in the living room. Her face is flushed, her nose is red, and her eyes are swollen.

"Simon?" I ask, sitting down next to her as gently as I can.

"I hate him," she says, eyes flashing and then filling with tears.

"What happened?"

Haisley sniffs once and explains. "We had a fight the other night, but I was still hoping... I don't know, and it doesn't matter now because I ran into them in the lobby. Simon and *Brittney*," she says, sneering.

"Damn. I'm sorry. Did they say anything?"

"Yeah, they said, 'Hi Haisley! How's it goin', Haisley?'" Haisley herself says this in a high-pitched, mocking voice, as she flips her hair and swings her shoulders exaggeratedly. I can't help but let a tiny smile slip through.

"I was so startled, all I could do was stare at them like a big, stupid cow, and then *Brittney* says, 'I love your *hair*, Haisley' (switching back to the high-pitched voice for this last). God, I hate her. I hate them both."

"What a bitch," I agree.

"Don't tease me, I'm not in the mood," she gives me a sidelong glance, but lets her own tiny smile slip through.

"I'm not, I swear. But as a matter of fact, I love your hair too. She's probably eaten up with jealousy." Haisley has a few strands of glittery fairy hair that accentuate not only her own beautiful auburn color but her deep green eyes as well.

"Thank you." Haisley sits back miserably. "She's not jealous of me." The way she said it breaks my heart. I feel for Haisley, and for myself, and then, powerfully, for both Wryan and Izzie. They'd broken up, but each was starting to dream of another future, excited about the prospect. All for nought.

We sit together talking for over an hour. Haisley tells me about her and Simon, how they'd been so perfect for each other at first, and how impressed he was that she was getting her PhD, which boosted her own confidence and motivated her to finish. Everything was rosy, and she daydreamed about the two of them together, doing romantic things, getting married, etc., etc., etc.

"Honestly, I did sometimes sense that Simon was bored when I talked about my work. But I pushed that out of my head. I'd ask him, and he'd say all the right things, and I lapped it up. What an idiot!"

She also started to notice Brittney constantly there, hovering in the background, but she dismissed that too. She'd pegged Brittney as a party girl, always with the FOMO, had to insert herself into everything. Haisley had been so enamored with Simon she couldn't, wouldn't, see anything that might spell danger for their continued relationship. Despite the big fight, Haisley had been certain they'd get back together and make up. That is until she was confronted by the sight of Simon and Brittney together, definitively a couple.

"That's when I texted you guys that we're broken up. I wanted to make it official. I never want to have anything to do with him ever again. I hate him."

For the most part, I sat and listened, either murmuring support or empathetically echoing her disdain, but my mind was still with Wryan and Izzie. Ardor turning into contempt, accompanied by hurt, helplessness, and fury—these are things that drive people to go crazy, to do things they would never do if they were in their right mind. Haisley's plaintively furious *I hate him* reverberates in my mind. Unrequited love can turn on a dime into hate. Was Izzie seeing Romin? Was he jealous of Wryan? Or was the secret busted, and Romin's wife jealous of Izzie? Was the money some kind of payoff—or, a related thought occurs to me: was it blackmail? Celeste told the entire team that Izzie was pregnant—had that belief been a closely guarded secret, one that turned out to be the last straw for someone? What if whoever it was found Izzie in that hot tub and tried to force her underwater? If she'd had too much of the St. Sava tea, she might not have been able to put up a struggle. What if Wryan had looked out and seen Izzie in trouble, and rushed to her aid? In a rage, in a panic, and Wryan hampered by the wetsuit he was wearing, a reasonably strong person could have grabbed hold of the long nylon cord attached to the back zipper. Strangling him with it would not have taken a lot of brute strength. All it would require is to hold on tight. I remember my thought earlier that we might be looking at this the wrong way around.

Maybe Izzie, not Wryan, was the intended victim.

Chapter 31

A Hunch Pays Off

I wake up later than I meant to the next morning and have to hustle to make it to our meeting place by the appointed time. Phyllis and Tessa are already waiting for me when I zoom over on my e-bike at top speed, but they assure me they only just arrived themselves. I'm nervous because the only running I've done since college is my 20-minute warmup jog on the treadmill when I use the gym in our apartment; but I'm also excited because I remember I used to enjoy it. Tessa assured me I'd do fine, that the plan for today is a relatively easy four-mile run out and then walk back. We jog the short distance from the car to the Capital Crescent Trail, and I relax into the familiarity of the old rhythm. At first, Tessa and Phyllis chat while I hang back, listening and observing. I'm amazed at them both, for different reasons. Tessa runs like she swims: her gait is smooth and efficient, and she doesn't appear to be exerting any effort as she strides along. Phyllis runs stiffly, with short, jerky steps and unquestionable effort. Nevertheless, she finds her tempo and goes and goes—considering her age, the speed and stamina she has is remarkable. We all settle in at Phyllis' pace, which ironically is slow for Tessa, near the maximum for Phyllis (who doesn't want to hold us back), but perfect for me.

The trail takes us through a tunnel and past a water plant, and eventually down to the Potomac, where we parallel the canal towpath. It's getting harder for Phyllis to talk, so Tessa drops back to run alongside me and asks about Aspire. I've already told her that Izzie's body has been found, and now I elaborate on the meeting with Gail yesterday and the death of Duke's cousin Faye.

"What a sad story," Tessa sighs. "By the way, talking about the team reminded me of something. I've been meaning to tell you that my colleague Jodie went to the trade show for WhereGear."

"Really? What did she say? Did she meet Nathaniel Tau?"

Tessa works part-time as a fashion buyer for a company that represents a number of sports apparel brands. She's mentioned her friend Jodie, with whom she shares an office, many times over the years, but until now I didn't know that WhereGear is one of Jodie's accounts.

"Not Nathaniel himself, unfortunately, because he wasn't there when she stopped by the booth. She went to take a look at their samples and pick up their marketing literature, but she told me she was also just curious because I'd told her about you and everything that's been going on. She did see Duke and Nahla.

"Interesting. I wasn't sure they'd still go after all this. Did she talk to them?"

Tessa nods and tells Phyllis to keep straight when the path splits before returning to my question. Jodie mostly spoke to Nahla, who was reserved initially but opened up somewhat when Jodie explained she was aware of what had happened to their team. She confirmed much of what Jodie already knew from Tessa, and while this was obviously still a shock, to Jodie she'd also come across as frustrated and even angry about it.

"Angry that they're dead? Angry at the police?"

"Jodie said she sounded angry at Wryan and Izzie. At least, maybe not them, exactly, but angry that the team's path forward had been so clear, and now it's all up in the air. They're not sure what happens next, and Nahla is worried that nothing will happen if they don't pull themselves back together."

"In-ter-esting." The way she said this makes Nahla sound cold, but that's not necessarily fair. Next to Duke, Nahla is the most ambitious and the one with the greatest prospects. According to Redd, she is also practical and smart. She can mourn her friends but still be worried about what happens to her own aspirations if the team can't perform. She has worked toward these for years, overcoming immense challenges to get this far. Of course she's worried about what will happen now. "I hadn't thought about the team's future, but they all must be wondering about it. Even if they're grieving and freaked out about two friends being murdered, it's not as if they can just forget about everything else. I mean, all that preparing, training... everything they've been working toward individually and as a team has been a huge part of all their lives for a long time."

"That's true, Lily. Those things don't just turn off, even in tragedy. It's human nature to keep wanting and striving, no matter what," Phyllis surprises me by interjecting, turning her head back toward us so that we can hear her before plowing ahead again.

Bemused, I look over at Tessa, who shrugs and then nods. "The people left behind still have to move forward."

"And Duke? How did he seem?"

"Smooth," Tessa grins, but then turns serious again. "She said he was pleasant and very attentive, especially when he heard she buys for WhereGear. You can't tell from his demeanor that anything is wrong, but he might be avoiding his own grief and anger by focusing his full attention on the present."

"Oh, yes!" Phyllis breaks in again, turning her head just long enough to make another comment. "People do that. Especially A-type personalities. They take comfort in working."

Tessa and I do the same bemused look-shrug-nod thing, and then we all fall silent until we reach our four-mile mark and slow to a stop. We give each other high-fives as we catch our breath and turn around to walk back. As my heart rate slows to its normal rhythm, I can't help feeling elation and a certain pride in having managed the run so comfortably.

As we walk, I consider Jodie's impressions of Nahla and Duke, and wonder about the other members: Max and Carlo, Celeste, and even Gail. None of them are putting in the kind of effort that keeps them at the elite level of athletic competition for the sheer fun of it. They're putting in a lot of hours on top of their jobs, studies, and personal lives. They all had big dreams and very specific goals. Are those goals in jeopardy? Or do they think they can bury their feelings and continue on without missing a beat? And is it possible that while the loss of Wryan and Izzie is a terrible blow in most ways, it's a good thing for someone? I'm back to my original quandary: were they murdered for passion? Or for greed?

The route is mostly flat, and while the canal is stagnant and covered with green algae, it doesn't detract from the prettiness of the scene. On the contrary, the park, which incorporates the towpath and the canal, has a pleasant ambiance of summery idyll. Trees line both sides of the path, and we're treated to occasional glimpses of the river through the leaves. It's already hot and humid, though, and rapidly getting hotter. My tank top is soaked, and I take long gulps of water from the bottle I've been carrying. I'm a wreck, but I feel good. I'm seriously considering adding regular runs to my schedule. It occurs to me that if I do that, I will be swimming, biking, and running. *Shoot, maybe I need to get into triathlon.*

"You're smiling." I look up to see Phyllis' sparkling blue eyes on me.

I tell her not to laugh and then describe my thought process. Both she and Tessa cheer.

"Come train with us anytime!"

"I'd love to! But I don't know. You guys are going to be doing mega distances. I need to start small."

"Well, how about hiking?" says Tessa. "Part of our program is to do some long, slow hikes to get used to being on our feet for hours without all the pounding."

"Count me in! I love hiking, and I haven't been in a long time!" I grin back at both of them. It's a nice feeling to be included, and despite the sadness of the past few days, I feel my spirits lift.

As I'd told Haisley I would, on the way home I stop at the big Castlevine hotel downtown. I take off my bike helmet and fluff my hair, although I know it's in vain. I swapped my tank top for a clean t-shirt while in the parking lot with Tessa and Phyllis, but I still look pretty raw. I figure I can freshen up in the restroom of the hotel before I do anything else, and that will have to be that. I take a deep breath and walk inside.

There are posters and electronic boards advertising the various events of the day and where they're taking place, but that's not what I need to know. After washing my face and re-fluffing my hair, I start walking toward reception but notice a bored-looking lady at an information desk and decide to try her first.

"Excuse me. I was wondering if you have a list of events that were held here last week?" I can't think of an explanation for asking, so I don't give one.

"Hi there," she says, sitting up straighter and pulling her screen closer. "There were quite a few; is there one in particular you wanted to know about?"

"I'm not sure. Was there something related to health?"

"Not seeing anything like that," she shakes her head, reading down her screen.

"How about sports? Especially this past Friday?"

"Not seeing that either. Unless... do you mean like esports?"

I would have laughed if I hadn't felt so discouraged. I'd been convinced that this was the reason Wryan was unexpectedly back in town the day before the race, but I can't figure out why. My shoulders fall as I capitulate to myself that this has turned out to be a dead end, but then I straighten them again, refusing to be defeated. The lady takes my gesture as a "maybe." She clicks on something and leans in to read.

"There was a pinball convention with competitions. That's kind of like an esport, right?"

"Uh, yes. That's the one," I squeak.

The lady consults her screen again and now reads out loud, " *The Mid-Atlantic Pinball Convention will showcase hundreds of machines and host various tournaments, free-play games, and a kids' zone. A full range of guest speakers and panels will provide opportunities to meet pinball designers, programmers, and sound engineers.* That one opened Thursday evening and ran through Sunday."

"Thank you. You don't happen to have any brochures or anything with more information about it, do you?"

"I'm sorry, I don't, but I remember it was popular. The place was packed all three days."

"Do you know if any of the machines were for sale?"

"Oh, I don't know about that... Jamal! Hey Jamal!" she breaks off and starts waving to a young man pulling a load of chairs on a dolly. "Jamal was there, taking care of the rooms and doing setup and stuff," she explains to me.

"Hey, Shona, wassup?" Jamal leaves his dolly and comes over to the desk.

"Yeah, hey, you remember the pinball convention? This lady wants to know if they had machines for sale."

"Mm hm, sure did. There were a LOTTA pinball machines. Some of them were for display only, you know, but most of them were for sale. I'm pretty sure there was an auction, too."

"Sounds fabulous!" I beam at him. "Do you happen to know if the ones for sale were all new ones, or were any of them refurbished?"

Jamal takes off his baseball cap and rubs his head. "You looking for a used pinball machine? 'Cause definitely they had a bunch. All kinda people looking to plug their stuff and looking for deals." He breaks into a grin. "Not just inside, either. You'd see 'em go out to the parking lot, selling out the back of their trucks! Too bad you just missed it. Check our website next year; I bet they come back."

"Great! I will, thank you! You've been super helpful."

"No problem." He gives me a smile and goes back to his dolly. I thank Shona for her help, too, and practically waltz across the floor, barely able to contain my excitement. I feel triumphant, equal parts exhilarated and relieved. Maybe I ought to feel disheartened because I've just uncovered yet another innocent explanation for what had potentially been the reason for Wryan's murder, but I'm not. Wryan had no secret life; he was exactly who and what he said he was all along. I'm so happy to know this, to realize that I wasn't duped, and that the guy I knew didn't have some evil alter ego into criminal activity. This confirmation alone makes it seem as if the murkiness is beginning to dissipate. It's as if I've found solid ground. Grinning to myself, I move to a quiet corner and take out my phone.

"Ah, Lily, to what do I owe the pleasure?" Dan Ridley answers, sounding more like Dr. Ben than his usual self, but there's a grain of sincerity behind the jokey tone.

"I think I know why Wryan might have had all that money in cash on him," I say, and sense his mood change immediately from casual to alert and professional.

"You have my attention."

"I think he sold a pinball machine."

I tell Ridley about Wryan's fascination with pinball, his pastime of restoring them, and that he was always on the lookout for ones in need of repair. He'd told me people would pay good money for some of the older ones. When Jamal talked about selling in the parking lot, a memory had come back clear and unabbreviated.

***

"You mean people do this as a job?" I asked, incredulous.

"Some do. For most of us, it's a secondary gig, but if you can get a sought-after machine working, and it's otherwise in good condition, you can make a nice profit. A lot of people pay in cash, too, so there's no paper trail." Wryan leaned in and pretended to look around, as if checking to see if anyone was spying on us. "Some of these old guys, they're a little rough around the edges. They don't do *Venmo*; they don't do *PayPal*. Cash on the barrel."

His histrionics made me laugh. "Really! The dark underbelly of the pinball trade. Do I need to notify the IRS about the black market in Monster Bash going on here?"

He laughed too and shook his head, but despite my kidding around, I was interested. Here was a whole world I'd never imagined existed. I asked if he was working on anything at the moment, and he showed me a picture of a pre-World War II electromechanical machine that he said could be worth thousands to the right customer if he could get it working again.

***

I explain all of this to Ridley, along with my discovery of the pinball convention at the downtown Bethesda Castlevine the same weekend as the triathlon.

"I did a quick check on the web, and ten thousand dollars wouldn't be out of the ballpark for the one he showed me."

"Well, well, well. You continue to amaze me with your nose for detecting, Ms. Piper. It's an intriguing theory. But I have to say, his father and some of his teammates did mention Wryan's hobby, and they were all adamant that he only worked on circuit boards, not whole machines, and that it brought him very little income. Any idea why the disconnect?"

"They're mostly right—he rarely worked on a whole machine, and he hadn't considered buying one since his mom got sick."

"But...?"

"He happened to come across one up for auction and figured it wouldn't hurt to put in a bid."

"I see."

"And there's no way Wryan would miss out on an event like this if he was going to be in the same city, because he'd have a ton of customers right on the spot who could take it away with them.

No shipping or delivering or coordinating for it to get picked up to worry about."

"Even so, it surprises me that no one else we spoke with mentioned the convention. You'd think it would be the first thing that came to mind for at least one of them."

"I doubt he'd tell any of his teammates. He wouldn't want them thinking that he was letting some esoteric hobby distract him from their big event. He wouldn't want them to blame pinball if for some reason he didn't perform as well as everyone hoped."

He's quiet for a moment. "A pinball machine is pretty big."

"It is, but he was pulling the bikes on a trailer, plus he had the whole back of his truck. He would have had space."

"Interesting. Very interesting. We'll look into it."

I feel invincible. I know I'm right. And even if it's only to eliminate a few rat holes, I'm helping. This morning's run and my discovery of the pinball machine sale have catalyzed my mind and my body. My brain fog is gone and I'm on fire now, my perspicacity positively fizzing. As soon as I hung up from the call with Ridley, another idea about Izzie and that hot tub came to me. I need to flesh it out a little, though, before I call him back.

Chapter 32

Lily's Theory

When I get home, there is a note on the kitchen counter from Haisley.

Just sent my final draft to my advisor!!! Needed to get out and take a break! Come to the Iguana when you get this—Redd is coming too! PS: Don't worry about Otto, I took him out at noon. -H

I take a quick shower and put on "real" clothes, then check that all the furries have plenty of water before racing back down the elevator and over to the shopping center. Haisley must be totally stoked, and I want to be there for her. She's girding herself for the last push once her advisor provides his comments, but for now there's nothing to do but relax and wait.

"You made it!" calls Haisley from a small table by the window. She jumps up when I come over, and we dance in a quick circle, hugging each other.

"Congratulations!"

"Oh, no, don't say that—it's bad luck. But I'm so relieved it's out the door and off my plate for a little while," she smiles.

"Fair enough. I'll just say good luck, then, and help you enjoy the day."

Redd comes in, and he gives Haisley a big hug. "Way to go, girl!"

We're all surprised to see Star come over to take our order, since she's not usually on during the day, and when she hears why we came in, she, too, gives Haisley a hug.

"Happy birthday!" she tells her with a wink. If you come on your birthday, you get a free dish of ice cream, and Haisley bounces up and down joyfully.

"Thank you! Thank you!" she says, taking in all of us.

It turns out to be a nice break; everyone relaxed, not feeling the need to rush off anywhere. Haisley jabbers happily about her post-thesis hopes and possibilities; she's already thinking ahead to when she's completely finished and has her PhD. She wants to take a long vacation somewhere fun, and she's going to apply for a post-doctoral position at a number of universities. She laughs at herself for being "boring," but the one she most hopes to get is right here at the University of Maryland.

"More research? You must be a glutton for punishment," Redd says, shaking his head but smiling to see her so excited.

"I know. It's crazy, but it's what you do when you want a career in academia, and that is what I want. I love the atmosphere, and I have so many ideas for new research projects!"

"Good for you, Haisley! I'm sure you'll get something great," I tell her, and I mean it. Wherever she lands, I know she'll be perfect.

We order lunch, and when it comes, we take our time, talking about everything and nothing. When Haisley's ice cream arrives, we sing happy birthday, and she carefully stops to make her wish before blowing out the candle.

"Thanks for coming today, guys. This has been wonderful. I kinda feel like you've been holding back, though, Lily. You look like you're bursting to say something."

She knows me so well it can be alarming, but of course, she's right. I tell them about the pinball convention, and while it's only a theory, I'm sure it explains the cash in Wryan's bag. Now it's my turn to be congratulated, and I revel in their praise. What can I say? It feels good to be admired. Scratch that; it feels amazing.

"There's another thing," I continue when everyone is quiet again. "I've been thinking about Izzie. She may have snuck into the hot tub to meditate. She may have slipped under and not come back up."

"On purpose? Mm mm mm. Doesn't sound like Izzie. What put that in your head?" asks Redd.

"Oh, no!" I assure Redd with a vehement shake of my head that I didn't mean suicide. Not at all. "It's other things that I remembered that are making me put two and two together," I say, and tell them about a conversation we had the night we first met.

As the Iguana (and our table in particular) became increasingly loud, Izzie and I had had to huddle to be able to converse, so that for some time it was just the two of us in a sea of background noise. She'd been telling me about the sport of freediving, of which I knew almost nothing, and why she liked it so much.

"When you go down deep, and it's absolutely quiet, and you're still a long way from being out of breath, it's as if the whole world has stopped and you get a perfect moment. The pressure keeps you in place, so you don't have to fight to stay down, and it feels as if Mother Earth is swaddling you."

I'd loved her description, the peace and oneness that it evoked, and asked if you can get that feeling in shallow water. She had to think about it, but then nodded, telling me that surfers sometimes meditate underwater, probably for exactly that reason.

"It's a way to practice holding your breath while taking your mind off the fact that you're holding your breath," she'd said, and we'd both laughed—not at the concept, just at the way she'd phrased it. Then she'd turned more serious, explaining, "I've been thinking of trying it. Being underwater calms you. You know how a thunder jacket quiets dogs? Even if it isn't deep, that little bit of pressure is soothing, like a hug."

I look around the table and say, "She may have seen the hot tub from the window of the Airbnb and thought it would be a way to settle her nerves, and it may have worked too well."

Haisley sits back and looks at me skeptically, one eye open and one eye closed. "It's *possible*, I suppose. I've heard of surfers drowning that way. But in a hot tub? Her first time meditating, and nerves a wreck about the race? Hard to imagine she'd zonk out to that extent." She leans forward again and puts her elbows on the table, resting her chin in her hands. "And what would it have to do with Wryan being murdered? I assume you still think their deaths are too much of a coincidence not to be related."

Redd nods agreement, but they both look at me as if they believe I have a good answer.

I put my hands in the air, palms toward them. "Hear me out. There's a mushroom tea they make in St. Sava. I looked up the side effects, and they can be really severe." I open my phone to the screen shot I've taken of the warnings about use of this type of mushroom, and read out loud, "...*seizures, central nervous system depression, sleepiness, confusion, loss of consciousness or even coma...*" I pass the phone to Redd, who reads and then passes it to Haisley. "The active ingredient is called muscimol, and you can buy it in capsules, too. I think someone who knew about this particular tea could have given it to Izzie, and maybe pulled apart some extra capsules to dump the powder in. It would really ramp up the potency, but the flavor would be the same, especially with a lot of added honey."

"How on Earth do you know that? Hey, did you learn that in your tea classes?"

I grin and nod and explain the story about bumping into Madame Klimenkova in the international grocery. Then I tell them that I fell asleep in the hot tub myself the other day, and how disorienting it was.

"If you'd had a lot of this muscimol, it would be much worse—and Izzie could have gone unconscious or been paralyzed by it. Even if she woke up, she might not have been able to move her arms or legs to get her head back above water."

"And there'd be no signs of a struggle with another person," adds Haisley.

"Nope."

"Now, wait a minute. You think it was Izzie they wanted to kill?" Redd lifts his eyebrows, to which I give a half-shrug in reply. It's a possibility.

"It's a great theory, but I'm not sure it really works. Like, how would that person even know about the hot tub?" frowns Haisley, and I don't have a good answer.

Star has noticed how quiet we've become and comes over to check on us, then pulls up a chair to sit next to her when Haisley explains our theory.

"I do think it might work," she enthuses. "What if Izzie mentioned to the wrong person that she intended to try the hot tub later that night? As for why... no one's answered that for Wryan yet, either, have they?"

We all shake our heads "no."

"But it might be jealousy," I say, noting that both Romin and his wife had a reason to be jealous. "The wife might have been enraged if she found out about Izzie, but what if Romin knew about the tea? What if he heard about Izzie being pregnant and knew it wasn't his? He may have been hurt and jealous enough to want to kill her."

"Maybe, maybe," Haisley nods slowly. "But giving her tea and waiting is a very cool-headed, thought-out plan. I'd have thought that killing someone in a jealous rage would be exactly that—fast, furious, hands-on."

"Like strangling Wryan," says Star.

The electricity that runs through the table almost crackles. We gape at Star and then at each other.

"Sweet Jesus," Redd says.

We all jump when my phone rings. I grab it where I'd laid it on the table, intending to silence it, but then I see that it's Gail calling.

"Hey! What's up?" I whisper to the others that it's Gail. They watch me while I speak, but it's too loud in the restaurant to use the speakerphone, so they can't hear what she's saying.

"Thought you'd like to know you guys might be right about Izzie and Romin. Apparently, his wife drove all the way down from Pittsburgh that night."

"Really? Where did you hear that?"

"I was on the phone with one of my friends from the aquatic center. The gossip is running rampant up there."

"Did she confront them?"

"That's the question. Romin isn't answering his phone, so we can't ask him what's going on. My friend says the police up here questioned both of them, though. Romin and his wife."

Gail doesn't have any more details, so I thank her for the call, and when we hang up, I fill in the others.

"Does that blow our hot tub theory away?" Star asks.

"If it's the wife? I'm not sure," I say slowly, absorbing the news that Romin's wife had driven all the way down from Pittsburgh, on her own, the night before the race. That is not a cool, level-headed action.

"It's jealousy, like you said, just of Izzie, not Wryan," Redd reads my mind.

"True. But Wryan is the one who gets strangled, while Izzie's death has to be pre-planned. It's backwards."

"Don't get discouraged, Lily. Discarding a theory that doesn't work is all part of the process. The act of thinking through it can lead us to the right answer." Haisley smiles at me and takes a swallow of her drink. She puts it back on the table and leans back.

"Our problem is that we're making an awful lot of assumptions to try to make a theory fit," she says. "That's always a big mistake. It's a big no-no in scientific research to assume without checking the facts, even when an assumption really seems valid."

"You're right about that," agrees Redd. "There have been wrong assumptions here right from the start: the people who found him assumed Wryan had drowned at the start of the race, everyone assumed Wryan and Izzie were still together, and what's more, they assumed Izzie was pregnant, and we all assumed at first that Wryan's bundle of money was due to something illegal... You know what? What if there's something we're all taking as a given that we shouldn't be?"

I look over at the two of them; my turn to be in awe. "You guys are right! What else comes to mind that we've just assumed is true?"

We're all quiet, thinking.

"Is there really no inheritance money at stake?" asks Haisley.

"Were Romin and Izzie really having an affair?" asks Star.

"Is it only Izzie and Wryan?" I add, and their eyes open wide.

"Damn," Redd says quietly.

Haisley is right, and these are all good questions. It's time to get the facts.

Chapter 33

Frank

The first thing I do when Haisley and I get back to the apartment is call Frank, Tessa's husband, who happens to be a realtor. If anyone can help me get to the bottom of what's really at stake regarding Duke's inheritance, it's him.

"Lily! How's it going, kiddo? You trying to find Tessa? She's at work, but she should be answering her cell."

"Hi Frank. Actually, today I'm looking for you. I have a land ownership question."

"Oh! In that case, you've come to the right place. At least, I think you have. What's your question?"

I explain about the Hilander estate in St. Sava, and tell him I'm wondering who owns it, what's likely to happen to it if the owner dies, and how much it's worth in U.S. dollars.

"Yikes! Overseas. I'm not sure you've come to the right place after all."

"I know, not your usual bailiwick, but I thought you might know someone who would know how to find out?"

"Tell you what. Let me do a little digging. Can I call you back?"

"Sure! Thank you! Anything you learn would be helpful."

I hang up smiling. Frank is not only a very nice guy; he's a nice guy who can't resist a real estate challenge.

Since it's hot, I decide to go up to the pool and hang out there for a while. It's the middle of the day and almost empty, so I lay my towel and pool bag on a chair underneath a big umbrella and wade in. I'm not planning on swimming laps; I just want to cool off a bit, so I go under to get myself completely wet and float over the "edge" to the glass portion looking down on the sidewalk. I love how my heart gives a little leap when I first catch sight of the sudden drop. It's a microscopic adrenalin jolt, just enough to wake me up and bring me completely into the present.

It reminds me of the day I thought Star was the murderer following me in Wryan's truck, which gave me a big adrenalin jolt. Did the murderer get what he wanted with the deaths of Wryan and Izzie? Or can his plan—whatever it is—still be thwarted? Gail has been passing on to me all the rumors she encounters; surely the others are doing the same with their friends. Is the murderer listening in, keeping tabs in case one of them hits the mark? If so, he might well strike again; he'd have nothing to lose at this point. It comes down to motive, I decide. We have to know for sure. If we could follow the murderer's reasoning, we would know if anyone else is in danger. So, now it's not only about Wryan's death, it's no longer about finding Izzie, it's about people who are still here, still alive, and keeping them that way. My heart beats faster, but not because of the lane drop-off. It's the realization of how high the stakes really are to figure out that motive.

I continue to float, trying to nudge my thoughts in the right direction, but no definitive answers come to mind, so I get out to dry off and try to relax under the umbrella, lying back on the lounge chair with my eyes closed.

I'm very nearly fast asleep when my phone rings. It's Izzie.

Chapter 34
Phone Calls

"**H**ello?" I sit bolt upright, squeezing the phone to my ear and holding my hand against the other to block out the faint outdoor sounds wafting across the deck.

"I'm sorry to surprise you like this. This is Jessica Walker. Izzie's mom. I'm contacting my daughter's friends and saw your name in her phone. She spoke of Lily from Bethesda, and I thought this might be you?"

"Oh! Yes, Mrs. Walker, I... hello," I stumble, trying to keep my voice steady until my heart stops thudding through my chest. They must have found the phone when they found Izzie. "I'm so sorry about your daughter. I didn't know her very long, but she was fun, and funny, and she was... a really special person." I manage to finish smoothly, if lamely.

"Thank you for saying that. She was very fond of you too. I could tell whenever she mentioned you. That's why I wanted to call."

"Of course! Is there something I can do?" I ask her, wishing fervently that there is. There's no taking away the pain, but even distraction can help get you through the first and hardest days.

"No, dear, but I appreciate you asking. I wanted to tell you myself that we're holding her funeral service at our church, First Presbyterian of Sanders, on Tuesday. I know it's far for you to come and I really don't expect you to make the trip, but I wanted you to know that you are welcome. Izzie would have wanted you to know that."

There's a catch in her voice in the last sentence, and I'm swept by a sudden, fierce desire to hug this woman I've never met. I tell her how touched I am by her thoughtfulness. I can't take more time off work, so I don't plan to go, but I want to send flowers. When I ask if Izzie had a favorite, her mother tells me, "I don't think so, but send lilies! It'll be as if her friend is here," which makes me tear up and smile both at the same time.

"Thank you, Mrs. Walker. That's exactly what I'll do! Is there anything else? How are you holding up?"

"I wake up in the morning and for the briefest moment I forget, and then I remember, and it's just... so awful I don't ever want to wake up again. Her dad is the same. But everybody, Kam in particular, has been very kind. He's been checking in constantly, bringing us groceries, helping us cope with arrangements."

"It's good that you have support. Um, I'm sorry, Kam is...?"

"No, I'm sorry. I thought Izzie might have mentioned him. Kamran Anjani, her coach's brother. They brought him on as an assistant coach a few months ago, and the two of them had become quite friendly. He was terribly broken up when Izzie went missing, and then when they found her, well, it's like he can't stop hovering. To be honest, ever since the police told us Izzie had broken up with Wryan, I've wondered if maybe she and Kam had been, you know, in a relationship."

"Oh! Ah, she mentioned she was seeing someone, but never told me his name."

"She never told me anything about either of them." We're both quiet, she grappling with a new wave of grief and loss, me trying to think what to say.

"I'm sure she would have. She and Wryan were both waiting until after the ultra to tell anyone," I stutter. Then, totally ham-handed, I say what is probably the stupidest, most inane comment under the circumstances. "I had no idea there was a Kam. Who she was seeing was such a big secret I actually thought it might have been her coach Romin." Ugh. As soon as the words come out, I cringe in horror. What was I thinking? Stupid, stupid, stupid. But Izzie's mom surprises me again. She gives a kind of sad laugh.

"I can't blame you. The aquatic center is quite the Peyton Place, if that allusion means anything to you, although I'm certain your guess is wrong in this case. Kam confided to me that Romin has been having an affair with Celeste."

I almost drop the phone.

"Holy... I mean, I had no idea." My voice sounds to me like a yelp, but Mrs. Walker doesn't seem to notice.

"No, well, everything has been so hush-hush, but none of it matters now, does it? Not to me, anyway. And I have to say, Celeste, the whole team, has been absolutely lovely to us these past few days. They're all good people trying to find their way, just like Izzie." She sounds wistful, mournful, and also a bit disconnected. I do believe none of it matters to her now. Some of it matters to other people, though, of that I have no doubt. I reiterate my sympathies along with my sincere fondness for her daughter, and soon we hang up.

My brain is exploding at Mrs. Walker's revelation. I never saw it coming, but as the fireworks start to die down, it occurs to me that all this means is that the whole Romin-wife-jealousy theory of Wryan and Izzie's murders probably goes out the window. Star nailed it—*were Izzie and Romin really having an affair?* The police must know, because neither Anjani has been arrested (I'm certain the gossip line would have alerted Gail, who would immediately have told me if that had happened). They must still be looking for someone else. Redd is so right: we keep making all kinds of assumptions, not knowing our own blind spots. I stand up and then sit down again on the edge of my lounge chair, shell-shocked and at a loss for how to approach coming up with a new theory. I need to talk to someone, but right now, not the Bears. I want to make another call first.

Talking to Mrs. Walker, wanting to hug her, has left me yearning to get in touch with my own mom and give her a hug, too. Barring that, I want to hear her voice over the phone. Is it comfort that I want, or do I want to give my own mom what I could not give Izzie's—the comforting assurance that her daughter is alive and well? I'm not quite sure, but either way, before I do anything else, I need to talk to my mom.

She picks up sounding surprised and asks if I'm all right. I feel bad for worrying her, so I quickly assure her I'm fine, just in a mood to chat. I ask her what's going on with her and Dad, and listen as she goes through various wonderfully ordinary, nothing-and-everything activities that make up their usual routine.

"We've been watching lots of murder mystery miniseries lately. They suck you in, and your dad doesn't seem to have any problem following the plots." She reels off the names of a few of these shows and asks if I've seen any of them. It's as good an "in" as any, and I tell her all about how I'm mixed up in a very real murder mystery. Sure enough, it turns into a long conversation, with Mom appalled but also attentive, sympathetic, and everything else I needed her to be at that moment. She is a good listener, and it feels so good to talk.

"And did you really like this Wryan? Was it turning into more than just a few dates?" She asks at one point.

"I did really like him. I don't know if it would have become more serious or not, but it might have. I like his friends, too; I especially liked Izzie. And I feel so sorry for his cousin Duke." I tell her about the multiple tragedies that have afflicted the Wells family in the past year, including the death of his other cousin, Faye, in a fire. This leads me down the rambling road of explaining Wryan and Duke's connection to St. Sava and the Hilander racehorse training center.

"St. Sava... I've heard of that. Is it off the coast of Africa?"

"Close! I'm impressed! But it's not an island; it's on the border between Botswana and South Africa."

"Of course! Now I remember. It came up in an article I read a few years ago about the new rules of succession to the throne."

I should mention that my mom is a fanatical royal watcher. How many evenings have I called her, only to hear, "I'm sorry, Lily, I'll have to call you back. I'm watching The Crown!" (or some such show). Really, Mom? You can't hit pause? But of course, I don't mind. I want her to enjoy herself.

"You did? No way! It was about St. Sava? What did it say?" I can't quite believe that I've once again come across this tiny country so randomly.

She tells me it was one of those fascinating little glitches that come to light unexpectedly when something changes. In this case, it turned out that the letters patent for the Hilander duchy are nearly unique for hereditary peerages in that they specify "heirs" as opposed to "male heirs" (among other things). The article explained that for titles of nobility with those letters, the new laws of succession would apply.

"Just another example of small differences having unintended consequences," she finishes.

"What new laws? What changed?"

"It's a change in how they determine who's next in line to become king or queen. The main thing is that girls don't lose their place to boys anymore. It went into effect right before William and Kate had their first baby, so that if it was a girl, she would be the next monarch." Mom chuckles, "It was quite a big deal back then, but as it turned out, their first baby was a boy, so it probably won't make a difference until at least the next generation."

"Sorry, Mom. Very boring of them. I hope you're not too disappointed."

"I guess I can live with it," she says airily. "And it's not a total washout: at least Prince Michael of Kent is back on the list!"

It's a bit of a family joke that my mom has a thing for Prince Michael, but I'm surprised he might be king one day. If it hadn't been for Mom, I'd never even have heard of him.

"Oh, no, nothing like that," she laughs when I say this. "There's probably fifty or a hundred people ahead of him, but at least he's on it!"

"Mo-o-om!" I groan. She'd had me going, and now I realize she's just been teasing me.

"Anyway, your friends were all born well before the act was passed, so it wouldn't affect them, even if there were any girls," she says, finally back on topic.

"Good to know. I guess," which gets another chuckle. Mom knows I don't remotely share her interest in royal minutiae, and that I really don't need to know this at all.

The one thing our wandering through that little tangent did was to lighten our conversation again. While it had gotten understandably melancholy, we end things with both of us smiling, which, when I think about it, is exactly what I wanted when I phoned.

Cheered and energized, I grab my bag and my towel and race down the stairs to our apartment. Haisley is in the kitchen, and I call to her, "I have news! Back in a sec!" as I race by to take a shower and put some clothes on. When I come back out, she's still in the kitchen, sitting on a stool at the counter. She's sipping coffee, and I see she's already poured me a cup and left it sitting next to her at the ready.

"Is that for me? Thanks!" I slide onto a stool myself.

"Is it about Celeste and Romin?" she asks innocently.

I freeze with my coffee cup halfway to my mouth. "You know about that? How?" I squawk.

"How did you find out?" She asks, and we grin at each other before comparing notes. I tell her about the call from Izzie's mom, which sobers us both.

"I called Miller and told her about our convo at the Iguana. She called Karen to tell her, and then Miller called me back a little later," Haisley says. "Karen told her she'd been talking to Dr. Ben and he slipped up."

"Do tell!"

When Karen and Dr. Ben passed in the hall, she told him that she'd heard about Romin's wife driving all the way down and that we'd been theorizing she wanted to confront Izzie. Dr. Ben had corrected her without thinking ("You mean Celeste"). He tried to backtrack, but Karen wasn't having it. She turned and walked with him back to his office to get the rest of the story, which Dr. Ben had himself heard from Dan Ridley. He figured we'd eventually hear it from Aspire anyway, so gave Karen the gist.

Our guesses had been fairly accurate initially: the wife had discovered the affair, and when Romin didn't come home for dinner, she figured he'd gone to be with Celeste. Enraged, she left their baby with her mother so she could make the drive down immediately. Her mother was worried, and called Romin to warn him, and to beg him to stay calm. What ensued would have been a comedy of errors if it hadn't been so pitiable.

Romin was not with Celeste; one of his junior swimmers had knocked his front teeth out goofing around on the diving board, and Romin had driven him to the hospital. He couldn't get ahold of the boy's parents, and had therefore stayed with him until past dinner time.

"He didn't call his wife to let her know?"

"She didn't believe him."

"Oh, jeez."

When the boy's mother finally arrived at the hospital, Romin was frantic. He called, but his wife didn't answer her phone, so he drove to Hillandale to try to dissuade her from whatever she was intending to do. His wife, however, had gone to Bethesda, assuming they were all still at the Castlevine hotel. It was only after she arrived and discovered that neither Romin nor any team member was there that she finally got in touch with him. It was so late, he ended up staying at the Hillandale hotel, while she stayed at the Castlevine. At sunrise on the morning of the race, Romin turned around and drove back to Bethesda to speak with her, promising to end things with Celeste, hoping they could make up. They followed each other home in a state of relative peace, both of them exhausted.

"Unbelievable. So, no confrontation."

"No confrontation. In the end, no one knew anything about any of it. If you're wondering about the juniors' race, apparently Romin's brother Kam is an assistant coach, and he was there to coach the kids through it."

"I know about Kam. Mrs. Walker told me about him," I look significantly at Haisley, whose eyes grow huge.

"It was Kam? He was Izzie's boyfriend?"

"The very one."

"And he has an alibi, because he was at the swim meet in Pittsburgh. Holy moly, as Karen would say. If it isn't some jealous love triangle, and it's not some drug deal or whatever else you illegally use cash for these days, what the hell did happen?"

I shake my head. "I don't know. But in eliminating both those possibilities we just got a lot closer to finding out."

Chapter 35
Conversations

After dinner, I call both Karen and Miller to sort of close the circle on the Romin thing and discover that Haisley has already filled them in on my suspicions about the Amanita muscaria tea from St. Sava. Karen is astounded that I'd even discovered it, never mind that I'd made the connection to Izzie having drowned without a struggle, which is gratifying, but Miller's reaction is even better.

"Describe the box."

"Um... the one from St. Sava? It was kind of mossy green, and it had a black-and-white picture of a mushroom on it."

"I've seen it before. Izzie had some."

"No way! You're sure? The same one? When did you see it?" I squeeze my phone to my ear as if afraid I'm mishearing her. I can't believe it.

"Yeah, green with a drawing of a mushroom. She pulled it out of her purse and gave a few individually wrapped bags to... Nahla,

I think. Maybe she gave them to other people too, but definitely Nahla."

"Did either of them say anything?"

"Not that I remember. From the way they did it, I guess I assumed they'd pre-arranged for Izzie to give her some. Maybe she wanted to try it or something."

"Oh my God. I mean, I thought there was a connection, but now I'm kind of floored. Do you think I'm right? That Izzie went under because she'd had too much?"

"Yeah, I think maybe you are. Who's ever even heard of it before, and Izzie has some? Walks like a duck."

"I wonder where Izzie got it."

"I dunno. Where did you get yours? All I know is, that tea was there."

My head barely stops spinning from this conversation when Frank calls me back.

"That was fast!" I tell him.

"If you know the right people to ask, you can find out just about anything, and to that point, how would you feel about being connected into a conference call? I've got a friend of mine on the line who specializes in international finance and real estate. His name's Mark, and if anyone can answer your questions, he can."

"Fantastic! Definitely put him on!"

Frank opens the line, and the three of us go through the rigmarole of "Are you there? Can you hear?" ultimately ascertaining that all three of us are indeed connected. Mark sounds upbeat and confident, seemingly enjoying his role as The One Who Can Help. Frank had given him the gist about Wryan's murder, his connection to me, and his relation to St. Sava, but I fill in more details about what I want to know and why. I can hear him tapping his keyboard, and his tone suggests he can definitely supply pertinent information. It turns out that Mark's niche is third-world and developing countries, and he is very familiar with the area I'm asking about.

"The Hilander estate, which includes all the grounds, buildings, and accouterments—as in, anything contained in or on the property—is jointly owned by one Alistair Wells, Duke of Hilander, and a Ms. Manou Kotze. Since they both have the same address, I presume they're living together."

"That's right, they are. They've been together for a long time and have a daughter named Chloe. Since they own it jointly, what happens if Alistair Wells passes away?"

"Oh, that's pretty straightforward. According to St. Sava law, when a person dies, the surviving owner automatically takes sole possession of anything held jointly, superseding any instructions that might be contained in a will. So, Manou will immediately own everything outright. Is that what you wanted to know?"

"Yes, that's it. Wryan was under the impression that his cousin Duncan would get the title of Duke upon the death of his uncle, but no money. I just wondered whether he could have been mistaken, and Duncan might inherit some after all, but it doesn't sound like it from what you said."

"I couldn't tell you about the title, but he won't inherit anything from the estate; and since Manou is joint owner of the property, it's likely she's also joint owner on their bank accounts and other financial holdings. Even if Alistair kept a bank account in his own name, he would likely bequeath it to his girlfriend in his will, and if there were no will, the money would still go to his daughter before it would go to his nephew."

"Maybe he has money solely in his name that he bequeaths to Duke in his will?"

"It's certainly possible, but there's no way to find out until the will is opened."

"Makes sense. Is the estate worth a lot?"

"That depends on your perspective. Right now, the land estate could be worth in the ballpark of five million U.S. dollars, but it would be difficult to sell and could take a very long time. There aren't many buyers lining up for something on that scale in that location. Someone would have to keep the training center running while it was on the market, too, to maintain the value."

"Got it. Sounds like a lot of money to me, but it's not something you'd cash in on easily."

"That's about the crux of it," Mark says cheerily. I'm not sure what else to ask, but I don't want to let my "expert" go just yet, so I say the first thing that pops into my head.

"Do you know if Alistair Wells is very wealthy?

Mark chuckles to himself and says that that, too, is a matter of perspective. Alistair would certainly be considered rich compared to many residents of St. Sava and its surrounding countries. He lives a European lifestyle, and his family wants for nothing. "That said, Lily, he's carrying a significant debt load, with Hilander as collateral, so his position is more precarious than it might seem on the surface."

"You should tell her why you laughed just then," breaks in Frank. "I'll bet she'll find it interesting!"

Mark chuckles again and says, "Yes, well, I don't know this as absolute fact, but locally it's common knowledge that the Duke of Hilander is a private money lender. He takes out a personal loan at one rate and lends it at a higher one. As long as his debtors pay him, he's able to pay back his own loans and make a profit."

Mark explains that there is an unspoken practice among some financial institutions in the UK to offer those with aristocratic titles preferential rates, especially if there is a history of patronage. Alistair was known to take advantage of his family's long-standing relationship with certain banks to borrow significant amounts and still be able to offer a reasonable rate to his own clients. The practice isn't illegal, Mark stresses, but it can be risky. In answer to my question of why anyone would go to Alistair rather than a formal lending establishment, Mark responds that in cases where a company or corporation is already in debt or underwater, Alistair might be either their only, or only affordable, option.

"Companies? Like Tau Activewear, for example?"

"That's an excellent example. I happen to know that Tau has been stretching to increase production and enter new markets. It's a company that might well require a loan on top of a loan."

I thank him profusely for the information, and after Mark drops off the call, I do the same to Frank, who laughs it off with an easy, "Always a pleasure!"

After we hang up, the first thing I do is write down what I learned. Then I sit back and ponder. Carlo's joke from the memorial gathering comes back to me: *no bill is too high for Uncle Tau and the bank of Hilander*. Did Alistair Wells lend Nathaniel money? I'm betting the answer is yes, but I'm not sure where that gets me.

There's money all around Aspire, but it's not Wryan's and it never would be, so why would someone murder him? Ditto for Izzie. And why that night? If the motive has something to do with the big master plan, wouldn't it make sense to wait until after the race? To me, the timing smacks of a desperate move from someone who thought it had to happen right away. Or has someone been biding his time, waiting for an opportunity, and the triathlon offered one? That's a possibility, too—what better setup to make it look like an accidental drowning? Damn. Figuring this out requires a higher level of brainpower than my own, and it flits into my head to call Ridley and tell him what I learned from Mark. Then I remember his caution not to ask too many questions and nix the idea. The police probably know all this already anyway. Of course, they haven't made an arrest yet. Maybe my brainpower, or lack thereof, isn't the problem. What we all need is a way to connect these disparate pieces into a coherent story, one that leads to the murderer.

Dee Dee paws me softly, and when I look down, she gives me an enormous yawn. I pick her up and cuddle her, rubbing my cheek on her soft head.

"You know what, Dee? My master plan to solve this case is a lot like Aspire's: all they have to do is get to the Olympics; all I have to do is connect these random clues. Easy peasy, right?"

I turn her head to face me, but she has no answer other than to blink slowly and commence purring loudly. It's soothing, but not helpful.

Chapter 36

Aha!

Mindless YouTube surfing fills the rest of the evening as I consider what to do next. The team is leaving town tomorrow, and for some reason their departure equates to failure for me, as if I didn't find the answer quickly enough; and once they're gone all possibility for answers will disappear, too. It's ridiculous, of course. The police are the ones investigating, and they will continue to investigate until they get to the bottom of it; but it still bothers me.

I end up going to bed at a reasonable hour, but after a lot of tossing and turning, it's close to midnight and I still can't relax. I pick up my phone and start fiddling, ordering lilies to be delivered to Izzie's church, scrolling through Instagram, playing games. I buy a pair of sandals, some makeup, and a pack of cat toys online before giving up. Sometimes you need to step back in order to step forward. For me, yoga is one of the best ways to stop the spin of everyday life and empty my head of everything except mastering a particular position and my own breath. Since I'll never get to sleep at this rate, I go up to the rooftop patio and peer over the edge to the city below, its sidewalks completely empty. It's warm and humid, but the oppressive mugginess of the day is gone.

I look up at the stars, composing myself, and then stand perfectly still, pressing my feet down and rolling my shoulders back to set myself in mountain pose. I relax my face, rest my tongue on the roof of my mouth, and breathe deeply into my belly. I concentrate on the slow rhythm of my breath, allowing the whirling distractions of my thoughts to dissipate. I practice inhaling and exhaling from each nostril, then move into child's pose, resting my forehead on the ground and remaining there for some time. When I'm ready, I change to half butterfly. My aim is to force my third eye chakra to open a little more, and with that in mind, I rest my forehead on an upended kickboard as I round into a forward fold. I need no cheat sheet as I move from position to position, each one chosen to keep pressure on the same spot in the middle of my forehead. When I finish and lie back in corpse pose, my entire body sinks heavily as the last vestiges of tension recede. I stop trying to think and allow my mind to disengage. When I stand up again, I feel serene and sleepy. I go down the elevator and straight into bed.

An hour later, I sit bolt upright. I had been sound asleep, dreaming some bizarre, slightly macabre dream featuring a man with a handlebar mustache, when a question popped into my head and woke me up with its urgency. *Why is Prince Michael back on the list?*

Yes, that is the question that has me wide awake at two o'clock in the morning. I don't know myself why it suddenly seems important, but I have a feeling, like I've remembered something, like I'm on the brink of a breakthrough. *Trust your gut.* I ignore its absurdity and focus instead on the question itself. Nothing changed for Prince Michael's generation, and any royal women born since the change in rules would surely bump him down or off the list, not back on, wouldn't they? I can't call my mom at this hour, so I grab my phone and start searching for more details about the Succession to the Crown Act.

Wikipedia confirms what my mom already told me: for those in the line of succession born after 28 October 2011, the eldest child, regardless of gender, precedes any siblings. There are other elements of the act, too, though, like the fact that while a Catholic is still disqualified from succession, this is no longer true for a person who marries one. Who even knew that *was* a disqualification?

I switch to AI summaries for a layperson's explanation of it all, and find one that lists specific things that have changed now that the legislation is in force, and sure enough, Mom is right: *Prince Michael of Kent, the Queen's first cousin, is now back in the line of succession... He was removed in 1978 when he married his Catholic wife*. Aha! That settles that. Nice for him, I guess, although hardly life-altering.

Now, the big question is: why did I need to know this so badly that it woke me from my slumber? What deliberations were going through my subconscious brain that made it alight on this particular fact?

I stay still and prod my memory toward this question. I find myself thinking back to Wryan's phone call telling me the team would be back in town for the ultra, and that he hoped we could have dinner. I was flattered that getting together with me seemed so important to him, but as we talked, I could tell something was bothering him. I remember asking if he was sure he wanted to do the race.

He sounded part way between resolute and wistful when he said, "The race, yes. I've been dreaming of this one for a long time. But you're right. The timing is pretty bad with my mom. I hate to leave her; she's so weak now. The priest came to visit today. That's a bad sign."

It had been said lightly, almost joking, and he'd gone on to explain that his mother had been a "good Catholic girl while her parents were alive," but had pretty much lapsed for over a decade.

"She had me baptized and got me through confirmation, and she still attends the occasional Easter mass, but that's been about it, so it was nice of the guy to remember her at all, never mind come around in person. It's unsettling, though, like a harbinger of the end."

There was nothing categorically different in his mother's state from the way she had been for several weeks already, and Wryan had been looking forward to the ultra for almost a year—not to mention the fact that the team was counting on him. He made up his mind to come, so the decision was made. Much of the rest of our conversation had been about what we'd like to do when he was here, and I could tell he really was looking forward to seeing me again. This was what I remembered most about that call, how gratifying it was to have someone so enamored of me. What can I say? I haven't been in a relationship for a long time, at least not one that had the potential to last. I'd forgotten the remark about the priest until just now. Wryan's father had married a Catholic. Could it possibly matter?

I spend an hour searching the internet for more information, absorbing it all, wondering at the back of my head whether we had once again made an assumption without checking the facts. Was Duke really going to be a duke? *Facts*, I tell myself whenever my mind starts to jump ahead, *just get the facts*. It's complicated, no doubt about that, and I don't think I know enough about Wryan's family to figure out if any of it matters. Or do I?

I have my notes to consult, and memories are coming back fast and furious now, snippets of different conversations beginning to line up in a coherent story. As quietly as I can, I slip into the kitchen and put a coffee pod into the Keurig. When it's done, I take my mug back to my room, quietly close the door, and turn on the light. There is a glass whiteboard on the wall next to the desk, so I uncap a marker and write the name of Wryan's grandfather at the top of the board: George Wells (Deceased). Here goes.

Before I have time to write anything else, there's the sound of bumping at the door. Looking over, I see a paw reach under and scratch along the bottom. Shoot. I turn the lights off and open the door for Dee Dee, and use the gentle glow of my phone screen to check if there are any more interlopers waiting in the wings. Otto is fast asleep in his bed, and after I close the door and once again turn on the light, I realize that Dexter has been here all along, stretched out on top of my basket of freshly cleaned clothes. I pick up my marker and start again.

As I make notes and draw lines, I'm astounded at how much I know about the Wells family tree. The current duke is Alistair Wells, Wryan's Uncle Alistair, obviously the oldest son of George. I know Alistair had a daughter by his first wife—Faye, who died in the barn fire—and that he has another much younger daughter, Chloe, by his long-term girlfriend Manou Kotze. So far, so good. Duke's father—or rather, Duncan's (to use his proper name) was Callum Wells, the one who died from a riding accident, and his mother I know is Helen, because Wryan referred to them a few times as Uncle Callum and Aunt Helen. Wryan's biological father was Barrett Wells, and it occurs to me that he, rather than

Duncan's father, was probably the next eldest (*"they named their kids alphabetically,"* Wryan said his mom used to quip). That brings me to Wryan's mother, whom Duncan calls "Aunt Eden," and her partner, the man Wryan truly considers his dad, Fred Burley. I put an asterisk by Eden's name to denote that she is Catholic.

Next to each name, I write the order of succession to the duchy according to the old rules. Since Alistair had no sons, the next oldest brother would inherit it upon his death. Barrett Wells (Wryan's father) would have lost his place by marrying a Catholic (Eden), leaving Callum (Duncan's father) as the only option. I pause and consider here. If Callum pre-deceased Alistair, would the duchy then go automatically to Callum's son Duncan? My research from the last hour tells me maybe not. If Barrett were older than Callum, even though he himself was excluded, his son, Wryan, would be next in line. Interesting. Wryan didn't seem to think this could be the case, but why not? Maybe Callum was the older of the two after all. I sip my coffee and ponder. *Ah,* I think and add an asterisk to Wryan's name because he, too, is Catholic—he'd mentioned being baptized and going through confirmation—rendering him disqualified. Therefore, Duncan eventually does become the next duke.

Now for round two, where I check if the new rules change anything. Even if Faye had lived, she was born before they came into effect, so she would still have been out of the running.

Since Alistair and Manou never married, their daughter Chloe is technically illegitimate and thus ineligible, too. If Barrett was the next oldest brother, though, he (like Prince Michael) would no longer be disqualified by marrying a Catholic and so would be back on the list ahead of Callum. In theory, upon Barrett's death the title would therefore go to his son, Wryan, but in this case it can't, because Wryan himself is Catholic and still disqualified. Duncan still becomes the next duke.

Nothing changes.

It's a relief to finish up and reach a conclusion, but I can't help my sense of frustration at having put so much effort into this—to have thought I'd had some brilliant breakthrough—only to find there's nothing there.

Dee Dee has joined Dexter snoozing atop my clean clothes, and I'm starting to feel sleepy again too. I set my coffee mug on the desk, turn off the light, and crawl back into bed, my mind still drowsily churning over the scribbles on the whiteboard. Duke is still duke. Disappointment turns to relief, as I realize what it might have meant were that not so. I fall into a lucid dream in which I decide to take up triathlon and Wryan asks me to come to Pittsburgh to join Aspire...

I sit up so fast I startle Dexter, who hisses and leaps down from the laundry to hide in the closet.

"Shhh... shhh..." I whisper soothingly as I more carefully get out of bed again and turn on the light.

The team. What did the team think? Everybody thought Izzie was pregnant by Wryan, and that they were in a hurry to get married. I go back to the board and add more lines to show Wryan married to Izzie, and their baby. Izzie was not Catholic—her funeral was going to be at a Presbyterian church—and Wryan was in no way devout, so it is exceedingly unlikely they'd have had their baby baptized Catholic. Therefore, the title passes through Barrett and Wryan down to the baby, regardless of whether it is a boy or a girl. I stare at the board, my sleepiness gone, my mind racing.

Can this be it? Was it about the duchy, the all-important tinge of nobility? It was Duncan's "in" to the circles he needed to influence, his introduction to potential sponsors, his connection to a world of power and money that was unique to him. He'd figured out how to leverage it, exploit it, and monetize it to an extraordinary degree; and while the network he'd built already would likely remain, the future potential (and who knows what other ambitions he had?) would be lost, wasted on a 100% American baby and its oblivious parents.

I want to wake up Haisley to show this to her, and ask her if I'm out of my mind or if she sees it too, but I stop myself. There is no rush, no reason not to let her get a good night's rest. There are assumptions here that may be false: Callum may be the older brother after all, or perhaps I've misunderstood the rules. For now, it's just an interesting hypothesis, a possibility among other possibilities. Even so, if I'm right, it explains both deaths. Wryan and Izzie about to marry; Izzie pregnant with what would then be born a legitimate child. They both had to die for Duncan to remain d uke.

I take a picture of my whiteboard so I'll have it on my phone.

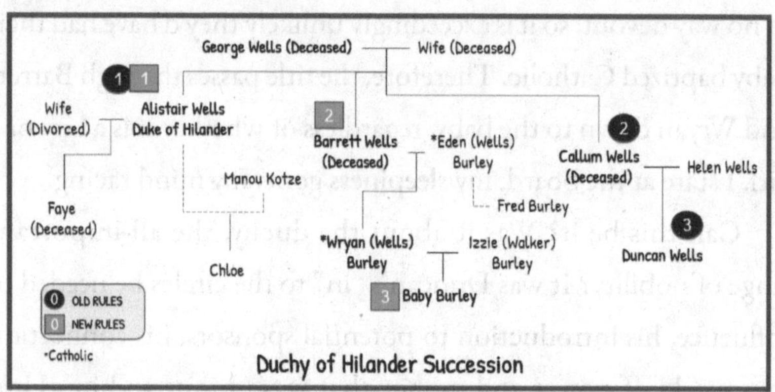

Duchy of Hilander Succession

I can't believe it, but I can't get it out of my head. I'm freaking out, and I know I won't sleep for the rest of the night, so I go back to the kitchen to make another mug of coffee—I can't be any more wired than I am already—and sit down on the couch. Dexter eventually forgives me and joins me on my lap. Together, we watch the sun come up and wait for Haisley to emerge from her bedroom.

Chapter 37
Validation

Around eight in the morning, it occurs to me Haisley might not be up until much later. I can't stand it anymore; I have to do something, so I text Karen.

Me: I got something. It's either way off base or important. Are you free?
Karen: Sounds VERY interesting! I'm at the hospital — come on by!
Me: On Saturday?
Karen: Yes but not working exactly
Me: On my way [smile]

I toss on some clothes and hop on my e-bike. The hospital isn't far, and I'm keyed up, but I'm trying not to get ahead of myself. There may be holes I can't see. Maybe all I have is an irrelevant family tree. Either way, I'm dying to hear someone else's take on it. I lock my bike and, after a quick, hopeful glance at the coffee kiosk (closed), I head to the elevators and push the button for the administrativ e office floor.

The hallway is quiet and empty; all the office doors are shut except for Karen's. She must hear my footsteps coming, because she pokes her head out and then comes to meet me halfway.

"Come on in," she greets me with a smile. "I can't wait to hear what it is you've got."

"Thanks," I say and do a doubletake when I walk through the door and see Dr. Ben there, too. "Hi!" I yip in surprise.

"Good morning, Lily," he crows as Karen hurriedly adds, "I didn't think you'd mind—I ran into Dr. Ben at the vending machines earlier and he offered to help me with my little, um, project." Karen has mentioned before that since his wife left him, Dr. Ben has started coming to work almost every weekend. She suspects he's lonely and doesn't know what to do with himself in his newly bachelor apartment.

"Of course I don't mind—in fact, this is great!" I beam at both of them. Then I look around at Karen's normally neat office awash in paper, with small piles lying on every flat surface and across much of the floor. "Is this your project? Are you sure I'm not disturbing you? You look busy."

Karen waves her hand dismissively. "I'm using the copy machine here to make a bunch of programs for my daughter. She's doing that summer theater thing." She flashes me an exaggeratedly toothy grin, adding, "Don't tell anyone."

Dr. Ben gives me a wink and says, "I'm her Acting Collator-in-Chief."

"Nice." I mime zipping up my lips and throwing away the key.

Karen moves a pile off the guest chair for me and then one off her desk chair so she can sit down and says, "Sooo? Don't keep us in suspense!"

I start by telling them about talking to my mom and wondering idly if anything has changed with regard to St. Sava and the Hilander dukedom. Then I tell Karen to check her email, as I've sent her the picture of my Wells family tree, and she pulls it up on her computer. Dr. Ben and I go around to her side of the desk, and he leans against the bookshelf behind Karen's chair, while I sit on her desk next to the computer so we can all look at it together.

I go through the various names, who each is in relation to the others, and how I'd learned them. Next, I point to my original succession hierarchy and trace through the tree to show how I'd calculated it. Then I point to the new succession, and this time I explain the changes in the law as I understand them, to show how I reached the new order. They stare at the screen, nodding as I speak but not interrupting.

For Dr. Ben's sake, I explain that Celeste is a classic busybody, and that as soon as she thought Izzie was pregnant, she would have told everyone else on the team—except, of course, Wryan. I also tell him about Izzie's ring, the simple one from her grandmother, that she had started wearing on her right ring finger, and about the St. Sava tradition of women wearing their wedding rings on that fin ger.

"If someone knew about that tradition, they might have thought it was either a wedding or engagement ring, and that Wryan asked Izzie to wear it on that hand as a nod to family."

"Would the whole team have known about that particular custom?"

"Maybe, maybe not. But Duke would," says Karen soberly. "If Duke suddenly noticed the ring while they were all sharing the Airbnb and thought Wryan and Izzie were either secretly engaged or even that they'd already sneaked off and gotten married, and that they were likely going to have a legitimate baby before his uncle dies, he might have panicked."

"Fascinating," mutters Dr. Ben, who has been pondering Karen's screen for several minutes.

"Meaning... I've definitely gone off the deep end? Or is this actually something suspicious?"

"Meaning you're incredible," says Karen. "I'd never have thought to look into this, but it's definitely suspicious. It's the timing that's just so..."

"Yeah."

"But do you really think Duke—Duncan—killed Wryan? And probably Izzie too?" Karen looks at me aghast.

"No! No way. We all saw them together at happy hours and stuff; they really did come across as close. And what about Wryan's parents? He loved them practically as much as Wryan did. How could he do that to them? No way. We must still be missing something."

"It certainly bears considering," says Dr. Ben, chewing on his glasses, still frowning at the screen.

My gut tightens seeing the two of them take my theory seriously. I let out a long, slow breath. There can be big disconnects between the heart and the brain, and I'm experiencing the throes of that conflict right now. My brain acknowledges the rational conclusion that Duke is potentially a murderer; in fact, very likely a murderer. My heart, for reasons unfathomable, is not yet ready to let go of its affection for Wryan's cousin. Wryan himself had loved and revered him, for one thing, and he is so impressive in every way—dashing, talented, and accomplished, but also sympathetic, having suffered loss after loss. Could he be so diabolical? So cold hearted?

I stare out the window reviewing in my mind every interaction I've ever had with Duke. What did I miss, and how did I miss it? Some evil vibe, something off—I should have had an intimation, but nothing like that comes to mind. My heart sends my brain signals of hope for some other explanation; my brain tells my heart to snap out of it.

Dr. Ben mercifully puts pause to my deliberations. "Among us chickens, I don't mind telling you that it still bothers me that there's absolutely no evidence to suggest your friend Izzie's death was anything but an accident." He smiles ruefully at me.

"There were no signs of a struggle whatsoever. If the motive here was indeed for Duncan to remain the heir to the duchy, Wryan's murderer took a big chance that the two of them hadn't already secretly married by not killing Izzie too, and her dying by accident would have been a remarkable stroke of luck. One that begs credulity a little too much." He looks again at the screen and back at me. "Don't get me wrong, Lily. You made an extraordinary leap here, and the results are quite titillating; there's no doubt about that."

Karen and I look at each other. "You need to tell him about the tea," she says.

Dr. Ben's eyebrows go up, and he looks a question at me.

"It's another one of those too good to be true coincidences," I say. I pull out my phone, where I've taken screenshots of the mushroom tea and of the description of the potential side effects of its active ingredient, muscimol. "I mean, they make this in St. Sava, of all places. And Izzie definitely had some, because Miller saw her with it, and she was sharing it with her teammates, so at least some of them knew about it, too. Any one of them could have given her a really big dose without her knowing it, especially if they also had capsules to pull apart and mix in with her tea. Maybe they knew about her using the hot tub, or maybe they were planning to strangle her too, or maybe they just wanted to make sure she couldn't put up a fight."

Dr. Ben touches his brow lightly with one hand, and then covers his mouth as he studies the pictures on my phone. "I don't know what to say," he declares, giving it back to me with a look of wonderment, which causes me to flush scarlet. Trying to hide it, I shrug my shoulders and fiddle with my purse, putting the phone away.

"Tell you what. Karen, why don't you email me a copy of this picture? Then let's finish up here so we can all go visit our good friends the Ridleys and see what they're up to this fine morning."

We both nod, Karen emails the picture, and the two of us start scrambling around her office, finalizing her programs while Dr. Ben calls Dan Ridley. He looks at us over the phone and gives a thumbs up and a smile before hanging up.

"Is that it? Are we ready? Our hosts await us."

This is getting exciting. I leave my locked bike at the hospital and ride with Karen, who follows Dr. Ben in his car.

"You keep coming up with the most mind-boggling ideas, Lily. I really am beginning to wonder if you should consider something in law enforcement."

I flash her a quick grin, appreciating the compliment but not able to revel in it too much because I'm extremely nervous. There's something about the idea of barging in to talk to Detective Ridley—in his home, no less!—that puts me on edge. My hands are clammy when we get out of the car and join Dr. Ben on the doorstep.

Chapter 38
Saturday Morning

Toni Ridley, wearing cutoff jeans and a t-shirt, greets us warmly and ushers us into the living room, where her husband is sitting perusing a file. He glances up at us briefly over his glasses, but doesn't say anything as he continues to read. Toni tells us all to have a seat, she'll be right back, and disappears.

"You've painted the wall blue," remarks Dr. Ben from the sofa, not sounding completely happy about it.

"Well spotted! Maybe you should be a detective," Ridley responds without looking up.

"It's a different blue from the kitchen. You don't think it clashes?"

Ridley sighs—or was that a growl?—stops reading, pulls off his glasses and looks over at Dr. Ben. "You can't see the kitchen from in here."

"No, but if you go into the kitchen, you'll notice that it's a different blue and wonder if maybe it clashes. Won't you?" He sounds serious, but his eyes are twinkling mischievously.

"Mm-hm. You're right. Tell me, what color would you like us to paint our living room?"

Dr. Ben is smiling now, but he's not giving up. "You could make it beige again. Or maybe a light yellow. That would be cheery."

"Good idea. How about this: let's forget this detecting stuff altogether and head down to the paint store. You can pick out a bunch of color cards, see which one you like best."

Dr. Ben throws his head back, about to laugh, but stops himself when Toni emerges from the kitchen, where she'd gone to make coffee. She's holding the pot in one hand and has a bunch of mugs hooked on the finger of the other. As she starts to place these on the table, Dr. Ben tells her, "We were discussing your new wall color in here."

Toni beams at him. "Oh, yeah! We just did that! Do you like it? We're going to do the kitchen next..." she drifts off slightly, noticing the subtle 'cut' sign her husband is making in her direction. I can see she's confused by this, not sure why he wants her to stop, and so continues, "...in a soft yellow."

Dan Ridley sags in defeat. Dr. Ben flashes them both a beatific smile and exclaims, "Well! I think that sounds beautiful!"

I peek over at Karen, who is doing the same to me. We've seen this before, and always enjoy it: the easy way in which they like to tease each other, even in the midst of working serious crimes. For her part, Toni is oblivious to the badinage, as she goes about setting milk and an assortment of sweeteners next to the coffeepot. We all make our way over to get a mug, and for a few minutes no one speaks, all of us busy fixing the coffee how we like it and resettling ourselves in our seats. Dr. Ben is once again the first to break the silence.

"I don't suppose you have any cookies? Or maybe some chocolate?"

Ridley positively glares at him and says, "I'm sorry. I didn't realize we were having a tea party," but Toni is unfazed.

"We might have some Nutter Butters left. Let me check." It's said innocently, accommodatingly, but there's something there that makes me wonder if she's really so oblivious after all. It occurs to me she's enjoying teasing her husband a little too, and is playing along. I glance over at Ridley, and sure enough, he rolls his eyes, but he can't keep the slight smile at bay.

Toni returns with the promised Nutter Butters, and we each take two as she offers them around to her guests, but as she is about to set the rest of the package on the table, Dan says, "Hey! Gimme one of those!"

We all laugh, and now I'm relaxed, feeling safe among friends, my nervousness gone. This might even be kind of fun.

***

"And you figured this out on your own? Out of the clear blue sky, you decided to verify the succession to the Hilander duchy?"

Dan Ridley is looking at me with eyebrows raised high, his demeanor suggesting something between awe and stupefaction. When I went through the diagram of the family tree (which Dr. Ben had helpfully forwarded to both Ridleys), he and Toni kept glancing at each other. While I'm not sure of the exact meaning of their silent communications, this was clearly new to them. It was the Ridleys who believed I could help find Wryan's murderer before I did, and they'd asked me to see what I could remember. None of us, of course, expected this.

"We'd been talking about assumptions," I tell him, "And how we've gotten a lot of our assumptions wrong over the past few days. You know, like how Celeste had jumped to conclusions about Izzie being pregnant, and all the wrong assumptions that spread across the Aspire team from her information." I stop to unstick a piece of Nutter Butter with my tongue and wash it down with coffee. "Duke—Duncan—needed his title; he used it to meet people and stuff..." I decide at the last minute not to mention his uncle's involvement in a loan operation, as I don't want to explain how I know about it. Instead, I finish off telling them that I'd made the diagram more as a way to test my assumptions and only then realized the importance of Izzie being pregnant.

"Which brings us to the tea," says Dr. Ben. Both Ridleys look at him in confusion, but all he does is smile and cock his head in my direction. The Ridleys look back at me, and once again I go through my spiel about the potential side effects of muscimol.

"Izzie talked about meditating underwater and how comforting it could be. If she was meditating in the hot tub after ingesting muscimol, she could have become paralyzed and unable to lift her head up again. Even if she just went in to relax, she could have fallen unconscious and... drowned."

"Lily found a brand of that tea from St. Sava in the international grocery in Bethesda, and Miller noticed Izzie had the same box. Who would have introduced her to it? It has to be Duke," says Karen.

I've come to the same conclusion, rationally, although it's still wrenching to hear it said out loud. It's a scary thought, to have been so taken in by someone so vile.

"It does look like that," I say.

"Remember what you said about jumping to conclusions," Toni smiles at both of us. "Not a good idea. But this is intriguing, isn't it?" She adds this last to her husband, who nods energetically.

"It certainly is. You've identified some very interesting and unexpected connections, Lily. It really is impressive."

"Um, thanks." I mutter.

"Your arrival was timely," Ridley adds to Dr. Ben, picking up his folder and giving it a wave. "They delivered this to me last night, thank you very much. Another piece of the puzzle."

From his seat in the chair across the room, Dr. Ben bends forward to take a little bow. "Ever at your service."

Karen and I look from each other to each of them, but no one volunteers what's in that folder, and neither of us dares ask. There's nothing more to say; the coffee and cookies are long gone, and both Ridleys are clearly anxious to get to work, so we make moves to be on our way.

"As always, it has been an education and a delight!" Dr. Ben calls to us from the rolled-down window of his car as he backs down the driveway. Karen and I climb into her SUV, so she can give me a lift back to the hospital to reclaim my bike. We immediately start speculating about what could have been in that file and how it fits into the case.

Chapter 39
Final Farewell

During a lull in our conversation, I decide it's high time to let the others know, so while Karen drives, I send them a text.

Me: Izzie's baby would have become the new duke not Duke
Miller: Not if it was Kam's???
Redd: So she WAS pregnant?
Haisley: No I think you do capitalize the title

"What's everyone saying?" asks Karen, because every time a text comes in, both our phones buzz. When I read out their comments, she starts laughing.

"I don't know why we bother. Our text strings only confuse things," I moan, laughing too.

"True, but I love it. It's fun when we all get together and iron it all out," says Karen, and I can't disagree.

I look down when the phone buzzes yet again. This one is from Gail, texting the news that their plane has been delayed for four hours.

I know it's crazy but you wouldn't like to come join for coffee? National Landing hotel in Crystal City right by the metro

If I take the metro, I could be there in less than 45 minutes, and I realize how much I do want to see her one more time. I ask Karen if she wants to come, but she says she needs to get home.

"You should definitely go, though. I can drop you off at Bethesda station if you want."

I accept, and in no time I'm on the platform. I still need to pick up my bike from the hospital, but it's safe for the time being, and I can take an Uber over there when I'm done. Since it's Saturday, there isn't much of a crowd, and when the train arrives, I easily find a seat. I take out my phone to review my diagram, pondering what else it could mean and why it was pertinent to Ridley's file.

No longer inclined to feel sorry for him, I consider Duke in light of what I already know. He's leveraged his slight connection to the royal family to the hilt, inserting the eye-catching title into introductions whenever it might open a door. All he needed was an opening, a greeting, a chance to make an impression, and he could charm his way wherever he wanted. One admirer, or even a minor acquaintance, led to another—he made sure of it. In relative light-speed, he'd wheedled his way into the Olympic organizing circles where he could influence the decision about adding a new sport to the games. He also had his uncle's example for a very nice side hustle: taking loans at a favorably low rate and lending the money out at a higher one. Because he, too, would one day be the Duke of Hilander. He had a lot to lose if he was suddenly plain old ordinary Duncan-no-cool-nickname Wells.

Another question from the fuzzy corners of my brain now comes to the fore in alarming clarity: is the Wryan-Izzie-baby rumor the first time he'd come up against the possibility of not inheriting the duchy after all?

Chloe, Alistair and Manou's daughter, is young enough to have been born after the new succession rules came into effect. What if Alistair Wells was contemplating marrying Manou? Would that legitimize Chloe's claim to the title ahead of Duke's? Last year, when Duke was home for the triathlon in South Africa, his Uncle Alistair may have mentioned it to him. Was Duke responsible for the fire that killed his cousin Faye? Had Chloe been his intended victim? He was there when it happened, and it would likely be his only chance. He may have missed his target, but did getting away with it strengthen Duke's sense of his own invincibility? Could this be the information in Ridley's file? If it is, Duke truly is a cold-blooded killer. The thought repels me.

I hadn't stopped to consider whether Gail would be by herself or not; I'd assumed so, but of course, I was wrong. When I arrive at the hotel bar, Gail rushes over to give me a big hug and lead me toward the couches and low tables where they're all gathered. It's the whole team; even Nathaniel Tau is there, and while I'm discomfited for a moment, I must admit it's nice how enthusiastically they welcome me. Max shoots me a smile as Celeste calls out, "Uh-oh, there goes the neighborhood." Carlo follows Gail's example, lifting me off my feet in a big bear hug. Duke is there too, but is thankfully trapped between a wall and Nahla (who nods sedately, gracing me with a whisper of a smile). He doesn't get up but flashes me his own dazzling smile and lifts both hands in greeting. I wave back to be polite, but follow close to Gail as she guides me to sit next to her, across from Max and Celeste.

Nathaniel asks me what I'd like, and I scan the table to see what everyone else has ordered. It's an interesting mishmash: half of them seem to have gone for coffee drinks while others have started on cocktails. I tell Nathaniel a latte would be great, thanks.

Gail leans close and says, "I'm so happy you made it. I know it's way out of your way."

"I'm really glad you texted! It's not that far by metro," I say in reply, adding in a low voice, "Anele isn't here?"

Gail shakes her head, rolls her eyes, and mouths, "Shopping."

I'm half disappointed, as I've been curious about her and what she'd be like in person. On the other hand, I'm relieved; I don't want the tumult of this particular new person in the mix on our very last day together.

"Ah! Lily! Here is your coffee!" calls Nathaniel, smiling broadly and pointing to me for the benefit of the server. I smile back at his good-humored face, and I take the latte in both hands.

"Are you all on the same flight?" I ask, to no one in particular.

"Mostly," answers Celeste, "except for our fearless leader (she nods toward Duke), who is driving the truck back with the bikes. Oh, and Nahla is from Baltimore, so she's going to visit her family and then fly out of BWI tomorrow. Nathaniel is flying home to Botswana, also out of BWI tomorrow, so he's her ride up."

"You're a local! I had no idea." I open my mouth and then smile at Nahla.

"She tries to keep that quiet. Pittsburgh isn't easy on Ravens fans!" says Carlo, getting a laugh.

"I was going to drop the guys off at the airport on my way when we heard about the delay, so we made a detour here and decided to inveigle Nathaniel into coming to pay for drinks while we waited with the girls," Duke adds, with a "what-can-you-do" shrug.

"Oh! That's why you asked me to come? And here I thought you all just liked me," Nathaniel pretends to sound hurt, and the others call out "aww" and "we do!" Nahla, on his left, gives him a playful kiss on the cheek at which Carlo, on his right, does the same, to roars of delight.

"Ugh! Get away from me!" Nathaniel screws up his face and pushes lightly at Carlo, but then he, too, roars with laughter.

Despite these hijinks, there is a subdued aura to the group, everyone trying to avoid the topic of going home without their two teammates, and without knowing why. Nevertheless, we're all so comfortable with each other by now that the lapses into silence don't bother us. I feel like I've known everyone here for years, and my throat tightens at the thought that this is likely the end of the road for us. They might come to Bethesda again, but they might not. They may not even survive as a team.

Poignancy makes the time pass quickly, and soon Gail is checking her phone and telling the others they should probably head back over to the airport. While I'm feeling teary-eyed, Aspire are all focused on their trip now, so I swallow hard and hide behind a huge smile as we hug each other one more time. I'm the first to leave, since the others need to go back to reception to get their luggage, which the hotel has stored for them while they were in the bar.

After the dim light inside, the bright sunshine and heat of the day almost blind me, and for a moment I'm disoriented. I'm looking back and forth, trying to decide which is the way to the metro, when Duke calls my name. The sound coming from right behind me makes me jump.

"It's hot! Let me give you a lift home," he says with a friendly smile.

It's hard to believe that this time yesterday I would have been delighted to accept his offer, but now everything is different. My mind has finally made the switch from "friend" to "foe," and I want nothing more to do with him. I don't trust his bonhomie, and even in broad daylight, I'm nervous. I'm also discombobulated by the fact that my own "watch out" radar is still so off, still not pinging on any intimation that this guy is anything but nice. It's as if I have to consciously put my "fight or flight" instinct into high gear, because my brain knows I need to be wary of him even if my gut does not.

"Um, ah…" My adrenalin surges and I can't come up with a single good reason why I'd prefer to take the metro rather than accept a lift. My mouth goes dry, and my heart starts to pound. I don't want to get in the car with him, but I'm starting to feel trapped. Will refusing to go signal to him that I know? What would he do?

"Don't be absurd. You need to pick up Anele and get on the road; you have a long day ahead. I can take Lily home."

Sweet, smiling Nathaniel has unwittingly come to my rescue. I never thought I'd be so happy to see someone I barely know.

"Thank you so much! I mean, both of you, but, yeah, I don't want to delay you any longer, Duke. It's what, about a four-hour drive?" I grab hold of Nathaniel's reasoning like Otto grabs his squeaky toy: full force, no surrender.

"Doesn't matter, it's no problem," Duke insists, but my new hero doesn't back down.

"No, you go! Come, Lily, my car is right here," Nathaniel points with his key and clicks it, and a nearby car gives a short honk and blinks its lights.

"Okay, thank you very much. And thanks, Duke! Have a safe trip back!" I call to him, backing toward the car.

"Take care of yourself," Nathaniel says to Duke, giving his arm a gentle squeeze, and then comes over to open the door for me. Before I know it, the motor is on, the air conditioning is on, and we're moving.

"Thank you!" I say yet again, "You're a lifesaver!"

Nathaniel laughs a little at this exaggeration and replies, "It is always a pleasure to have a charming travel companion."

He drives through the overhang of the front entrance and stops, allowing the car to idle.

"I'm waiting for Nahla, to drive her up to Baltimore. Yes, here she is."

He gets out of the car to put Nahla's luggage in the trunk, and I roll down the window and ask if she'd like the front seat, since she's going farther, but she shakes her head. "This is fine," adding with a grin at Nathaniel, "I don't mind the chauffeur treatment."

I hear him laughing when my phone buzzes. I glance down and see a text from Karen.

Karen: Where are you?
Me: Just leaving CC—Tau giving me a lift

She doesn't respond, and I assume that's the end of our exchange, but as Nathaniel climbs back into the driver's seat and buckles his seat belt, I get another message.

ASK HIM TO GO TO THE HOSPITAL TO GET YOUR BIKE

Strange. Karen never uses all caps. Is it a mistake? Or is something else going on? Stranger still, my "watch out" radar, dead silent with Duke, just emitted a faint ping.

"You live near the Iguana, yes? Shall I head that way?" asks Nathaniel.

"I left my bike at Austin Hill Hospital. Would it be possible for you to take me there?"

"Certainly."

I "like" Karen's last post, and she in turn sends me a thumbs up emoji followed by three exclamation points. Something is definitely up, but I don't know if it's some kind of joke, or just another meetup, or what. That's the exasperating part of our ambiguous messages.

Making conversation, Tau sighs and says, "I had a bad feeling about this week. Nothing specific, you know? Just a feeling. Do you believe in intuition, Lily?"

"I do," I answer heartily, because I had just been thinking about intuition. "But I have a hard time distinguishing it from either generally being a worrywart or unfounded wishful thinking. Sometimes I wonder if it's only intuition if you happened to guess right." I check the rearview mirror to see if Nahla is listening, but she's using her phone as a mirror to reapply her lipstick. "Are your intuitions usually right?" I ask, and Nathaniel smiles wryly.

"I trust my feelings, as they never turn out to be unfounded, but I can never guess beforehand what exactly will go wrong, so it is not always helpful."

"What did you think was going to go wrong?" I'm interested now, curious as to how he wrestles with his own vague intimations of danger.

"I'm not sure, but probably an injury. Something like that can set the whole team back." Nathaniel glances at me, his grave expression a complete contrast to every other interaction I've had with him. "I had a similar feeling when Duke and Nahla raced in the Durban triathlon. It was such a perfect opportunity to showcase ourselves so near to home, I started to worry it would turn to bad luck. Which it did."

He has my full attention now. Does he mean the one last year? When Duke's cousin Faye died? Is that what went wrong? I try to sound casual as I ask, "Why? What happened?" In the mirror, I see that Nahla has put away her phone and lipstick and is paying attention, too.

"It is a very popular and well-known race in Africa, and I built an advertising campaign around it and Aspire—my competitors and my brand were getting a lot of attention. It was wonderful."

Nathaniel pauses to negotiate a tricky lane change between two large trucks, and I hold my breath, waiting for him to continue.

"I was in Gaborone and had too many commitments there to go to Durban myself. It was my assistant who called me with the news: Duncan and another athlete had been neck and neck, part of the lead group on the bike leg, when they both took a curve too quickly on a downhill. They skidded and crashed into each other, and that was the end of the race for both of them."

"Oh no. But they were okay, weren't they?"

"Duncan broke his collarbone; the other athlete broke his jaw. They spent the rest of the weekend at the hospital, and it took months for them to recuperate fully."

I'd had no idea. There's no way Duke could have returned to St. Sava in time to cause that fire. Am I completely wrong? Or is my timing off?

"Was that the same time Duke's cousin was killed? I thought that happened while he was racing in Africa."

Nahla makes a sound like a "tsk" and I turn my head briefly to look at her. She gives me a hard stare, making me wonder if this is not a topic I should have brought up with Nathaniel. I tell myself to keep quiet, to stop putting my foot in it every time I open my mouth. Nathaniel, however, doesn't seem put out in the least.

"Ah, you know about that, do you? You are right; it was the next day." He pauses for a minute and then adds with a rueful smile, "Duncan told me later that he was glad I'd sponsored him for that race. If I hadn't, he probably would not have made it back for the funeral. Not what I intended, but life is not always what we intend it to be, is it?"

"No, it isn't." His comment strikes me as profound in its simplicity, and I take advantage of it to change the subject. I tell him that I myself am doing things I never thought I'd do, and give him the example of teaching yoga instead of finishing college, and now taking lessons in tea, of all things.

He gives me a quick glance, making sure I'm not joking. "Now that is something unusual. What do they teach you in these lessons?"

"All kinds of things: history, growing climates, my teacher's own life story, but mostly it's about the effects of different types of tea on our overall health and well-being. Actually, one of the sessions was on teas made from mushrooms, and it made me wonder if Izzie took too much of one of those. She had a tea made in St. Sava that contains a substance that can cause paralysis and coma. It occurred to me that if she'd been drinking that tea, she might have drowned in the hot tub because of it."

Nathaniel and Nahla both gasp.

Nathaniel bursts out, "Lily, where did you get this idea? I have not heard this!"

"That's insane. She gave that tea away anyway; she didn't like it all that much," adds Nahla more levelly.

My relief at having successfully evaded Duke has made me loose and talkative. I jump in immediately to defend myself, to demonstrate that my ideas are not outlandish at all. I blurt out how I've been wondering whether the succession of the Hilander duchy is at the base of it all, and whether, determined to kill Wryan, the person who murdered him made sure Izzie drank enough muscimol to incapacitate her in case they'd already eloped and she had to be killed too. Only when I've spat it all out do I stop and assess my audience.

Nahla may have taken umbrage at being contradicted; she's giving me the death stare in the rear-view mirror. Nathaniel's expression is no more encouraging; his eyes open wide, staring forward but unseeing and the car slows, as if he's forgotten he's driving. Then he seems to come to himself, checking traffic and maintaining speed, but he's frowning deeply.

"I had no idea you or anyone was thinking along these lines."

My faith in my own theory begins to waver. Part of me had wanted—even expected—them to confirm its soundness by revealing something about Duke that might indicate ruthless singlemindedness, but their reactions are quite the contrary. Nahla's glare looks like outrage to me, or defensiveness, or even fury. Is this loyalty to Duke? Or is it...

My stomach drops. Memories that I've been trying to coax gently forward for the past week come back to me in full force now. *Having a title opens doors.* These things worked in Duke's favor, but they also worked in Nahla's. I hear Redd's words: *Nahla's got a lot going on in that head of hers. She's as ambitious as hell.* She'd been to the Olympics for Botswana, but wanted the fame (and compensation) that comes to American Olympians. Nahla would have been among the first to hear Celeste's gossip about Izzie's "pregnancy." Nahla was right there in the Airbnb with Wryan and Izzie, with easy access to both of them, and she had that tea—Miller saw Izzie give her some. Duke helped her put together the seed money for her charity; was it Nahla, not Nathaniel, who'd gotten a special Hilander loan?

The more I think about it, the more things come to mind that until now I'd pretty much disregarded. No one knew exactly how Nahla had gotten to the start of the race. She claimed she was on the competitor shuttle, but she could just as easily have driven over in Wryan's truck late at night, offloaded his body in the Chesapeake, and remained until morning. Goosebumps tingle on my neck as the pennies continue to drop. Nahla was in St. Sava with Duke, and would likely have heard about the ring tradition. She was there the night of the barn fire, while Duke was still in the hospital in Durban. Do I have this wrong? I've been thinking Duke was a fiend for killing his cousin, but what about Nahla? Same motive, same knowledge, same access, and no tight family ties with the victims to stay her hand.

I risk another peek at her in the mirror. She's looking out her window with brows furrowed and arms folded tight against her.

Is she angry with me? Or is she getting nervous that I suspect her? She turns back to look sternly at me in the mirror and gives an infinitesimal shake of her head, her expression impenetrable. I quickly lower my eyes, my heart beating fast.

I'm wrestling with this lightning bolt when my phone lights up for a second. It's a text from an unknown number, and it says, "Shut up."

Nathaniel's eyes move from the road to me and back, waiting for a response. I'm so freaked out now it's hard to think, but I breathe in, hold my breath for a few seconds, and breathe out. *Calm down. You have to think.* Whoever sent the text knows what's happening in the car, and it obviously isn't from Nathaniel. It has to be from Nahla. I don't dare risk trying to look at her or answer back, but my mind is whirling. Is this a threat? Or a warning? Wait a minute. Could Nahla be trying to warn me?

Oh, shit. I'd completely forgotten: Nathaniel was there too, in the hotel right down the street from the Airbnb when Wryan was killed. I hadn't even considered his interests, but I should have. Duke was the visionary, the natural promoter, while Wryan was the loyal henchman who was destined for the life of a medical practitioner. If Wryan had a legitimate child while his uncle Alistair was still alive, and the title passed to the baby instead of Duke, Nathaniel would lose his royal mascot, his titled automatic "in" to the circles of money and influence he coveted. His company had even adopted the advertising slogan "sporting attire royalty," and he could be deeply in debt to Alistair. Duncan would certainly renew the loan agreement, but could, or would, anyone else? Un likely.

I *know* I've known all along that Duke could never hurt Wryan, who was practically his brother, and not Izzie either. I'd leaped immediately to Nahla, a fellow competitor, but what about Nathaniel Tau? Not only was he in the same town the night of the murder and would have been a welcome visitor to the Airbnb, he (and his no doubt many henchmen) were also right nearby when the fire that killed cousin Faye started. Smiling, solicitous, kindhearted Nathaniel. Who knows what cold determination lies beneath his expansive friendliness? They say psychopaths are often very charming.

Which one is it? Nahla? Or Nathaniel?

"Oh, well, the Bears and I have been thinking about all kinds of crazy things. You know how it is when you don't have the whole picture," I answer with a helpless shrug. I want to allay their worries while making it clear that I'm not the only one who knows about the implications of the duchy inheritance. Yet another sickening possibility has occurred to me: what if they're in it together?

Nathaniel grunts and returns his eyes fully back to the road. I turn to Nahla and ask innocently, "You still okay back there?" using this courtesy as a way to check her face and body language. Nahla briefly checks the rearview mirror, where she can see

Nathaniel's face, and then says, "Fine, thanks," followed by a scintilla of a nod. What does that mean, and who was meant to see it? Is she helping me or Nathaniel? I consider texting her back, but Nathaniel suddenly veers across a crowded traffic lane to take an exit. I grab the car's armrest, and my phone slides off my lap and down under the seat. I reach for it, but can't get it.

We are now traveling not on the highway, but along a road I don't know. I look at Nathaniel in surprise, and he tilts his head to point toward his own phone, which is on a holder attached to the armrest of his door.

"I am sorry. We are coming to a long red line, and Waze suggests this route instead. I had to take the exit right away. You are both all right?" He checks Nahla in the mirror and then smiles over at me apologetically, his concern and benevolence shining through.

"How much longer 'til we're there?" asks Nahla coolly.

I'm awash in confusion. Nahla? Nathaniel? Both? And what about Duke—is he part of this too? They all had means and motive. Are Nahla and I a team, working together against Nathaniel? Or is she the wrongdoer, her text an attempt to shut me up before Nathaniel became suspicious of *her*? My intuition, my third eye, is dizzy from all the rationalization and gives me no help. I don't know who to trust.

"Not long, but we need to backtrack a little to get on a different road."

This is weird. We're heading back toward DC, and I don't see any other particularly dense traffic to indicate that anyone else is doing the same thing. I reach under the seat again to try to get my phone, but still can't find it. Damn.

"I really need to use the ladies' room. Can we pull over somewhere?" says Nahla. I look back at her, and she opens her eyes wide at me, lifting her eyebrows. I make a flash decision that it is indeed me she is trying to help, and add, "I need to too. I don't think I can wait."

Nathaniel grunts again, but he is too polite to refuse. "I will see what I can find."

Nahla consults her phone and says, "There's a park with restrooms nearby. Take the next left, and you'll see the entrance pretty soon."

Nathaniel doesn't answer, but he does take the left and fairly quickly turns into a parking lot. Nahla and I scramble out of the car and head for the plastic Jiffy Jon.

Nahla opens the door to go in first, but before she does, she says to me quietly, "Stall. Keep stalling as long as you can."

Nathaniel has lowered the window of the car, and I stand by the Jiffy Jon waiting for Nahla, who is taking her time in there. The stupid thing is, now that we're here, I really do need to pee, and it's starting to get urgent for real. I'm not sure why we're stalling. Did I guess wrong? Is Nahla up to something?

"Is she all right?" calls Nathaniel from the car.

I lift my hands to signal I don't know, but knock on the door as if I'm checking.

"Nahla? I really do need to go."

She opens the door and glares at me, but lets me through. "Take as long as you can," she again exhorts me with quiet irritation.

Inside, the plastic cabin smells sickly antiseptic, but it's quiet, and I make use of the privacy to collect myself. I'm more and more inclined to trust Nahla, but she's so smart, it might be a trick. *Why are we stalling?* Is Nahla waiting for someone? Could someone else be coming—someone with a gun, or... something? In the sweltering heat of the port-a-cabin, my hands go cold and I shiver. I don't know what to do.

If Nathaniel is the killer, or they're together, the worst thing to do would be to get back into the car with them. I can't stay in here forever, and I can't call anyone, as my phone is still in the car. Not only does that leave me without means of communication, I hate to leave it. Maybe I can tell Nathaniel I just need to get the phone and I'll get myself home from there and then take off running. It's a plan, but not a very good one. I stand up, shaking, and ready myself to open the door.

"What's wrong? Are you both sick?" I hear Nathaniel call, concerned. Is he a good guy? Or a bad guy?

"We're fine. She's coming," Nahla calls back, and I hear her footsteps move away.

I have my purse with me—that's something, at least. I'd placed it on the floor of the car next to my feet and had had to grab it in order to get out. *Forget the phone; just start walking.*

I go outside into the blissfully fresh air and call to the car, "I have a friend who lives near here. I'm good. Thanks for the ride." I wave vaguely over to them and start walking toward a small footpath leading who knows where. Under normal circumstances I would never act so rudely, but these aren't normal circumstances.

"Lily!" calls Nathaniel, but I don't dare look back. I'm afraid that if I do, I might lose my resolve and actually return to the car, as dumb as that sounds. I move forward as if I know exactly what I'm doing and where I'm going (which I absolutely do not). I listen for Nahla's footsteps coming up behind me—if she's a murderer, she might try to tackle me and... strangle me. I walk faster. If she's not, and she's as afraid of Nathaniel as I am now, she could use coming after me to ask what's going on as an excuse to get away herself. I keep walking, hearing no footsteps, and take heart in the fact that there are a few people around: some moms with kids, some walkers. I can hear a dog barking and, in the distance, a siren.

The siren strikes me as an odd sound for the middle of the day in this leafy suburban park, and I focus on it. Is it getting nearer? It's definitely getting nearer. I stop walking, and the siren is suddenly very loud. It must have made the same turn we did. Curiosity gets the best of me, and I turn around to see red lights coming up the drive. I can't believe it, but sure enough, two police cars pull into the parking lot. They shut off the sirens, but the flashing lights continue to turn. I creep back to the start of the footpath and watch. Nathaniel and Nahla had started to drive off, but they were stopped and told to get out of their car.

One of the officers looks over toward me and approaches.

"Are you Lily Piper?" she asks when she gets close.

"Yes," I gawk at her.

She relays this information into her radio and gets what sounds to me like a garbled response; it's loud but barely intelligible to me, although the officer acknowledges it as if she heard it clear as day.

"Your friend is coming to pick you up. She'll be here any minute, but I'd like to ask you a few questions if that's okay." She doesn't wait for me to respond before asking the first one, taking me through the day from when Karen dropped me off at the metro to how and why I ended up here in this park. I can see over her shoulder that other officers are doing much the same with Nathaniel and Nahla. As she's finishing up, I see Karen's SUV come around the curve. I can't help the manic grin that splits my face, and when Karen stops and races over to me—not even bothering to close her door—we give each other a huge hug, laughter bubbling up from relief.

"Thank God!" She looks me up and down, no longer hugging, but holding me by both shoulders at arm's length.

"I'm fine, I'm fine," I wiggle free and start to laugh at her again, but for some reason the laugh turns to tears. I wipe them away when another officer jogs across the road toward us, saying, "Is this your phone?" I nod, taking it gratefully and slipping it into my purse. The second officer jogs back across the road. The first one says I can go, and Karen ushers me into her car. Through the window, I watch Nahla, Nathaniel, and the other police officers continue talking until we turn onto the main road and head home.

Chapter 40
The Culprit

"Thank God you're okay," Karen says for the hundredth time. "We've been so worried."

"Why? What happened? How did the police know how to find us?" I ask, this last being almost the most unfathomable. I myself didn't know exactly where we were.

"Remember that file of Ridley's? It was about the murder weapon that killed Wryan. It wasn't the zip pull from his own wetsuit; it was Nahla's."

"What? How do they know? Oh my God. It was Nahla? All along?" Now that it's out there, I can't believe it. In my gut, I'd decided Nahla and I were on the same side back there in the park. How did I get it so wrong again? I lean back against the seat and press my hands to my cheeks and drag them slowly downward and then look over at Karen, who is shaking her head.

"Nope."

I sit up straight, my entire face an agonized question. "Then who? And seriously, how are you here? Please help. I'm brain dead."

Karen smiles over at me and takes pity, giving me the whole story as she drives carefully along streets that are now comfortingly familiar.

"In all the excitement, I forgot to bring my daughter's programs with me when we left the hospital, so I went back to get them. Turns out Dr. Ben also went back to the hospital to do some more work."

She tells me that Ridley had tried to get ahold of me, but I was probably in the metro and the call didn't go through. He wanted to warn me to stay away from Aspire because they were on the brink of an arrest, and when I didn't answer, he called Dr. Ben to see if he could contact Karen. When they realized they were both at the hospital, they called Ridley back together and told him about me going to Crystal City to meet up with Gail, which worried him. Then, when she got my text saying I was in the car with Nathaniel and relayed the news to Dr. Ben, the look on his face scared her.

"Ridley can try to find their car. Tell Lily to have Nathaniel bring her here," he'd said. Karen didn't know why Ridley wanted to find the car, since up until then she thought Duke was the evildoer, but that scared her even more; hence the all caps.

"Did he ever tell you what was up? He must have said something if you know about Nahla's wetsuit. And why are you so sure it wasn't her?"

"He told me everything while we were waiting for you," Karen says quietly.

It turned out that the logo on Nahla's regular wetsuit had almost worn off, so Nathaniel brought her a new one for the big race. He thought there might be TV and social media coverage, and wanted to make sure it was visible on his star athlete. His prints, and only his prints, were on it, along with Wryan's DNA on the cord that had strangled him.

"The evidence was still there because Nahla never used it. At the last minute, she agreed to do the bike portion of the relay instead of the entire individual triathlon, remember? But Nathaniel didn't know that."

I close my eyes and nod my head in comprehension.

"Celeste let him in; he laid the wetsuit on a chair for Nahla to find, and the two of them sat in the kitchen chatting."

"And she told him Izzie was pregnant, right? She'd told the rest of the team and just had to tell Nathaniel."

"Something like that. Then Izzie came in and joined them for a few minutes, and Nathaniel may have seen the 'new' ring on her finger and really started to get alarmed."

Karen explains that he didn't have a lot of time to work out a plan, because he was leaving for Botswana after the trade show and might not get another chance, so he had to use whatever was available. When he travels, he drinks the mushroom tea from St. Sava to help him sleep. It was Nathaniel who gave Izzie her box of tea — Celeste confirmed that—and Celeste also told the police he'd invited them to join him in a cup of tea when he was with them that evening. Celeste got a phone call and went to her room to take it (Karen shoots a quick grin at me and I shoot one back. Probably Romin.), but Izzie stayed. Nathaniel went out to his car where his suitcase with his stash of tea was still in the back. It is highly likely that, as I'd suggested, he dumped the contents of multiple capsules into the box to add to the mug he'd served to Izzie.

"But why? If he was going to kill Wryan, why did he need to dope up Izzie?" I ask.

"Because you were right! Since they were a 'couple,' he assumed they'd be sleeping in the same room, and he didn't want Izzie to be able to help Wryan."

I lean my head back with a moan. Poor Izzie. Killed for no reason at all, for so many assumptions that were all so very wrong.

"Nathaniel's prints were also on the back door of the Airbnb. He had what sounded like a reasonable explanation at first, but now they think he unlocked the back door of the Airbnb and returned later, when he thought everyone would be asleep."

"It must have been a shock to find Wryan awake and in his own wetsuit."

Karen sighs over at me. "I bet it was! But maybe it worked to Nathaniel's advantage. He could have told Wryan Izzie was sick in his car or something, knowing Wryan would walk out of his own free will to check."

"And then..."

"Yeah."

We fall silent, and another question comes to mind. I open my mouth to ask, but Karen's phone rings and Dr. Ben's name appears on her car display. She gives me a sidelong glance and answers on speaker.

"Karen! Glad I caught you. Is Lily home safe and sound now?"

"She's safe enough and sound enough, but she's still with me. I'm taking her to the hospital first to get her bike. We're actually pulling into the parking lot now."

"You're here? That's perfect! I just got off the phone with Dan. We three can meet in the Nook for a few minutes if you'd like."

Karen lifts her eyebrows in my direction, and I nod energetically. We definitely want to hear what Ridley had to say.

"See you in a few!" she sings out before hanging up.

Even though the kiosk is closed, there are a number of people taking advantage of the Nook's comfortable chairs, so Dr. Ben stands up when he sees us and signals us to follow him. We go down a corridor, through some double doors, and end up in one of the staff break rooms, empty at the moment.

"Lily, you're a sight for sore and worried eyes. I'm glad to see you both. Sit down! Sit down! I'm sure you're curious to hear what's happening." He smiles his twinkly smile, and despite everything, my spirits lift, and I smile back as Karen and I take seats opposite him at the break table.

"So! Questions?"

I give a laugh and drop my head back for a moment. "Well, jeez. I have so many questions, I don't know where to start."

Karen laughs too and gives Dr. Ben a rundown of our conversation in the car, which allows me to get my bearings and decide what to ask first.

"I still don't understand how the police found us. How did they know?"

"An excellent place to start!" Dr. Ben bobs his head up and down, smiling. "It's fairly straightforward: Nahla shared her location with us."

I look from Dr. Ben to Karen and back, bemused. "She did?"

Karen nods and takes over because she had a role in this part. Nahla had Redd's number and texted him; Redd texted Karen, who passed along the information to Dr. Ben, who passed it to Ridley. The police were planning to intercept Nathaniel quietly as he was nearing the hospital, but when he suddenly diverted back toward DC, they helped Nahla guide him to the park where they eventually caught up with us, right on the edge of Montgomery County.

"So, Nahla *was* trying to help me. I mean, both of us. What was she afraid was going to happen?" My goosebumps return with a vengeance, along my arms this time as well as the back of my neck.

"She told the police that as soon as you explained your suspicions about Duke, and your reasoning, she knew that it was Nathaniel," Dr. Ben says.

Nahla had seen the calculated, take-no-prisoners side of Nathaniel and was aware there was much more to him than the ebullient persona he presents to the world. She knew he'd do anything to keep hold of the contacts and influence he got through Duke. She even wondered, as I had, about the fire at Hilander. At the time, she had no reason to think it wasn't an accident, but afterward something changed in her relationship with Nathaniel. She couldn't put her finger on it, but it was as if he'd pegged her as someone who was part of team Nathaniel, not just team Aspire. She put it down to her Botswana roots and their shared skin color, but it hadn't felt chummy, like his relationship with Duke. It had felt conspiratorial. Then, on hearing my suspicions, she wondered again about the fire. She wondered if Nathaniel thought she knew all along, and that she was helping him on purpose with her "silence."

Nahla had tried to warn me without signaling to Nathaniel that she wasn't on his side. *Stall* I hear her quiet command again. She knew the police were coming. She'd been wrestling with everything I had been; in fact, she'd had the horrifying certainty that we were in a car with a man who could kill without compunction, and who would be leaving the country very soon. Yet, she'd still kept her head and come up with a plan.

"When Nathaniel changed direction, she thought he might be heading back to the airport or, more likely, to the interstate that would take them directly to BWI to fly back to Botswana immediately," Dr. Ben is saying now. "She was afraid of two things: one, that he would get away; and two, more importantly, that he would do something drastic on the way to you to keep you from asking questions and voicing your theories to anyone else."

He looks at me gravely, and Karen covers her mouth with her hand, a whispered "Lily" escaping before she falls silent.

I swallow, my mouth dry. "What about Nahla herself? Did she think he'd hurt her too?"

Dr. Ben holds my gaze but wags his head slowly from shoulder to shoulder. "She was scared; that's for sure. But she thought she might be able to act as if she wanted to help Nathaniel get away with everything. After all, it was still in her interest, too, for Duke's status to remain unchanged, and she wanted to imply that it was the two of them against you. That's why she didn't want Tau to see you two talking."

"Woah. She was good." I shake my head in wonder. "I honestly couldn't decide myself whose side she was on. She may have saved my life." This last comes out in a nasally quiver, tears having sprung from nowhere, and I can't hold them back. I press my fists to my eyes, but it doesn't help. Karen puts her hand on my shoulder and Dr. Ben leaps up, looks around for tissues but doesn't find any, so he grabs some paper towels for me to blow my nose. I take deep breaths and, eventually, calm down.

"Hang on a sec." I go over to the sink to splash water on my face and blow my nose into more paper towels. "Sorry," I say shyly, sitting down again.

"Don't be," Dr. Ben smiles kindly. "You've had quite a day."

Chapter 41

August

At first, I wasn't sure I was ready to go back to work on Monday morning, but I was glad I did. The old routine swept me up, and normalcy returned remarkably quickly. My clients were so happy to see me back; their sympathy and kindness raised my spirits and renewed my sense of optimism. It's not that I didn't grieve the loss of Wryan and of Izzie—I did and I do; but concentrating on my clients and on all the daily details that consumed me before their deaths provides a little bit of a buffer so that my outrage and sorrow don't overwhelm me. I'm acutely aware of an unexpected upside to all that has happened, which I cherish as a final, lasting gift from them both. That nagging feeling that I'm standing still, stuck in mud when I should be whizzing along a highway, no longer plagues me. My anxiety over both the present (*am I doing what I'm supposed to be doing?*) and the future (*what's the goal and will I get there in time?*) has mostly abated. When it does raise its growling head, I just smile at it and remember my conversation with Dr. Ben the day we walked together to the main building. I see his eyes shining and hear his earnest observation. "There's nothing wrong with that third eye of yours, Lily. Sounds to me like you're right on target." And it's true. I feel it in my gut. What drives me is helping people find peace and well-being, and I have a whole lifetime ahead of me to figure out a myriad of interesting, exciting, and as yet unforeseeable ways to do that.

I visit Tessa often, and I've gone running with her and Phyllis several times now. As my confidence and comfort grow, so does my appreciation of this surprisingly meditative sport. My footsteps and my breath form a quiet rhythm of their own accord, while my mind flies wherever it will. I love it when I settle into the same state of relaxed but focused flow that I get when I'm swimming—only the scenery is better. I'm not saying I'm hooked (yet!), but I enjoy it more than I thought I would.

I've also been in touch with both Gail and Nahla since they got back home. It's funny how comfortable I've become with Gail. I enjoy her camaraderie in a way that is similar to Izzie's, although their personalities are very different. Gail is an old soul; Izzie was a firecracker. Nevertheless, we've developed a lasting rapport. As for Nahla... we have a bond now. Did she save my life? We'll never know for sure, but she planned and acted thinking it might come to that, and that is enough. There's something about going through an intense experience together, with the stakes that high, that razes all the usual barriers and leaves you both appreciating the other in a very special way. I tried to tell her thank you, but she stopped me.

"You know, Lily, sometimes you help people, and sometimes you hurt them, and you don't even know you're doing it. It just happens."

"Yeah, but... you didn't hurt anyone. You mean Nathaniel? He brought it on himself!"

"No, not Nathaniel..." she drifts off, and I wait silently, giving her time. "It's Duke's cousin, Faye. I think the fire and her death were my fault."

I can't imagine what she's talking about. How could Faye's death be her fault? But I don't say anything dismissive out of hand. She would never accept such easy absolution.

"What makes you think that? Were you ever even in that barn?"

"No, but she told me that her parents might be getting married, and if they did, she'd be the next Duchess of Hilander. I think she was just trying to impress me, you know? Like she wanted me to think of her as somebody important, not some stupid little kid."

"Okay." I wait for her to tell me why this matters.

"I figured she was probably wrong about that. Not lying, just mistaken. But it made me wonder, especially since Duke had pretty much embodied the role already, and I asked Nathaniel about it.

I told him how I was helping her gather blankets and pillows to take to the barn so she could sleep there and she told me that her parents might get married. Then that very night, there's a fire."

"Oh Nahla. I'm so sorry. You couldn't possibly have foreseen anything like what happened. It was a perfectly innocent conversation. Just like Celeste telling everyone Izzie was pregnant. She couldn't have had any idea that it would lead where it did. It's Nathaniel's fault, not yours."

"Maybe. You're right that it's not Celeste's fault; I hadn't thought about it that way. But even so, as soon as you mentioned the succession thing, I knew. I knew he'd intended to have Chloe killed, but got poor Faye instead. And I knew he'd killed Wryan and Izzie. I couldn't let it happen again. I didn't know where he was taking us or what he was thinking in that car, but there's no way I was just going to sit on my hands and leave you in danger too. No way."

I smiled into the phone. This is the Nahla I've come to know: serious, determined, invincible. But not a soothsayer. I meant it when I said there was no way she could have known the havoc such a simple question could unleash. I hope one day she will fully come to terms with that and forgive herself.

Before we hung up, I asked her what was happening with the team. Surprisingly, they've stayed together for the most part, still training with Romin Anjani, although Celeste has moved to a new team in Texas. When I asked what they're doing about sponsorship, her voice shone coyly down the phone. Duke turned the full force of his powers of persuasion onto WhereGear, and it worked; they couldn't wait to sign Aspire, and even added Nahla's foundation to the roster of charities they support. Nahla herself is on the brink of a modeling contract for their triathlon line.

"That's fantastic! I'm so happy for you," I told her sincerely. "I can't wait to see you in a commercial!"

At this, Nahla gave one of her rare laughs, but we both knew I wasn't completely joking. It could definitely happen.

From Gail I heard the sad news that Wryan's mother died a few days after their return. Apparently, she went peacefully, holding her husband's hand. She never knew her son had predeceased her. Wryan's dad is now in the throes of loss and loneliness, but Duke goes to see him almost every day. Gail said they are both supporting and leaning on each other in their mutual grief.

"Speaking of Duke, I saw Anele at the aquatic center the other day, and she mentioned you."

"She did? Why?" My eyes opened wide in surprise, not only that she'd mentioned me, but that she knew who I was in the first place.

"She said she wished she'd had a chance to meet you. Duke told her you're very smart, and you ended up helping the police. He said you're quite something."

That got me. Not only that I'd made an impression (albeit by proxy) on Anele, but that Duke had said such a thing. I knew immediately that it was true, too, because while the rest of us might use words like "awesome," or "cool," or "amazing," Duke would always use the phrase "quite something." Back then it was one of the charming nuances that made him stand out, and it was all the more charming because when he said it, his accent came through very clearly: *quoi-tt something*. When Gail told me that, I positively glowed for the rest of the day, reveling in the fact that I, stubby, provincial Lily Piper, has managed to impress both the beauteous Anele and the great Duke Wells. Right at that moment, I surprised myself with the surge of goodwill I felt for both of them.

After all the furor died down, the Ridleys invited me, Karen, and Dr. Ben over for a barbecue. Toni said they wanted to thank me for my help identifying the implications of the duchy succession, but when I told this to Dr. Ben, he shook his head with a knowing smile.

"I'm sure they do, but Dan's a big softie underneath the granite. He wants to see you in the flesh to satisfy himself that you're all right."

Either way, I was touched and looked forward to the barbecue. It was a very relaxed evening, all of us sitting around the Ridley's patio table eating chicken and corn on the cob and potato salad. At first, no one talked about the case, but truly, when a huge woolly mammoth is sitting right in the middle of everything, you can only tiptoe around it so much before acknowledging its presence. Karen broke the ice by asking if there'd ever been a final determination on Izzie's death.

Dr. Ben hesitated for a moment, but then sighed at her resignedly. "Autopsies in Maryland are public record, so if you went through the steps to put in a request, you'd be able to find out for yourselves anyway," he shrugged, wiping his lips and fingers free of the worst of the sauce. He told us that he relayed my tea theory to the medical examiner in Hillandale, who agreed it made sense to have toxicology test for muscimol in Izzie's remains. Upon finding it in very high concentration, he amended her manner of death from "accidental" to "undetermined."

"But not murder?" I asked, wavering between swelling with pride that my premise had had even this much of an impact, and disappointed that it wasn't enough.

"No, not homicide, although manslaughter is still a possibility," Ridley broke in. "The body of evidence and interviews paint a remarkably clear picture, one that might just sway a jury." Karen and I both stopped eating and looked up expectantly, waiting for him to tell us exactly what happened.

Ridley took a swig of beer and looked down at the table, lost in thought. "We don't know exactly what happened, of course," he said, either not noticing or not acknowledging the chagrin on our faces. "It's entirely possible that Tau's intent really was only to incapacitate her, and he couldn't have had any idea that she'd go get into a hot tub. The problem is that we don't have hard evidence he even did that, though. A good defense lawyer would argue that Izzie could have taken too much muscimol all on her own."

I knew he was right, but I still felt deflated, and Ridley seemed to read my mind. "We'll just have to wait and see, but I'll tell you this much," he added, "The fact of Wryan's murder was never in doubt, and Izzie having muscimol in her system and drowning, too, makes it highly likely it was premeditated, no matter how hastily conceived the plan. And of course, we have a compelling motive for them both." He gave a quick glance around his audience, adding, "If you end up going to trial, it's always best to be able to lay out the motive."

"Thanks to Ms. Piper with her change of succession diagram!" Dr. Ben threw his head back for one of his famous hoots, accompanied by intense blushing on my part.

Both Ridleys smiled and mumbled something like "Uh, huh," to this, but they were careful not to say too much about the case against Tau while it was still pending trial. Dan Ridley did admit that things would have gotten complicated indeed had Nathaniel managed to get on a plane and depart the U.S.

"We have general agreements with Botswana, but they're vague. Nathaniel Tau is a very rich and very important business owner over there. They may have extradited him, but they may have balked—Tau probably had a number of strings he could have pulled to delay things indefinitely," he said. He's seen situations where negotiations drag on for years while a criminal continues to walk free overseas.

Toni grinned at us, disclosing that they'd had information indicating Tau was planning to fly to Pittsburgh with the team and depart from there to Botswana. "They'd alerted Pittsburgh International to look out for him, but not Baltimore. The change in plans threw everyone for a loop."

"Yeah, yeah," her husband said. Then he turned his grim smile on me and added, "I wanted you anywhere but in that car with him, but in the end you and Nahla did help us get him before he slipped away."

Karen clapped me on the back, and I grinned bashfully down at my plate. I felt simultaneously praised and scolded, and didn't know where to look. Dr. Ben finally put me out of my misery by declaring that the dinner was delicious, and standing up to gather paper plates and dump them in the trash. Toni started to cover up the leftovers, and together, she and Dan brought the food into the kitchen to put in the refrigerator. When they joined us again, we all sat comfortably in the shade of their backyard pergola, sipping our drinks at the now-clean table.

"What about Alistair's daughter Faye, though?" I asked, recounting to them what Nahla had told me. "Was that murder or truly an accident?"

"Now that's a sad one," Ridley shook his head. "If Tau was involved, which wouldn't surprise me, it's not likely ever to be proven."

"But they decided not to marry?" prodded Dr. Ben.

Ridley shook his head again. "I asked Wryan's dad about it. According to Fred Burley, it was never that serious a consideration, although Duke told him he discussed it with Manou and his uncle when he and Nahla were there. Here's the irony: it was Duke who first brought up the idea to his uncle. He'd just seen Wryan's mom hit with a frightening diagnosis, and it made him worry what would happen to Manou and Chloe if something happened to Alistair."

"*Duke* wanted them to get married?" I squeaked, unable to believe how wrong I'd been.

"He put it to them as a solution, but Manou was not keen on marriage. Even so, the discussion may have been what prompted them to move everything into joint ownership."

"It's the worst kind of irony when you really think about it," frowned Toni. "Tau was so worried about losing his precious titled athlete promoter, but if he'd simply sat tight and done nothing, the team would still be intact and the whole master plan still marching forward."

"That's true," added her husband. "Tau caused so many people so much grief. He even sacrificed two of his key athletes, and all it did was bring about his own demise."

There wasn't much more to say, but so much to think about and to mourn: lost youth, dreams, potential, friendship, and family. Nevertheless, when Dan and Toni disappeared into the kitchen and then reappeared bearing a cake with the words "Good Job, Lily!" inscribed in blue icing, everyone cheered. Dr. Ben returned to the refrigerator to retrieve a bottle of champagne, which he popped to more clapping and whistling.

When we all raised our glasses, I was the one who spoke first, saying, "This is for our late fellow Iguanas, Wryan and Izzie, and also Faye, who I feel in my bones is just as much a part of all this. I hope now they can rest in peace."

"To Wryan, Izzie and Faye!" they repeated, more or less together, and we all drank.

As Toni started cutting the cake and passing pieces around, Dr. Ben leaned over to Dan, saying sotto voce, "I love the new paint in your kitchen."

***

It's the very end of August before we Bears find ourselves once again all together at the Iguana for happy hour. Haisley has submitted her thesis to the degree committee and is preparing for her viva voce exam. Rather than feeling drained and sick to death of the whole ordeal, she tells us she is invigorated and excited that the end is so near. As she's talking, I send her a quick, secret eye flick across the table. She's excited and full of energy for another reason, too, I happen to know, although we're both pretending I don't. She's tutoring a new PhD candidate as he starts his own journey. He's two years younger than Haisley, smart, cute, very tall—and the electricity between them is, as they say, palpable. For now, though, Haisley is insisting their relationship is purely business.

"Hey Lily, when are you going to air the podcast? You didn't forget it, did you?" Miller asks me.

"You know, guys, I've changed my mind. I appreciate all of you participating, but it was an awful lot of work, and I don't want to start it only to shut it down when I can't keep up."

"Oh, really? That's too bad. But you know what? At least you gave it a shot!" Miller says with unexpected equanimity. She must be mellowing with age.

"Is there anything you're thinking of doing instead?" asks Redd.

"As a matter of fact, there is." I can't help the ear-splitting grin that pops out. I'd gone on a long, fabulous hike with Tessa and Phyllis last weekend, and it had inspired me. "I've got an idea for a blog. It's going to be about hiking trails, but with an extra hook: a deep dive into whatever strange occurrences, disappearances, or other mysteries that have happened on them. It might even help with missing persons or cold cases. And guess what else: each episode is going to feature a signature drink—a recipe for how you could theoretically combine dried flora found along the trail to make a tea."

"That's perfect!" Karen claps her hands.

"Very you," acknowledges Miller.

"I can't wait to read it!" exclaims Haisley.

"It's gonna be terrific," Redd smiles and nods knowingly.

"Thanks." I'm embarrassed by their praise, but deep down I feel the same way. I'd been so excited about the blog, I'd even plucked up the courage to tell Madame Klimenkova about it after class. I asked if I could consult her now and again on those infusion ingredients. I'll never forget how her face lit up, and she clasped her hands to her chest, very nearly giving a jump of joy. "Oh, my heart! Of course! Lily, I help you make most tasty receipts."

Closure has a cathartic effect on the soul; even if it doesn't fix anything, it releases you to live again. We all feel it today, gathered around our regular table. We've barely touched our drinks, but somehow everything seems festive and funny, and we're laughing and teasing each other.

When Star comes by, Redd makes space and invites her to sit with us.

"Can't stop today," she shakes her head with a smile and a sweep of her arm that takes in the room. "Too busy. Just came to deliver this." She puts a pitcher of margaritas in front of us.

"Sure looks good, but that's not ours," Redd says ruefully. "Someone else must've ordered it."

"Someone else did order it. That guy at the bar? He pointed at Lily and said it's for the flying mermaid girl."

Everyone looks over at the guy, who turns for an instant to grin at us before going back to his beer. I open my mouth in wonder, shaking my head at the others, unable to fathom what's happening. Flying mermaid girl? No one has ever called me that.

"Don't just sit there like a dingdong! Go say 'hello!'" Miller urges me.

I slide slowly out of my seat, shy but very curious, and approach the bar.

"Uh, hi! Thank you for the pitcher," I tell the guy, more as a question than anything.

Good-natured hazel eyes in a tanned face that exudes both amusement and delight turn in my direction. There's something familiar about him, but at first, I can't place it.

"I was hoping I'd bump into you one of these days, and lo and behold! It finally happened. Can I buy you a drink?" He asks casually, indicating the stool next to his, and when I hear his voice, it comes to me. He is a park ranger. We ran into each other under decidedly precarious circumstances, and I never learned his name. I cover my mouth with my hand for a second, surprised and also, strangely, elated. I can feel my friends watching me from the table, so I flash them a gleeful show of teeth and wave my hand to signal that they should continue without me. Then, I climb onto the stool and ask the bartender for a Long Island Iced Tea. My partner watches as the bartender makes my drink and places it in front of me.

"H'm. Tea person," he murmurs into his beer, grinning.

I try to act normally, but I'm suddenly giddy, and, "My name is Lily, by the way," comes out in a breathless rush.

"Mitch," he says.

We shake hands formally and then laugh at ourselves. When we stop, he looks at me and I look at him, both of us smiling.

"I remember you."

Acknowledgements

So here we are—the acknowledgements! The section that no one ever reads, but it's important nonetheless. It is virtually impossible to write in a vacuum; somewhere along the line, someone has provided either the missing link to the story, or an idea of where to begin, or an unusual perspective. Here, at least, is a place to express gratitude for these invaluable contributions.

Thank you to my family and friends, and to their friends, who read book one and allege that they want to read this follow-on. I don't know if you're lying through your teeth, but the fact that you said it has motivated me to keep going, especially when I wasn't really feeling it, and that is priceless.

Thank you to all of my work colleagues over the years. You have inspired me with your names, your quirks, your hobbies, and your sense of humor. Without you, the characters in this series would not have come to life in the way that they did, and I feel they would be much the poorer had that been the case. Whether we worked together long ago or very recently, whether your role in my life was large or small, most of you are here somewhere (or at least, bits of you are!), and for that I am grateful.

I particularly want to acknowledge the inspiration of Oksana K., who introduced me to the mystique of *mukhomor*, and the teas and powders derived from the Amanita muscaria mushroom. It is also her mannerisms and exclamations that are very much at the heart of Madame Klimenkova's incarnation.

Special thanks to my editor, Paul Dinas, who received an original manuscript filled with too many threads, too many dead ends, and just too much irrelevant mush, but took on the project anyway. His detailed comments and suggestions were crucial to any coherence achieved in the final result; and as a bonus, I enjoyed our chats—I always came away from them with an idea for a way forward and a much-needed sense of hope.

And before we go, the biggest thanks of all goes to my husband, Ron. I am so, so happy that you are always there, always supportive, always ready to lend an ear (and a few extra brain cells). It can get pretty lonely when your wife has her head buried in her laptop at all hours, and it can be boring being a beta reader when you're not that big into fiction. You withstood it all with class and even—what?!—with enthusiasm. You have no idea what that means to me. But I do.

Born in Washington, DC, Anne Loiselle grew up in Bethesda, Maryland. She headed to Scotland for college, where she received both bachelor's and master's degrees in Russian from the University of St. Andrews, and then worked in Russia for several years. After moving back to the DC area, she completed another master's degree at George Mason University and had a career as a defense and intelligence contractor. Now she lives in the Blue Ridge mountains of Virginia, staying active, enjoying the surroundings, and focused on writing.